ONCE BURIED

(A RILEY PAIGE MYSTERY—BOOK 11)

BLAKE PIERCE

D1615990

BOOKS BY BLAKE PIERCE

RILEY PAIGE MYSTERY SERIES
ONCE GONE (Book #1)
ONCE TAKEN (Book #2)
ONCE CRAVED (Book #3)
ONCE LURED (Book #4)
ONCE HUNTED (Book #5)
ONCE PINED (Book #6)
ONCE FORSAKEN (Book #7)
ONCE COLD (Book #8)
ONCE STALKED (Book #9)
ONCE LOST (Book #10)
ONCE BURIED (Book #11)
ONCE BOUND (Book #12)

MACKENZIE WHITE MYSTERY SERIES
BEFORE HE KILLS (Book #1)
BEFORE HE SEES (Book #2)
BEFORE HE COVETS (Book #3)
BEFORE HE TAKES (Book #4)
BEFORE HE NEEDS (Book #5)
BEFORE HE FEELS (Book #6)
BEFORE HE SINS (Book #7)
BEFORE HE HUNTS (Book #8)

AVERY BLACK MYSTERY SERIES
CAUSE TO KILL (Book #1)
CAUSE TO RUN (Book #2)
CAUSE TO HIDE (Book #3)
CAUSE TO FEAR (Book #4)
CAUSE TO SAVE (Book #5)
CAUSE TO DREAD (Book #6)

KERI LOCKE MYSTERY SERIES
A TRACE OF DEATH (Book #1)
A TRACE OF MUDER (Book #2)
A TRACE OF VICE (Book #3)
A TRACE OF CRIME (Book #4)
A TRACE OF HOPE (Book #5)

PROLOGUE

Courtney Wallace felt a familiar burning in her lungs and her thighs. She slowed her jog down to a walk, then stopped, bent over with her hands on her knees, and gasped as she regained her breath.

It was a good, bracing feeling—a much better way to wake up than a cup of hot coffee, although in just a little while she'd have coffee with her breakfast. She still had plenty of time to shower and eat before she had to go to work.

Courtney loved the glow of early morning sunlight low among the trees and the lingering dampness of morning dew still in the air. Soon it would be a hot May day, but now the temperature was perfect, especially here in the gorgeous Belle Terre Nature Preserve.

She liked the solitude as well. She had seldom encountered another jogger along this trail—and never at this time of morning.

In spite of her satisfaction with her surroundings, a feeling of disappointment began to creep over her while she got her breathing back under control.

Her live-in boyfriend, Duncan, had promised yet again to come jogging with her—and yet again he had refused to wake up. He probably wouldn't get up until long after she'd gone to work at her own office job, maybe not until afternoon.

Is he ever going to snap out of this? she wondered.

And when was he going to get another job?

She broke into a gentle trot, hoping to shake off her negative thoughts. Soon she broke into a full run, and that invigorating burning in her lungs and legs seemed to sweep her worry and disappointment away.

Then the ground gave out from under her.

She was falling—a weird, suspended moment that somehow felt agonizingly slow.

She crashed and crumpled with a brutal thump.

The sunlight was gone, and her eyes had to adjust.

Where am I? she wondered.

She saw that she was at the bottom of a narrow pit.

But how had she gotten here?

She felt a terrible pain shooting up her right leg.

1

She looked down and saw that her ankle was bent at an unnatural angle.

She tried to move her leg. The pain sharpened and she cried out. She tried to stand up, but her leg collapsed beneath her. She could actually feel the broken bones rasping against one another. Nausea rose in her throat and she nearly blacked out.

She knew she needed help and reached into her pocket for her cell phone.

It wasn't there!

It must have fallen out.

It had to be here somewhere. She groped about to find it.

But she was partially entangled in a sort of rough, heavy, loosely woven blanket along with soil and leaves. She couldn't find the phone.

It began to dawn on her that she had fallen into a trap—a hole with the debris-strewn cloth stretched over to hide it.

Was it somebody's idea of a practical joke?

If so, it wasn't the least bit funny.

And how was she going to get out of here?

The walls of the hole were straight, with no footholds or handholds. Unable to even stand up, she would never be able to get out of here on her own.

And no one else was likely to come along this trail soon, maybe not for hours.

Then she heard a voice directly above her.

"Hey! Did you have a bit of an accident?"

She breathed a little easier at the sound.

She looked up and saw that a man was standing above her. His figure was silhouetted against pale light, so she couldn't make out his face.

Still, she could barely believe her luck. After so many mornings of seeing no one on this trail, this morning someone just happened to come by when she desperately needed help.

"I think my ankle is broken," she called up to the man. "And I've lost my phone."

"That sounds bad," the man said. "How did it happen?"

What kind of question is that? she wondered.

Although there seemed to be a smile in his voice, Courtney wished she could see his face.

She said, "I was jogging, and … there was this hole, and …"

"And what?"

Courtney was feeling more than a little impatient now.

She said, "Well, obviously, I fell in."

The man fell quiet for a moment. Then he said, "It's a big hole. Didn't you see it?"

Courtney let out a groan of exasperation.

"Look, I just need help getting out of here, OK?"

The man shook his head.

"You shouldn't come jogging in strange places where you don't know the path."

"I *do* know this path!" Courtney shouted.

"Then how did you fall in this hole?"

Courtney was dumbfounded. Either the man was an idiot or he was toying with her.

"Are you the dick that dug this hole?" she snapped. "If so, it's not funny, damn it. Get me out of here!"

She was shocked to realize that she was weeping.

"How?" the man asked.

Courtney reached up, stretching her arm as far as it would go.

"Here," she said. "Reach down and take my hand and pull me up."

"I'm not sure I can reach that far."

"Sure you can."

The man laughed. It was a pleasant, friendly laugh. Even so, Courtney still wished she could see his face.

"I'll take care of everything," he said.

He stepped away and out of sight.

Then she heard a rattling of metal and squeaking, grinding sounds coming around from behind her.

The next thing she knew, she felt a huge weight crashing down on her.

She gasped and sputtered until she grasped that the man had just dumped a load of dirt on her.

She felt her hands and legs getting cold—signs of panic, she realized.

Don't panic, she told herself.

Whatever was going on, she had to stay calm.

She saw that the man was standing with a wheelbarrow tilted over her. A few remaining clods of dirt tumbled out of the wheelbarrow onto her head.

"What are you doing?" she yelled.

"Relax," the man said. "Like I said, I'll take care of

everything."

He rolled the wheelbarrow away. Then she heard a dull, drum-like pounding against metal again and again.

It was the sound of the man shoveling more dirt into the wheelbarrow.

She closed her eyes, took a deep breath, opened her mouth, and let out a long, piercing shriek.

"Help!"

Then she felt a heavy clump of dirt hitting her directly in her face. Some of it got into her mouth, and she choked and gagged and spit it out.

His voice still sounding friendly, the man said …

"I'm afraid you're going to have to yell a lot louder than that."

Then with a chuckle he added …

"I can barely hear you myself."

She let out another shriek, shocked at the loudness of her own voice.

Then the man dumped the new wheelbarrow full of dirt onto her.

She couldn't scream again now. Her throat was clogged with dirt.

She was overcome by an eerie sense of déjà vu. She'd experienced this before—this inability to run from danger or even to scream.

But those experiences had only been nightmares. And she'd always woken up from them.

Surely this was just another nightmare.

Wake up, she told herself again and again. *Wake up, wake up, wake up …*

But she couldn't wake up.

This was not a dream.

This was real.

CHAPTER ONE

Special Agent Riley Paige was working at her desk at the BAU building in Quantico when an unwelcome memory swept over her ...

A dark-skinned man was staring at her with glassy eyes.

He had a bullet wound in his shoulder, and a much more dangerous wound in the abdomen.

In a weak, bitter voice, he told Riley ...

"I order you to kill me."

Riley's hand was on her weapon.

She ought to kill him.

She had every good reason to kill him.

Even so, she didn't know what to do ...

A woman's voice snapped Riley out of her reverie.

"You look like you've got something on your mind."

Riley looked up from her desk and saw a young African-American woman with short straight hair standing in her office doorway.

It was Jenn Roston, who had been Riley's new partner on her most recent case.

Riley shook herself a little.

"It's nothing," she said.

Jenn's dark brown eyes were filled with concern.

She said, "Oh, I'm pretty sure it's not nothing."

When Riley didn't reply, Jenn said, "You're thinking about Shane Hatcher, aren't you?"

Riley nodded silently. The memories were coming pretty often these days—memories of her terrible confrontation with the wounded man up at her dead father's cabin.

Riley's relationship with the escaped convict had been rooted in a weird, twisted bond of loyalty. He had been at large for five months, and she hadn't even tried to curtail his freedom—not until he began to murder innocent people.

Now it was hard for Riley to believe that she had let him go free for so long.

Theirs had been an unsettling, illegal, and very, very dark relationship.

Of all the people Riley knew, Jenn knew best just how dark it had been.

Finally Riley said, "I just keep thinking—I should have killed him right then and there."

Jenn said, "He was wounded, Riley. He posed no threat to you."

"I know," Riley said. "But I keep thinking I let my loyalty get in the way of my judgment."

Jenn shook her head.

"Riley, we've talked about this. You already know what I think about it. You did the right thing. And you don't have to take my word for it. Everybody else here feels the same way."

Riley knew that it was true. Her colleagues and superiors had heartily congratulated her for bringing Hatcher in alive. Their goodwill was a welcome change. As long as Riley had been in Hatcher's thrall, everybody here had been justifiably suspicious of her. Now that the cloud of suspicion had lifted, her colleagues' faces were friendly again, and she was greeted with renewed respect.

Riley truly felt at home here again.

Then Jenn grinned and added, "Hell, you even did things by the book for once in your life."

Riley chuckled. Certainly she had followed correct procedure in how she had apprehended Hatcher—which was more than she could say for many of her actions during the case she and Jenn had just solved together.

Riley said, "Yeah, I guess you got a real crash course in my … unconventional methods."

"I sure did."

Riley chuckled uneasily. She'd ignored even more rules than usual. Jenn had covered for her loyally—even when she'd broken into a suspect's house without a warrant. Jenn could have reported her actions if she'd chosen to. She could have gotten Riley fired.

"Jenn, I really appreciate—"

"Don't even mention it," Jenn said. "It's all in the past. Whatever comes next is all that matters."

Jenn's smile broadened as she added, "And I don't expect you to act like a Girl Scout. You'd better not expect me to either."

Riley laughed again, more comfortably this time.

She found it hard to believe that she had recently distrusted Jenn, had even considered her a true nemesis.

After all, Jenn had done much, much more for Riley than be discreet about her actions.

"Have I thanked you for saving my life?" Riley asked.

Jenn smiled.

"I've kind of lost count of how many times," she said.

"Well, thank you again."

Jenn said nothing. Her smile faded. A far-off look came over her.

"Did you want something, Jenn?" Riley asked. "I mean, why did you stop by?"

Jenn just kept staring down the hallway for a moment.

Finally she said, "Riley, I don't know whether I should tell you …" Her voice trailed off.

It was easy for Riley to see that something was troubling her. She wanted to reassure her, to say something like …

"You can tell me anything."

But that might be presumptuous.

Finally Jenn seemed to shiver a little.

"Never mind," she said. "It's nothing for you to worry about."

"Are you sure?"

"I'm sure."

Without another word, Jenn disappeared down the hall, leaving Riley with a distinctly uneasy feeling. She'd long sensed that Jenn harbored secrets of her own—perhaps some very dark ones.

Why won't she trust me? Riley wondered.

It seemed that one or the other of them was always a little distrustful. That didn't bode well for them working together as partners.

But there was nothing Riley could do about it—at least not yet.

She glanced at her watch. She was almost late for an appointment with her longtime partner, Bill Jeffreys.

Poor Bill was on leave these days, suffering from PTSD after a terrible incident during their last case together. Riley felt a pang of sadness as she remembered it.

She and Bill had been working together with a promising young agent named Lucy Vargas.

But Lucy had been killed in the line of duty.

Riley missed Lucy every day.

But at least she didn't feel guilty about her death.

Bill did.

Early this morning, Bill had called Riley and asked her to meet him at the Marine base that made up the largest part of the Quantico facility.

He hadn't told her why, which worried her. She hoped it was nothing serious.

Riley anxiously got up from her desk and headed out of the BAU building.

CHAPTER TWO

Bill felt a tingle of worry as he led Riley toward the Marine target range.

Am I ready for this? he wondered.

It seemed almost a stupid question. After all, it was only target practice.

But this was no ordinary target practice.

Like him, Riley was wearing a camouflage uniform and carrying an M16-A4 rifle loaded with live ammunition.

But unlike Bill, Riley had no idea what they were about to do.

"I wish you'd tell me what this is all about," Riley said.

"It's going to be a new experience for both of us," he said.

He'd never tried this new kind of range shooting before. But Mike Nevins, the psychiatrist who had been helping him with his PTSD, had recommended it for him.

"It'll be good therapy," Mike had said.

Bill hoped Mike was right. And he hoped it would take the edge off his nerves to try it out with Riley.

Bill and Riley took positions next to each other among upright four-by-four wooden posts, facing across a wide grassy field toward a paved area. On the pavement were vertical barriers marked with bullet holes. A few moments ago, Bill had talked to a guy in a control booth and everything should be ready now.

Now he spoke to that same guy through a little microphone in front of his lips.

"Random targets. Go."

Suddenly, human-sized figures appeared from behind the barriers, all of them moving about in the paved area. They were wearing the uniforms of ISIS-style fighters and appeared to be armed.

"Hostiles!" Bill called out to Riley. "Shoot!"

Riley was too startled to shoot, but Bill fired one shot and missed. Then he fired another shot that hit one of the figures. The figure bent completely over and stopped moving. The other figures turned to avoid the gunfire, some of them moving faster, others hiding behind the barriers.

Riley said, "What the hell!"

She still hadn't taken a shot.

Bill laughed.

"Stop," he said into the microphone.

Suddenly, all the figures were motionless.

"Today we're shooting at fake guys on wheels?" Riley asked with a laugh.

Bill explained, "They're autonomous robots, mounted on Segway scooters. That guy I talked to in the booth a minute ago is punching in programs for them to follow. But he doesn't control their every movement. In fact, he doesn't really control them at all. They 'know' what to do. They've got laser scanners and navigation algorithms so they can avoid each other and the barriers."

Riley's eyes were wide with amazement.

"Yeah," she said. "And they know what to do when the shooting starts—run, or hide, or both."

"Want to try it again?" Bill asked.

Riley nodded, starting to look enthusiastic.

Again Bill said into the microphone, "Random targets. Go."

The figures began moving as before, and Riley and Bill fired single shots at them. Bill hit one of the robots, and so did Riley. Both of those robots stopped and bent over. The other robots scattered, some gliding about capriciously, others hiding behind barriers.

Riley and Bill kept firing, but the shooting was getting harder. The robots that stayed on the move darted in unpredictable patterns at varying speeds. The ones who hid behind the barriers kept popping out, taunting Riley and Bill to shoot at them. It was impossible to tell from which side of the barrier they might appear. Then they either scurried around in the open or took shelter again.

Despite all this seeming chaos, it only took about half a minute for Riley and Bill to take out all eight of the robots. They were all bent over and motionless among the barriers.

Riley and Bill lowered their weapons.

"That was weird," Riley said.

"Want to stop?" Bill asked.

Riley chuckled.

"Are you kidding? Absolutely not. What's next?"

Bill swallowed, suddenly feeling nervous.

"We're supposed to take out hostiles without killing a civilian," he said.

Riley looked at him sympathetically. He understood her concern. She knew perfectly well why this new exercise made him feel uneasy. It reminded him of the innocent young man he had mistakenly shot last month. The boy had recovered from his wound, but Bill still couldn't shake off his guilt.

Bill was also haunted because a brilliant young agent named Lucy Vargas had been killed in the same incident.

If only I'd been able to save her, he thought yet again.

Bill had been on official leave ever since, wondering if he'd ever be able to get back to work. He'd completely fallen apart, lapsing into alcohol and even contemplating suicide.

Riley had helped him through it—in fact, she had probably saved his life.

Bill felt like he was getting better now.

But was he ready for this?

Riley kept eyeing him with concern.

"Are you sure this is a good idea?" she asked.

Again, Bill remembered what Mike Nevins had said.

"It'll be good therapy."

Bill nodded at Riley.

"I think so," he said.

They resumed their positions and raised their weapons. Bill spoke into the microphone. "Hostiles and civilian."

The same actions as before began to unfold—only this time, one of the figures was a female draped in a blue hijab. It certainly wasn't hard to distinguish her from the hostiles in their drab, brown outfits. But she was weaving among the others in seemingly random patterns.

Riley and Bill began to pick off the hostiles to the same effect as before—some of the male figures dodged the bullets, while others took shelter behind the barriers, only to dart out at unpredictable moments.

The female figure also moved as if frightened by the gunfire, hurrying to and fro frantically, but somehow never bothering to hide behind a barrier. Her simulated panic only made it harder not to accidentally hit her.

Bill felt cold sweat forming on his forehead as he fired one round after another.

Soon he and Riley had shot all the hostiles, and the woman in the hijab stood alone unscathed.

Bill breathed a slow sigh of relief and lowered his weapon.

"How are you doing?" Riley asked, a note of worry in her voice.

"Pretty good, I guess," Bill said.

But his palms felt damp against the weapon, and he was shaking a little.

"Maybe that's enough for now," Riley said.

Bill shook his head.

"No," he said. "We've got to try the next program."

"What's that?"

Bill gulped hard.

"It's a hostage situation. The civilian will be killed unless you and I take out two hostiles simultaneously."

Riley squinted at him doubtfully.

"Bill, I don't know …"

"Come on," Bill said. "It's only a game. Let's give it a try."

Riley shrugged and raised her weapon.

Bill spoke into the microphone, "Hostage situation. Go."

The robots came back to life. The female figure stayed in the open, while the hostiles disappeared behind the barriers.

Then two hostiles appeared from behind the barriers, hovering menacingly around the female figure, who wobbled back and forth with seeming anxiety.

Bill knew that the trick was for him and Riley to fire at both hostiles as soon as they had a clear shot.

It was up to him to call that moment.

As he and Riley carefully aimed their weapons, Bill said …

"I'll take the one on the left, you the guy on the right. Fire when I say 'Go.'"

"Got it," Riley said quietly.

Bill carefully monitored the movements and positions of the two hostiles. He realized that this was going to be hard—much harder than he'd expected.

The very second one of the hostiles drifted away, the other hostile placed himself dangerously close to the hostage.

Are we ever going to get a clear shot? he wondered.

Then, for just a fleeting moment, the two hostiles both drifted about a foot or so in opposite directions away from the hostage.

"Go!" Bill barked.

But before he could pull the trigger, he was seized by a rush of images …

12

He was dashing toward an abandoned building when he heard a shot ring out.

He drew his weapon and ran inside, where he saw Lucy lying prone on the floor.

He saw a young man moving toward her.

Instinctively, Bill fired at the man and hit him.

The man spun around before he fell—and only then did Bill see that his hands were empty.

He was unarmed.

The man had only been trying to help Lucy.

Mortally wounded, Lucy lifted herself up on her elbow and fired six rounds at her real attacker ...

... the man Bill should *have shot.*

A shot rang out from Riley's rifle, snapping Bill out of his flashback.

The images had come and gone in a mere fraction of a second.

One of the hostiles tilted over, dead from Riley's shot.

But Bill himself stood frozen. He couldn't pull the trigger.

The surviving hostile turned menacingly toward the woman, and a recorded shot rang out over a loudspeaker.

The woman buckled over and stopped moving.

Bill finally fired his weapon and hit the surviving hostile—but too late for the hostage, who was already dead.

For a moment, the situation seemed horribly real.

"Jesus," he said. "Oh, Jesus, what did I let happen?"

Bill stepped forward, almost as if he wanted to rush to the woman's aid.

Riley stepped in front of him to stop him.

"Bill, it's OK! It's only a game! It's not real!"

Bill stopped in his tracks, shaking all over and trying to calm himself.

"Riley, I'm sorry, it's just that ... it all came flooding back for a second and ..."

"I know," Riley said comfortingly. "I understand."

Bill slumped over and shook his head.

"Maybe I'm not ready for this," he said. "Maybe we'd better quit for the day."

Riley patted him on the shoulder.

"No," she said. "I think you'd better see it through."

Bill took a few long, slow breaths. He knew that Riley was

right.

He and Riley resumed their positions, and Bill again said into the microphone …

"Hostage situation. Go."

The same action resumed again, with two hostiles lurking dangerously close to the hostage.

Bill breathed slowly, in and out, as he peered through his sight.

It's only a game, he told himself. *It's only a game.*

Finally, the moment he was waiting for arrived. Both of the hostiles had moved ever so slightly away from the hostage. It was still a dangerous shot, but Bill and Riley had to take it.

"Go!" he said.

This time he fired instantly, and he heard the sound of Riley's shot a fraction of a second later.

Both of the hostiles buckled over and stopped moving.

Bill lowered his weapon.

Riley patted him on the back.

"You did it, Bill," she said, smiling. "I'm enjoying this. What else can we do with these bots?"

Bill said, "There's a program where we can advance toward them as we shoot."

"Let's give it a try."

Bill spoke into his microphone.

"Close quarters."

All eight of the hostiles began to move, and Bill and Riley advanced toward them step by step, firing in small bursts. A couple of robots fell, and the others scurried about, becoming harder to hit.

As Bill fired away, he realized that something was missing from this simulation.

They don't shoot back, he thought.

Also, his relief at saving the hostage felt strangely hollow. After all, he and Riley had merely saved the life of a robot.

It didn't change the reality of what had happened last month.

It certainly didn't bring Lucy back to life.

His guilt still haunted him. Was he ever going to be able to shake it off?

And was he ever going to be able to get back to work?

CHAPTER THREE

After their target practice, Riley was still worried about Bill. True, he'd recovered quickly after freezing up that once. And he'd actually seemed to enjoy himself when they started firing at close quarters.

He'd even seemed cheerful when he left Quantico to go back to his apartment. Still, he wasn't the same old Bill who had been her partner for so many years—and who had long since become her best friend.

She knew what he was most worried about.

Bill was afraid that he might not ever be able to come back to work.

She wished she could reassure him with kind, simple words—something like …

"You're just going through a rough stretch. Happens to all of us. You'll be over it sooner than you think."

But glib reassurances weren't what Bill needed right now. And the truth was, Riley didn't really know whether it was true.

She'd suffered her own spells of PTSD, and knew how hard recovery could be. She would just have to help Bill work through that awful process.

Although Riley went back to her office, she actually had little to do at BAU today. She didn't currently have an assignment, and these slow days had been welcome after the intensity of the last case in Iowa. She wrapped up the few details that needed her attention and left.

As Riley drove home, she was feeling contented at the thought of dinner with her family. She was especially pleased that she had invited Blaine Hildreth and his daughter to join them tonight.

Riley was delighted that Blaine was part of her life. He was a handsome, charming man. And like her, he was fairly recently divorced.

He was also, as it turned out, remarkably brave.

It was Blaine who had shot and badly wounded Shane Hatcher when he had threatened Riley's family.

Riley would always be grateful to him for that.

She had spent one night with Blaine so far, at his home. They'd been fairly discreet about it—his daughter, Crystal, had been away visiting her cousins during spring break. Riley smiled at the memory of their passionate lovemaking.

Was tonight going to end the same way?

*

Riley's live-in housekeeper, Gabriela, had fixed a delicious meal of *chiles rellenos* from a family recipe that she'd brought from Guatemala. Everybody was thoroughly enjoying the steaming, lusciously stuffed bell peppers.

Riley was feeling deep satisfaction with a very good dinner and wonderful company.

"Not too *picante*?" Gabriela asked.

It wasn't too hot and spicy for American taste buds, of course, and Riley was sure that Gabriela knew it. Gabriela always exercised restraint with her original Central American recipes. She was obviously fishing for compliments, which came quickly and easily.

"No, it's perfect," Riley's fifteen-year-old daughter, April, said.

"The best ever," said Jilly, the thirteen-year-old girl that Riley was in the process of adopting.

"Just amazing," said Crystal, April's best friend.

Crystal's father, Blaine Hildreth, didn't say anything right away. But Riley could tell by his expression that he was enchanted by the dish. She also knew that Blaine's appreciation was partly professional. Blaine owned an upscale but casual restaurant here in Fredericksburg.

"How do you do it, Gabriela?" he asked after a few bites.

"Es un secreto," Gabriela said with a mischievous grin.

"A secret, eh?" Blaine said. "What kind of cheese did you use? I can't place it. I can tell it's not Monterey Jack or Chihuahua. Manchego, maybe?"

Gabriela shook her head.

"I will never tell," she said with a chuckle.

As Blaine and Gabriela continued to banter about the recipe, partly in English and partly in Spanish, Riley caught herself wondering if she and Blaine might …

She blushed a little at the idea.

No, not going to happen tonight.

There could hardly be any graceful, discreet segue with

everybody here.

Not that there was anything wrong with things as they were.

Being surrounded by people she cared deeply about was pleasure enough for this particular evening. But as she watched her family and friends enjoying themselves, a new concern began to tug at Riley's mind.

One person at the table had barely said a word so far. That was Liam, the newcomer to Riley's household. Liam was April's age, and the two teenagers had been dating at one time. Riley had rescued the tall, gangly kid from an abusive, drunken father. He'd needed a place to live and right now that meant sleeping on the sofa bed in Riley's family room.

Liam was normally talkative and outgoing. But something seemed to be troubling him tonight.

Riley asked, "Is anything wrong, Liam?"

The boy didn't seem to even hear her.

Riley spoke just a little louder.

"Liam."

Liam looked up from his meal, which he had barely touched so far.

"Huh?" he said.

"Is anything wrong?"

"No. Why?"

Riley squinted uneasily. Something was wrong, all right. Liam was seldom monosyllabic like this.

"I just wondered," she said.

She made a mental note to talk to Liam alone later on.

*

Gabriela capped off the meal with a delicious dessert of flan. Riley and Blaine enjoyed after-dinner drinks while the four kids entertained themselves in the family room, and finally Blaine and his daughter went on home.

Riley waited until April and Jilly went to their rooms for the night. Then she went alone to the family room. Liam was sitting quietly on the still-closed sofa, staring off into space.

"Liam, I can tell something's wrong. I wish you'd tell me about it."

"Nothing's wrong," Liam said.

Riley crossed her arms and said nothing. She knew from

dealing with the girls that it was sometimes best to wait kids out.

Then Liam said, "I don't want to talk about it."

Riley was startled. She was used to adolescent moodiness from April and Jilly, at least from time to time. But it wasn't typical of Liam at all. He was always agreeable and obliging. He was also a dedicated student, and Riley appreciated his influence on April.

Riley continued to wait in silence.

Finally Liam said, "I got a call from Dad today."

Riley felt a sinking in the pit of her stomach.

She couldn't help remembering that terrible day when she'd rushed over to Liam's house to save him from being badly beaten by his father.

She knew she shouldn't be surprised. But she didn't know what to say.

Liam said, "He says he's sorry about everything. He says he misses me."

Riley's worry deepened. She had no legal custody over Liam. Right now, she was acting as a sort of impromptu foster parent, and she had no idea exactly what her future role in his life would be.

"Does he want you to come back home?" Riley asked.

Liam nodded.

Riley couldn't bring herself to ask the obvious question …

"What do you want?"

What would she do—what *could* she do—if Liam said he wanted to go back?

Riley knew that Liam was a gentle, forgiving boy. Like many abuse victims, he was also prone to deep denial.

Riley sat down beside him.

She asked, "Have you been happy here?"

Liam made a small choking sound. For the first time, Riley realized that he was near tears.

"Oh, yes," he said. "This has been … I've just been … so happy."

Riley felt her own throat catch a little. She wanted to tell him he could stay here for as long as he wished. But what could she do if his father demanded that he come back? She'd be powerless to stop it from happening.

A tear trickled down Liam's cheek.

"It's just that … since Mom went away … I'm all Dad's got. Or at least I was until I left. Now he's all alone. He says he's stopped drinking. He says he won't hurt me anymore."

Riley almost blurted out …

"Don't believe him. Don't ever believe him when he says that."

Instead, she said, "Liam, you must know that your dad is very ill."

"I know," Liam said.

"It's up to him to get the help he needs. But until he does … well, it's going to be very hard for him to change."

Riley fell silent for a moment.

Then she added, "Just always remember that it's not your fault. You know that, don't you?"

Liam gulped down a sob and nodded.

"Have you ever gone back to see him?" Riley asked.

Liam shook his head silently.

Riley patted his hand.

"I just want you to promise me one thing. If you *do* go to see him, don't go by yourself. I want to be there with you. Do you promise?"

"I promise," Liam said.

Riley reached for a nearby box of tissues and offered one to Liam, who wiped his eyes and blew his nose. Then the two of them sat in silence for a few long moments.

Finally Riley said, "Do you need me for anything else?"

"No. I'm OK now. Thank you for … well, you know."

He smiled at her weakly.

"Pretty much everything," he added.

"You're very welcome," Riley said, returning his smile.

She left the family room, walked to the living room, and sat alone on the couch.

Suddenly, a sob rose up in her own throat, and she started to cry. She was startled to realize how shaken she'd been by her conversation with Liam.

But when she thought about it, it was easy enough to understand why.

I'm so out of my depth, she thought.

After all, she was still trying to get Jilly's adoption settled. She'd rescued the poor girl from her own share of horrors. When Riley had found her, Jilly had been trying to sell her body out of sheer desperation.

So what did Riley think she was doing, bringing another teenager into the house?

She suddenly wished Blaine was still here to talk to.

Blaine always seemed to know what to say.

She had enjoyed the lull between cases for a while, but little by little, worries had started to creep in—worries especially about her family, and today about Bill.

It hardly felt like any kind of vacation.

Riley couldn't help but wonder …

Is something wrong with me?

Was she somehow just incapable of enjoying a quiet life?

Anyway, she knew she could be sure of one thing.

This lull wouldn't last. Somewhere, some monster was committing some heinous deed—and it would be up to her to stop him.

CHAPTER FOUR

Riley was awakened early the next morning by the sound of her phone buzzing.

She groaned aloud as she shook herself awake.

The lull is over, she thought.

She looked at her phone and saw that she was right. It was a text message from her team chief at the BAU, Brent Meredith. It was a call to meet with him, and it was written in his typical terse style …

BAU 8:00

She looked at the time and realized she'd have to hurry to make it to the hastily planned appointment. Quantico was only a half-hour drive from home, but she needed to get out of here fast.

It took Riley just minutes to brush her teeth, comb her hair, get dressed, and rush downstairs.

Gabriela was already making breakfast in the kitchen.

"Is coffee ready?" Riley asked her.

"Sí," Gabriela said, and poured her a hot cup.

Riley sipped the coffee eagerly.

"You must leave without breakfast?" Gabriela asked her.

"I'm afraid so."

Gabriela handed her a bagel.

"Then take this with you. You must have something in your stomach."

Riley thanked Gabriela, gulped down some more of the coffee, and rushed out to her car.

During the short drive to Quantico, a peculiar feeling came over her.

She actually began to feel better than she had during the last few days, even slightly euphoric.

It was partly an adrenaline boost, of course, as her mind and body prepared to embark upon a new case.

But it was also something rather unsettling—a feeling that things were somehow getting back to normal.

Riley sighed at the realization.

She wondered—what did it mean that hunting monsters felt more normal to her than spending time with people she loved?

It can't be ... well, normal, she thought.

Worse, it reminded her of something that her father, a brutal and bitter retired Marine officer, had told her before he died.

"You're a hunter. What folks call normal—it would kill you if you tried living it too long."

Riley wanted with all her heart for it not to be true.

But at times like now, she couldn't help but worry—were the roles of wife, mother, and friend impossible for her to fill?

Was it hopeless to even try?

Was "the hunt" the only thing she really had in life?

No, definitely not the only thing.

Surely not even the most important thing in her life.

Firmly, she put the unpleasant question out of her mind.

When she arrived at the BAU building, she parked and hurried inside and straight to Brent Meredith's office.

She saw that Jenn was already there, looking a lot more bright-eyed and awake than Riley felt. Riley knew that Jenn, like Bill, had an apartment in the town of Quantico, so she'd been in less of a rush to get here. But Riley also attributed some of Jenn's early-morning freshness to her youth.

Riley had been much the same as Jenn when she was younger—ready and eager to spring into action at a moment's notice, at any time of day or night, and able to go without sleep for extended intervals when the job demanded it.

Were those days slipping behind her?

It wasn't a pleasant thought, and it didn't brighten Riley's already uneasy mood.

Sitting at his desk, Brent Meredith cut a formidable figure as always, with his black, angular features, his broad frame, and his perpetual down-to-business attitude.

Riley sat down, and Meredith wasted no time getting to the point.

"There was a murder this morning. It happened on the public beach at the Belle Terre Nature Preserve. Are either of you familiar with the place?"

Jenn said, "I've been there a few times. A great place for hiking."

"I've been there too," Riley said.

Riley remembered the nature preserve pretty well. It was on the Chesapeake Bay, just a little more than a two-hour drive from Quantico. It had several hundred forested acres and a wide public beach on the bay. It was a popular area for outdoor types.

Meredith drummed his fingers on his desk.

"The victim was Todd Brier, a Lutheran pastor in nearby Sattler. He'd been buried alive on the beach."

Riley shuddered a little.

Buried alive!

She'd had nightmares about it, but she had never actually worked on a case involving this particular type of grisly murder.

Meredith continued, "Brier was found at about seven this morning, and it looked like he'd only been dead for about an hour."

Jenn asked, "What makes this an FBI case?"

Meredith said, "Brier's not the first victim. Yesterday another body was found nearby—a young woman named Courtney Wallace."

Riley suppressed a sigh.

"Don't tell me," she said. "Also buried alive."

"You've got it," Meredith said. "She was killed on one of the hiking trails at the same nature preserve, apparently also early in the morning. She was discovered later in the day when a hiker came across the disturbed earth and called park services."

Meredith leaned back in his chair and swiveled slightly back and forth.

He said, "So far, the local cops don't have any suspects or witnesses. Other than the locations and the MO, they don't have much of anything. Both victims were young, healthy people. There hasn't been time to find out if they were connected in any way, other than that they were both out there early in the morning."

Riley's mind clicked away as she tried to make sense of what she'd just heard. So far, she had too little to go on.

She asked, "Have the local cops closed off the area?"

Meredith nodded.

"They've closed the forested area near that trail and half of the beach to the public. I've told them not to move the body on the beach until my people get there."

"What about the woman's body?" Jenn asked.

"It's at the morgue in Sattler, the nearest city. The Tidewater District medical examiner is at the beach right now. I want the two of you to get down there as fast as you can. Take an FBI vehicle, something conspicuous. I'm hoping that if the FBI is visibly on the scene, it will at least slow this perpetrator down. My guess is that he isn't done killing yet."

Meredith glanced back and forth at Riley and Jenn.

"Any questions?" he asked.

Riley did have a question, but she didn't know whether she should ask it.

Finally she said, "Sir, I'd like to make a request."

"Well?" Meredith said, leaning back in his chair again.

"I'd like Special Agent Jeffreys to be assigned to this case."

Meredith's eyes narrowed.

"Jeffreys is on leave," he said. "I'm sure that you and Agent Roston here can handle this between the two of you."

"I'm sure we can," Riley said. "But …"

She hesitated.

"But what?" Meredith said.

Riley swallowed hard. She knew that Meredith didn't much like it when agents asked for personal favors.

She said, "I think he needs to get back to work, sir. I think it would do him good."

Meredith scowled and said nothing for a moment.

Then he said, "I won't officially assign him to the case. But if you want him to work with you on an informal basis, I've got no objection."

Riley thanked him, trying not to be too effusive lest he change his mind. Then she and Jenn requisitioned an official FBI SUV.

As Jenn started to drive south, Riley got out her cell phone and texted Bill.

I'm working on a new case with Roston. Chief says it's OK for U to join us. I want you to.

Riley waited for a few moments. Her heart beat a little faster when she saw that the message was marked "read."

Then she typed …

Can we count U in?

Again the message was marked "read," but there was no response.

Riley's spirits sank.

Maybe this isn't a good idea, she thought. *Maybe it's still too soon.*

She wished Bill would reply, if only to tell her no.

CHAPTER FIVE

As Jenn drove the SUV south toward their destination, Riley kept eyeing the text messages she'd sent on her cell phone.

Minutes passed, and Bill still didn't reply.

Finally she decided to give him a call.

She punched in his number. To her frustration, she got his voice mail.

At the sound of the beep, she simply said, "Bill, call me. Now."

As Riley set the phone down in her lap, Jenn glanced over at her from behind the wheel.

"Is anything wrong?" Jenn asked.

"I don't know," Riley said. "I hope not."

Her worry kept mounting during the drive. She remembered a text she'd received from Bill while she'd been working on her most recent case in Iowa …

Just so you know. Been sitting here with a gun in my mouth.

Riley shuddered at the memory of the desperate phone call that had followed, when she'd managed to talk him out of committing suicide.

Was it happening again?

If so, what could Riley do to help?

A sudden shrill, piercing noise chased these thoughts from Riley's head. It took a second for her to realize that Jenn had turned on the siren upon running into a patch of slow traffic.

Riley took the siren as a stern reminder …

I've got to get my head in the game.

*

It was about ten-thirty when Riley and Jenn arrived in the Belle Terre Nature Preserve. They followed a road to the beach until they found a couple of parked police cars and a medical examiner's van. Beyond the vehicles on a grassy rise was a barrier of police tape to keep the public away from the beach.

The beach wasn't immediately visible as Riley and Jenn got out of the van. But Riley saw gulls flying overhead, felt a crisp breeze on her face, smelled salt in the air, and heard the sound of surf.

Riley was dismayed but hardly surprised that a small group of reporters had already gathered in the parking area beyond the crime scene. They crowded around Riley and Jenn, asking questions.

"We've had two murders in two days. Is there a serial killer at work?"

"You've released the name of yesterday's victim. Have you identified this new victim?"

"Have you contacted the victim's family?"

"Is it true that both victims were buried alive?"

Riley cringed at that last question. Of course, she wasn't surprised that word had gotten out about how the victims had died. Reporters could have learned that much from listening to local police scanners. But she had no doubt that the media was going to sensationalize these murders for all they were worth.

Riley and Jenn pushed past the reporters without commenting. Then they were greeted by a couple of local cops, who escorted them past the police tape over the grassy rise onto the beach. Riley could feel sand seeping into her shoes as she walked.

In a moment, the murder scene came into view.

Several men surrounded a hole dug in the sand where the body still remained. Two of them strode toward Riley and Jenn as they approached. One was a stocky, red-haired man in a uniform. The other, a slender man with curly black hair, was wearing a white shirt.

"I'm glad you could get here so soon," the red-haired man said when Riley and Jenn introduced themselves. "I'm Parker Belt, the Sattler police chief. This is Zane Terzis, the Tidewater District medical examiner."

Chief Belt led Riley and Jenn over to the hole and they looked down at the half-uncovered body.

Riley was more than used to seeing corpses in various states of mutilation and decomposition. Even so, this one jolted her with a unique kind of horror.

He was a blond man, about thirty years old, and he was wearing a jogging outfit suitable for a cool summer morning's run along the beach. His arms remained sprawled in a statue-like state of rigor mortis from his desperate attempts to dig himself out. His eyes were shut tight, and his wide-open mouth was filled with sand.

Chief Belt stood next to Riley and Jenn.

Belt said, "He still had a wallet with plenty of identification—not that we really needed it. I recognized him the second Terzis and his men uncovered his face. His name is Todd Brier, and he's a Lutheran pastor in Sattler. I didn't go to his church—I'm a Methodist. But I knew him. We were good friends. We went fishing together from time to time."

Belt's voice was thick with sorrow and shock.

"How was the body found?" Riley asked.

"A guy came by walking a dog," Belt said. "The dog stopped here, sniffing and whining, then started digging, and right away a hand appeared."

"Is the guy who found the body still around?" Riley asked.

Belt shook his head.

"We sent him home. He was badly shaken up. But we told him he needed to be available for questions. I can put you in touch with him."

Riley looked up from the body over to the water, which was some fifty feet away. The waters of the Chesapeake Bay were a deep rich blue, with white-topped waves lapping softly at the wet sand. Riley could see that the tide was going out.

Riley asked, "This was the second murder?"

"It was," Belt replied grimly.

"Has anything like this ever happened here before these two?"

"Right here in Belle Terre, you mean?" Belt said. "No, nothing like it at all. This is a peaceful preserve for birds and wildlife. Local people use this beach, mostly families. From time to time we have to arrest some would-be poacher or settle an argument among visitors. We also have to chase away transients from time to time. That's about as serious as it gets."

Riley stepped around the hole to look at the body from a different angle. She saw a patch of blood on the back of the victim's head.

"What do you make of this wound?" she asked Terzis.

"It looks like he was struck by some hard object," the ME said. I'll study it better when we get the body to the morgue. But from the looks of it, I'd say it was probably enough to daze him, just long enough so he couldn't put up a fight while the killer was burying him. I doubt that he was ever completely unconscious. It's pretty obvious that he struggled hard."

Riley shuddered.

Yes, that much was obvious.

She said to Jenn, "Take some pictures and also send them to me."

Jenn immediately took out her cell phone and started snapping photos of the hole and the corpse. Meanwhile, Riley walked slowly around the hole checking the beach in all directions. The killer hadn't left a lot of clues. The sand around the hole had obviously been disturbed by the killer when he'd been digging, and there was a trail of vague footprints where the jogger had approached.

Vague, too, were any footprints left by the killer. The dry sand didn't hold the shape of a shoe. But Riley could see where the marsh grass she'd come through had been broken down by someone other than the investigative team.

She pointed and said to Belt, "Have your guys scour that grass carefully to see if any fibers might have gotten caught there."

The chief nodded.

A feeling began to creep over Riley—a familiar feeling that she sometimes got at a crime scene.

She hadn't felt it often during her most recent cases. But it was a welcome feeling, one that she knew she could use as a tool.

It was an uncanny sense of the killer himself.

If she allowed herself to let that feeling sweep over her, she was likely to get some insights into just what had happened here.

Riley moved a few steps away from the group gathered at the scene. She glanced at Jenn and saw that her partner was watching her. Riley knew that Jenn was aware of her reputation for getting into killers' minds. Riley nodded, and saw Jenn swing into action, asking questions of her own, distracting the others on the scene and giving Riley a few moments to concentrate her skills.

Riley closed her eyes and tried to picture the scene as it must have looked at the time of the murder.

Images and sounds came to her remarkably easily.

It was dim outside, and the beach was shadowy, but there were traces of light in the sky across the water from where the sun would later rise, and it wasn't too dark to see.

The tide was up, and the water was probably only an easy stone's throw away, so the sound of the surf was loud.

Loud enough so he could barely hear himself digging, Riley realized.

At that moment, Riley had no trouble stepping into a strange mind …

Yes, he was digging, and she could feel the strain of his muscles as he threw shovels of sand as far away as he could, feel the mixture of sweat and sea spray on his face.

The digging wasn't easy. In fact, it was a bit frustrating.

It wasn't easy to dig a hole in beach sand like this.

Sand had a way of trickling back in, partially refilling the space where he dug.

He was thinking ...

It won't be very deep. But it doesn't have to be deep.

All the while he kept glancing up at the beach, looking for his prey. And sure enough, he soon appeared, jogging along contentedly not far away.

And at the perfect time, too—the hole was just as deep as it needed to be.

The killer pushed the shovel into the sand and raised up his hands and waved.

"Come over here!" he shouted to the jogger.

Not that it mattered what he shouted—over the sound of the surf, the jogger wouldn't be able to pick out his actual words, just a muffled yell.

The jogger stopped at the sound and looked his way.

Then he walked over to the killer.

The jogger was smiling as he approached, and the killer was smiling back at him.

Soon they were within earshot of each other.

"What's up?" the jogger yelled over the surf.

"Come here and I'll show you," the killer yelled back.

The jogger unwarily walked over to where the killer was standing.

"Look down there," the killer said. "Look really close."

The jogger bent over, and with a swift, deft movement, the killer picked up the shovel and hit him in the back of the head, knocking him into the hole ...

Riley was yanked out of her reverie by the sound of Chief Belt's voice.

"Agent Paige?"

Riley opened her eyes and saw that Belt was looking at her with a curious expression. He hadn't been distracted long by Jenn's questions.

He said, "You seemed to leave us for a few moments there."

Riley heard Jenn chuckle from nearby.

"She does that sometimes," Jenn told the chief. "Don't worry, she's hard at work."

Riley quickly reviewed the impressions she'd just gotten—all very hypothetical, of course, and hardly a moment-by-moment sense of what had actually happened.

But she felt very sure of one detail—that the jogger had come over at the killer's invitation—and had approached him without fear.

This gave her a small but crucial insight.

Riley said to the police chief, "The killer is charming, likeable. People trust him."

The chief's eyes widened.

"How do you know?" he asked.

Riley heard laughter from someone approaching behind her.

"Trust me, she knows what she's doing."

She whirled around at the sound of the voice.

Her spirits brightened at what she saw.

CHAPTER SIX

Chief Belt stepped toward the man who was approaching.

He said, "Mister, this area is closed. Couldn't you see the barrier?"

"It's OK," Riley said. "This is Special Agent Bill Jeffreys. He's with us."

Riley hurried over to Bill and led him just far enough away so that they wouldn't be heard by the others.

"What happened?" she said. "Why didn't you answer my messages?"

Bill smiled sheepishly.

"I was just being an idiot. I …" His voice faded and he looked away.

Riley waited for his reply.

Then he finally said, "When I got your texts, I just didn't know whether I was ready. I called Meredith for details, but I still didn't know if I was ready. Hell, I didn't know if I was ready when I started driving down here. I didn't know if I was ready until just now when I saw …"

He pointed to the body.

He added, "Now I know. I'm ready to get back to work. Count me in."

His voice was firm and his expression looked like he really meant it. Riley breathed a huge sigh of relief.

She led Bill back over to the officials clustered around the body in the hole. She introduced him to the chief and the medical examiner.

Jenn already knew Bill and she looked glad to see him, which pleased Riley. The last thing Riley needed was for Jenn to feel marginalized or resentful.

Riley and the others told Bill what little they knew so far. He listened with a look of keen interest.

Finally Bill said to the ME, "I think it's OK to take away the body now. That is, if it's OK with Agent Paige."

"It's fine with me," Riley agreed. She was happy that Bill seemed like his old self now and eager to assert some authority.

As the ME's team began to extract the body from the hole, Bill surveyed the area for a moment.

He asked Riley, "Have you checked out the site of the earlier murder?"

"Not yet," she replied.

"Then we should do that," he said.

Riley said to Chief Belt, "Let's go have a look at your other crime scene."

The chief agreed. "It's a couple of miles into the nature preserve," he added.

They all managed to push past the reporters again without commenting. Riley, Bill, and Jenn got into the FBI SUV, and Chief Belt and the ME took another car. The chief led them away from the beach, along a sandy road into a wooded area. When the road ended, they parked their cars. Riley and her colleagues followed the two officials on foot along a trail leading through the trees.

The chief kept the group to one side of the trail, pointing to some distinct footprints here in the firmer soil.

"Just your everyday sneakers," Bill commented.

Riley nodded. She could see those prints going in both directions. But she felt sure they wouldn't offer much information except for the killer's shoe size.

However, some interesting marks were interspersed with the footprints. Two wobbly lines were dug into the soil.

"What do you make of these lines?" Riley asked Bill.

"Tracks from a wheelbarrow, coming and going," Bill said. He glanced back over his shoulder toward the road and added, "My guess is the killer parked about where we're parked now and brought his tools along this path."

"That's what we figured too," Belt agreed. "And he left again this way."

Soon they came to a spot where their path intersected a narrower one. In the middle of the smaller path was a long, deep hole. It was about the width of the path itself.

Chief Belt pointed to where the new path emerged from the surrounding trees. "The other victim seems to have come jogging along from that direction," he said. "The hole was camouflaged, and she fell into it."

Terzis added, "Her ankle was badly broken, probably from the fall. So she was helpless when the killer started piling dirt back in on her."

Riley shuddered again at the thought of that kind of horrible death.

Jenn said, "And all this happened yesterday."

Terzis nodded and said, "I'm pretty sure the time of death was identical to the murder on the beach—probably around six o'clock in the morning."

"Before the actual sunrise," Belt added. "It would have been quite dim. A jogger who came along here after dawn saw how the dirt had been disturbed and called us."

While Jenn started taking more photos, Riley scanned the area. Her eyes fell on some flattened brush that had been crisscrossed by the wheelbarrow tracks. She could see where the killer had piled up dirt about fifteen feet away from the trail. The trees were fairly thick beside these pathways, so a runner wouldn't have seen either the killer or the dirt as she'd come running in this direction.

Now the hole had been re-excavated by the police, who had piled the dirt right next to it.

Riley remembered that Meredith had mentioned this victim's name back at Quantico, but she couldn't recall it at the moment.

She said to Chief Belt, "I take it you were able to identify the victim."

"That's right," Belt said. "She still had plenty of ID on her, just like Todd Brier did. Her name was Courtney Wallace. She lived in Sattler, but I didn't know her personally. So I can't tell you anything much about her just yet, except she was young, probably in her early twenties."

Riley knelt down beside the hole and looked inside. Right away, she could see exactly how the killer had set his trap. At the bottom of the hole was a heavy, loosely woven blanket of erosion cloth, with leaves and debris tangled up in it. It had been spread out over the hole, unnoticeable to an unwary jogger, especially in the dim, pre-dawn light.

She made a mental note to call in a BAU forensics team to go over both of these sites. Maybe they could trace the origin of the erosion cloth.

Meanwhile, Riley was getting just a trace of the same sensation she'd had at the beach, of slipping into the killer's mind. The feeling wasn't nearly as vivid this time. But she could imagine him perched right where she was kneeling now, looking down at his helpless prey.

So what was he doing in those moments before he began to

bury her alive?

She reminded herself of her earlier impression—that he was charming and likeable.

At first he probably feigned surprise at finding the young woman at the bottom of this hole. He may have even given the woman the impression that he'd help her get out.

She trusted him, Riley thought. *If only for a moment.*

Then he'd begun to tease her.

And before long, he began dumping wheelbarrows full of dirt down on her.

She must have screamed when she realized what was happening.

So how did he respond to the sound of her screaming?

Riley sensed that his sadism fully emerged. He paused from his task to throw a single shovelful of dirt in her face—not so much to stop her from screaming, but to torment her.

Riley shivered all over.

She felt relief as that feeling of connection began to slip away.

Now she could get back to looking at the crime scene with a more objective eye.

The shape of the hole seemed odd to her. The end where she was standing was dug in a pointed wedge shape. The other end reflected that same shape, only inverted.

It looked like the killer had gone to a certain amount of trouble about it.

But why? Riley wondered. *What could it mean?*

Just then, she heard Bill's voice call out from somewhere behind her.

"I've found something. You'd all better come over here for a look."

CHAPTER SEVEN

Riley whirled around to see what Bill was yelling about. His voice was coming from behind the trees off to one side of the path.

"What is it?" Chief Belt called out.

"What did you find?" Terzis echoed.

"Just come here," Bill yelled back.

Riley got to her feet and headed in his direction. She could see broken-down brush where he had left the path.

"Are you coming?" Bill called out, starting to sound a little impatient.

Riley could tell by his tone of voice that he meant business.

Followed by Belt and Terzis, she waded through the thicket until they reached the small clearing where Bill was standing. Bill was looking down at the ground.

He'd found something, all right.

Another piece of erosion cloth was stretched over the ground, loosely held in place by small pegs at the corners.

"Good God," Terzis murmured.

"Not another body," Belt said.

But Riley knew that it had to be something different. For one thing, the hole was much smaller than the other, and square in shape.

Bill was putting on plastic gloves to avoid leaving fingerprints on whatever he was about to find. Then he knelt down and gently pulled the erosion cloth away.

All Riley could see was a circular piece of dark, polished wood.

Bill carefully took hold of the wooden circle with both hands and pulled it upward.

Everybody except Bill gasped at what he slowly brought out of the hole.

"An hourglass!" Chief Belt said.

"Biggest one I ever saw," Terzis added.

And indeed, the object was over two feet tall.

"Are you sure it's not some kind of trap?" Riley warned.

Bill rose to his feet with the object, keeping it perpendicular, handling it as delicately as he might handle an explosive device. He set it upright on the ground next to the hole.

Riley knelt and examined it closely. The thing didn't seem to have any wires or springs. But was anything hidden beneath that sand? She tilted the thing to one side and didn't see anything odd.

"It's just a big hourglass," she muttered. "And hidden just like the trap on the trail."

"Not an hourglass, exactly," Bill said. "I'm pretty sure it measures a longer period of time than an hour. It's what's called a sand timer."

The object struck Riley as startlingly beautiful. The two globes of glass were exquisitely shaped, connected together by a narrow opening. The round wooden top and bottom pieces were connected by three wooden rods, carved into decorative patterns. The top was carved into a ripple pattern. The wood was dark and well-polished.

Riley had seen sand timers before—much smaller versions for cooking that counted off three or five or twenty minutes. This one was much, much bigger, over two feet tall.

The bottom globe was partially filled with tan sand.

There was no sand in the upper globe.

Chief Belt asked Bill, "How did you know something was here?"

Bill was crouching beside the sand timer, examining it attentively. He asked, "Did anyone else notice something odd about the shape of the pit on the trail?"

"I did," Riley said. "The ends of the hole were dug in kind of a wedge-shaped manner."

Bill nodded.

"It was roughly the shape of an arrow. The arrow pointed to where the path curved away and some of the bushes were broken down. So I just went where it was pointing."

Chief Belt was still staring at the sand timer with amazement.

"Well, we're lucky you found it," he said.

"The killer wanted us to look here," Riley muttered. "He wanted us to figure this out."

Riley glanced at Bill, then at Jenn. She could tell they were thinking just what she was thinking.

The sand in the timer had run out.

Somehow, in a way they didn't yet understand, that meant that they weren't lucky at all.

Riley looked at Belt and asked, "Did any of your men find a

timer like this at the beach?"

Belt shook his head and said, "No."

Riley felt a grim tingle of intuition.

"Then you didn't look hard enough," she said.

Neither Belt nor Terzis spoke for a moment. They looked as though they couldn't believe their ears.

Then Belt said, "Look, something like this would surely have stood out. I'm sure there wasn't anything like it in the immediate area."

Riley frowned. This thing that had been placed so carefully just had to be important. She felt sure that the cops had somehow overlooked another sand timer.

For that matter, so had she and Bill and Jenn when they'd been on the beach. Where could that one be?

"We've got to go back and look," Riley said.

Bill carried the enormous timer over to the SUV. Jenn opened the back, and she and Bill put the object inside, making sure that it was braced and steadied against any sharp or sudden movement. They covered it with a blanket that was in the SUV.

Riley, Bill, and Jenn got into the SUV and followed the police chief's car back toward the beach.

The number of reporters gathered in the parking area had increased, and they were getting more aggressive. As Riley and her colleagues made their way through them and past the yellow tape, she wondered how much longer they would be able to ignore their questions.

When they reached the beach, the body was no longer in the hole. The ME's team had already loaded it into their van. The local cops were still combing the area for clues.

Belt called out to his men, who gathered around him.

"Has anybody seen a sand timer around here?" he asked. "It would look like a big hourglass, at least two feet tall."

The cops looked perplexed by the question. They shook their heads and said no.

Riley was starting to feel impatient.

It must be around here somewhere, she thought. She walked to the top of a nearby grassy rise and looked around. But she could see no hourglass, not even disturbed sand that would indicate something freshly buried.

Or was her intuition playing tricks on her? It sometimes happened.

Not this time, she thought.

In her gut, she felt sure of it.

She walked back and stood looking down at the hole. It was very different from the one in the woods. It was shallower, more shapeless. The killer couldn't have formed the dry beach sand into a pointer if he'd tried.

She turned all around and gazed in every direction.

All she saw was sand and the surf.

The tide was low. Of course the killer could have made some kind of wet sand-sculpture arrow, but it would have been seen right away. If it hadn't been destroyed, it would still be visible.

She asked the others, "Have you seen anyone else anywhere near here—aside from the man with the dog who found the body?"

The cops shrugged and looked at each other.

One of them said, "Nobody except Rags Tucker."

Riley's eyes widened.

"Who's he?" she asked.

"Just an eccentric old beachcomber," Chief Belt said. "He lives in a little wigwam over there."

Belt pointed farther along the beach where the shoreline curved away from the area where they stood.

Riley was getting a little angry now.

"Why didn't anybody mention him before?" she snapped.

"There wasn't much point," Belt said. "We talked to him when we first got here. He didn't see anything having to do with the murder. He said he'd been asleep when it happened."

Riley let out a groan of irritation.

"We're going to pay this guy a visit," she said.

Followed by Bill, Jenn, and Chief Belt, she started walking along the sand.

As they walked, Riley said to Belt, "I thought you'd closed off the beach."

"We did," Belt said.

"Then what the hell is anybody still doing here?" Riley asked.

"Well, like I said, Rags sort of lives here," Belt said. "There didn't seem to be any point in kicking him out. Besides, he's got no place else to go."

After they rounded the curve, Belt led them up across the sand to a grassy rise. The group waded through the soft sand and tall grass to the top of the rise. From there Riley could see a little makeshift wigwam about a hundred yards away.

"That's ol' Rags's house," Belt said.

As they approached, Riley saw that it was covered with plastic bags and blankets. Here behind the rise, it was safely out of reach whenever the tide was high. The wigwam was surrounded by blankets covered with what looked like a crazy assortment of objects.

Riley said to Belt, "Tell me about this Rags Tucker character. Doesn't Belle Terre have rules against vagrancy?"

Belt chuckled a little.

He said, "Well, yeah, but Rags isn't exactly your typical vagrant. He's colorful, and people like him, visitors especially. And he's not a suspect, believe me. He's the most harmless guy in the world."

Belt pointed to the things out on the blanket.

"He's got kind of a goofy business going with all that stuff he's got. He picks up junk off the beach, and people come around to buy stuff, or to exchange stuff they don't want anymore. Mostly it's just an excuse for folks to hang around and talk to him. He does this all summer, for as long as the weather here is comfortable. He manages to put together enough money to rent a cheap little apartment in Sattler for the winter. Then when the weather's good again, he comes back here."

As they got nearer, Riley could see the objects more clearly. It really was a bizarre collection that included driftwood, conch shells, and other natural objects, but also old toasters, broken TVs, old lamps, and other items that visitors had undoubtedly brought for him.

When they got to the edge of the outstretched blankets, Belt called out, "Hey, Rags. I wonder if we could talk to you some more."

A raspy voice answered from inside the wigwam.

"I told you before, I didn't see anybody. Haven't you caught the creep yet? I sure don't like the idea of a killer on my beach. I'd have already told you if I knew anything."

Riley stepped toward the wigwam and called out, "Rags, I need to talk to you."

"Who're you?"

"FBI. I'm wondering if maybe you'd run across a large sand timer. You know, like an hourglass."

There was no reply for a few moments. Then a hand inside the wigwam pulled aside a sheet that covered the opening.

Inside was a scrawny man sitting cross-legged, his big eyes staring at her.

And sitting right in front of him was a huge sand timer.

CHAPTER EIGHT

The man in the wigwam just stared up at Riley with wide gray eyes. Riley's attention snapped back and forth from the vagrant to the big sand timer in front of him. She found it hard to decide which was the most startling.

Rags Tucker had long grayish hair and a beard that hung down to his waist. His tattered, loosely fitting clothes suited his name.

Naturally she wondered …

Is this guy a suspect?

She found that hard to believe. His limbs were thin and spindly, and he seemed hardly robust enough to have carried out either one of these arduous murders. He fairly exuded a sense of harmlessness.

Riley also suspected that his scruffy appearance was something of a pose. He didn't smell bad, at least from where she stood, and his clothes looked clean in spite of all their wear and tear.

As for the sand timer, it looked much like the one they'd found back near the path. It was more than two feet tall, with wavy ridges carved on the top and three skillfully carved rods holding the frame together.

It wasn't identical to the other one, though. For one thing, the wood wasn't as dark—more of a reddish brown. Although the carved patterns were similar, they didn't look like exact replicas of the designs they'd seen on the first sand timer.

But those small variations weren't the most important differences between the two.

The greatest contrast was in the sand that marked passing time. In the timer that Bill had found among the trees, all of the sand was in the bottom globe. But in this timer, most of the sand was still in the top globe.

This sand was in motion, trickling slowly into the globe below.

Riley felt sure of one thing—that the killer had meant them to find this timer, as surely as he'd meant them to find the other one.

Tucker finally spoke. "How'd you know I had it?" he asked Riley.

Riley produced her badge.

"I'll ask the questions, if you don't mind," she said in a non-

42

threatening voice. "How did you get it?"

Tucker shrugged.

"It was a gift," he said.

"From whom?" Riley asked.

"From the gods, maybe. It dropped from the sky, the best I can figure. When I first looked outside this morning, I saw it right away, over there on the blankets with my other stuff. I brought it inside and went back to sleep. Then I woke up again, and I've been just sitting here watching it for a while."

He stared hard at the sand timer.

"I've never *watched* time actually pass before," he said. "It's a unique experience. Sort of feels like time is passing slowly and fast at the same time. And there's a feeling of inevitability about it. You can't turn back time, as they say."

Riley asked Tucker, "Was the sand running like this when you found it, or did you turn it over?"

"I kept it just like it was," Tucker said. "Do you think I'd dare change the flow of time? I don't mess with cosmic matters like that. I'm not that stupid."

No, he's not stupid at all, Riley thought.

She felt that she was beginning to understand Rags Tucker better with each bit of their conversation. This addled and ragged beachcomber persona of his was carefully cultivated for the entertainment of visitors. He'd turned himself into a local attraction here at Belle Terre. And from what Chief Belt had told her about him, Riley knew that he made a modest living at it. He had established himself as a local fixture and gained unspoken permission to live exactly where he wanted to be.

Rags Tucker was here to entertain and to be entertained.

It dawned on Riley that this was a delicate situation.

She needed to get that sand timer away from him. She wanted to do that quickly and without raising a fuss about it.

But would he be willing to give it to her?

Although she knew the laws about search and seizure perfectly well, she wasn't at all sure about how they applied to a vagrant living in a wigwam on public property.

She'd much rather take care of this without getting a warrant. But she had to proceed carefully.

She told Tucker, "We think it may have been left here by whoever committed the two murders."

Tucker's eyes widened.

Then Riley said, "We need to take this timer with us. It could be important evidence."

Tucker shook his head slowly.

He said, "You're forgetting the law of the beach."

"What's that?" Riley said.

"'Finders keepers.' Besides, if this really is a gift from the gods, I'd better not part with it. I don't want to violate the will of the cosmos."

Riley studied his expression. She could tell that he wasn't crazy or delusional—although he might sometimes act like it. That was just part of the show.

No, this particular vagrant knew exactly what he was doing and saying.

He's doing business, Riley thought.

Riley opened her wallet, took out a twenty-dollar bill, and offered it to him.

She said, "Maybe this will help sort things out with the cosmos."

Tucker grinned ever so slightly.

"I don't know," he said. "The universe is getting pretty pricy these days."

Riley felt like she was getting the hang of the man's game, and also how she could play along.

She said, "It's always expanding, huh?"

"Yeah, ever since the Big Bang," Tucker said. He rubbed his fingers together and added, "And I hear it's going through a new inflationary phase."

Riley couldn't help but admire the man's shrewdness—and his creativity. She figured she'd better settle a deal with him before the conversation got too deep for her to make any sense out of.

She took another twenty-dollar bill out of her wallet.

Tucker snatched both twenties out of her hand.

"It's yours," he said. "Take good care of it. I've got a feeling there's something really powerful about that thing."

Riley found herself thinking that he was right about that— probably more right than he could know.

With a grin, Rags Tucker added, "I think you can handle it."

Bill put on his gloves again and approached the timer to pick it up.

Riley told him, "Be careful, keep it as steady as you can. We don't want to interfere with how fast it's running."

As Bill picked up the timer, Riley said to Tucker, "Thanks for your help. We might come back to ask more questions. I hope you'll be available."

Tucker shrugged and said, "I'll be here."

As they turned to go, Chief Belt asked Riley, "How much time do you think is left before all the sand runs into the bottom?"

Riley remembered that the ME had said both murders had taken place around six o'clock in the morning. Riley looked at her watch. It was now nearly eleven. She did a little math in her head.

Riley said to Belt, "The sand will run out in about nineteen hours."

"What happens then?" Belt asked.

"Somebody dies," Riley said.

CHAPTER NINE

Riley couldn't get Rags Tucker's words out of her mind.

"There's a feeling of inevitability about it."

She and her colleagues were making their way back along the beach toward the crime scene. Bill was carrying the sand timer, and Jenn and Chief Belt flanked him to help him keep the timer steady. They were trying to avoid affecting the flow of sand in the timer. And of course that falling sand was what Rags had been talking about.

Inevitability.

Even as she shuddered at the thought, she realized that was exactly the effect the killer had in mind.

He wanted them to feel a tightening knot of inevitability about his upcoming murder.

It was his way of psyching them out.

Riley knew that they mustn't let themselves get too rattled, but she worried that it wasn't going to be easy.

As she trudged through the sand, she took out her cell phone and called Brent Meredith.

When he answered, she said, "Sir, we've got a serious situation on her hands."

"What is it?" Meredith asked.

"Our killer is going to strike every twenty-four hours."

"Jesus," Meredith said. "How do you know?"

Riley was on the verge of explaining everything to him, but thought better of it. It would be better if he could actually see both of the timers.

"We're on our way back to the SUV," Riley said. "As soon as we're there, I'll call you for a video conference."

Riley ended the call just as they got back to the crime scene. Belt's cops were still scrounging through the marsh grass searching for clues. The cops' mouths dropped open at the sight of Bill carrying the enormous timer.

"What the hell's that?" one of the cops asked.

"Evidence," Belt said.

It occurred to Riley that the last thing they wanted right now was for reporters to get a look at the timer. If that happened, rumors would really start flying, making the situation worse than it already was. And there would surely be reporters still lurking in the parking area. They already knew that two people had been buried alive. They weren't going to give up on that story.

She turned to Chief Belt and asked, "Could I borrow your jacket?"

Belt took off his jacket and handed it to her. Riley carefully draped it over the sand timer, covering it completely.

"Come on," Riley said to Bill and Jenn. "Let's try to get this to our vehicle without attracting too much attention."

However, when she and her two colleagues stepped outside the tape barrier, Riley saw that more reporters had arrived. They crowded around Bill, demanding to know what he was carrying.

Riley felt a jolt of alarm as they pressed against Bill, who was trying to keep the sand timer as steady as he could. The jostling alone might be enough to interfere with the sand flow. Worse still, someone might knock the timer out of Bill's hands.

She said to Jenn, "We've got to keep them clear of Bill."

She and Jenn pushed their way into the group, ordering them to back away.

The reporters obeyed surprisingly easily and stood around gawking.

Riley quickly realized …

They probably think this is a bomb.

After all, that possibility had occurred to her and her colleagues back in the woods when Bill had uncovered the first sand timer.

Riley cringed at the thought of the headlines that might soon appear, and the panic that might follow.

She said sharply to the reporters, "It's not an explosive device. It's just evidence. And it's delicate."

She was answered by a renewed chorus of voices asking what it was.

Riley shook her head and turned away from them. Bill had made his way to the SUV, so she and Jenn hurried to catch up with him. They got inside and carefully secured the new sand timer next to the other one, which was strapped in place and covered with a blanket.

The reporters quickly regrouped and surrounded the van, yelling questions again.

Riley let out a groan of frustration. They'd never get anything done with prying people all around them.

Riley got behind the wheel and slowly began to drive. An especially determined reporter tried to block her way, standing directly in front of the vehicle. She let out a blast of the vehicle's siren, sending the startled guy scurrying off. Then she drove the SUV away, leaving the gaggle of reporters behind.

After driving about half a mile, Riley found a fairly secluded place where she could park the vehicle.

Then she told Jenn and Bill, "First things first. We need to dust the sand timers for fingerprints right away."

Bill nodded and said, "There's a kit in the glove compartment."

As Jenn and Bill started to work, Riley got out her computer tablet and made a video call to Brent Meredith.

To her surprise, Meredith's wasn't the only face that appeared on her screen. There were eight other faces, including a babyish, freckle-faced visage that Riley was anything but happy to see.

It was Special Agent in Charge Carl Walder, Meredith's superior at the BAU.

Riley suppressed a groan of discouragement. She'd been at odds with Carl Walder many times. In fact, he'd suspended and even fired her on several occasions.

But why was he in on this call?

With a barely disguised growl, Meredith said, "Agent Paige, Chief Walder has been kind enough to join us for this conversation. And he's put together a team to help us on this case."

When Riley saw the annoyed expression on Meredith's face, she understood the situation perfectly.

Carl Walder had been monitoring the case all morning. As soon as he found out that Riley had asked for a videoconference with Meredith, he'd summoned his own group of agents to join in. Right now they were all sitting in their separate offices and cubicles at the BAU with their computers set up for conferencing.

Riley couldn't help but scowl. Poor Brent Meredith must have felt like he'd been ambushed. Riley was sure that Walder was grandstanding, as usual. And by bringing in a team of his own, he was brazenly signaling his lack of confidence in Riley's professionalism.

Fortunately, some of the people Walder had brought in were people she'd worked with and trusted. She saw Sam Flores, a nerdish and brilliant lab technician, and Craig Huang, a promising young field agent she'd helped mentor.

Even so, the last thing she needed right now was a team of people to manage and organize. She knew she'd function best working with just Bill and Jenn.

Looking quite pleased with himself, Carl Walder spoke.

"I hear you've got some information for us, Agent Paige. Encouraging news, I hope."

Riley swallowed her anger. She was sure he already knew otherwise.

"I'm afraid not, sir," she said.

She held her tablet so the group could see the sand timers that Bill and Jenn were deftly dusting for prints.

Riley said, "As you can see, Agents Jeffreys and Roston are here working with me. We found a sand timer at each of the two murder scenes. The one that's empty was hidden near the first body. We found the one that's still running not far away from where the second victim was buried. We estimate that it's going to run out at about six o'clock tomorrow morning."

Riley could hear audible gasps and saw the shock on all the faces on the screen—except for Walder's.

"What do you think it means?" Walder asked blandly.

Riley managed not to sneer with contempt. Walder was obviously the only person in the group who hadn't figured it out instantly.

Riley said, "It means, sir, that someone else is going to die when the glass runs out. And whoever it is will be buried alive, just like the first two victims."

Walder's eyes widened.

"That can't happen," he said. "I order you not to let it happen."

Riley's exasperation was rising. As usual, Walder was giving perfectly pointless orders—as if anybody here needed to be told that a third murder had to be prevented.

Walder turned his own computer to display the clock on his office wall.

He said, "It's now one o'clock. We're not going to let the clock run out. And we're not giving the media enough time to cause a panic. They're already moving on this story. I expect you to apprehend the killer before six o'clock tonight. And now I'll leave you to your work."

Carl Walder abruptly disappeared from the screen. Riley could see relief on all the other faces. She also knew that they were thinking exactly what she was thinking. Walder had made just

49

enough of an appearance to throw his weight around and seem to be in charge. Taking any real leadership responsibility wasn't his style.

And what about his six o'clock deadline?

Well, obviously, he wanted the case wrapped up before he went home to dinner. That way he could take full credit for solving it without a lot of trouble for himself.

Anyway, now they could get down to business.

Riley asked, "First of all, are there any questions?"

"What have you got in the way of a profile on the killer?" Craig Huang asked.

"Not much just yet," Riley said. "I've got a gut-level feeling about him. I suspect that he's personally quite charming, and that people might actually trust him when they first meet him."

Riley turned to Bill and Jenn, who were still dusting the timer and listening to the conversation.

"Do either of you have anything to add?" Riley asked them.

Jenn said, "The killer must be physically robust."

"That's right," Bill said. "These killings involved a lot of digging and carrying, and one of the victims was physically assaulted. He might not be especially big, but he's in pretty good shape."

Sam Flores, the technician, spoke up.

"I see that Agents Jeffreys and Roston are dusting for prints. Any luck with that yet?"

Bill and Jenn had almost finished dusting the first timer.

"None at all," Bill said. "It looks like the killer wiped it down carefully before leaving it."

Riley felt a flash of discouragement. If the killer had taken such care with the first timer, he'd surely done the same with the second. The only prints they'd find on it would be Rags Tucker's.

Sam said, "Could you give me a better look at the timers?"

Riley moved the tablet all around the timers so Sam could look at them more carefully.

Sam said, "Those are some pretty distinctive markings. Both timers are carved in the same style, but there are some interesting variations. Do you think they might be some kind of code?"

"That's a good thought," Riley said. "We'll take close-ups and send them to you. You can do some research, see if the marks mean anything. But I want you to do something before that, while the rest of us are talking. See if you can locate any hourglass makers in this general area."

"I'll do that," Sam said.

She could hear his fingers clicking on his keyboard.

Riley thought hard and fast, trying to decide how to deal with the others.

She said, "Agent Engel, I want you to get in touch with Parker Belt, the chief of police in Sattler. Get as much information as you can about the victims and their families, also the people who discovered the bodies. Share whatever you find out with the others here."

All the people on the screen were dutifully taking notes now.

Riley continued, "Agent Whittington, pay a visit to the first victim's family. Agent Craft, do the same with the second victim's family. Agent Geraty, see if you can interview the people who found the bodies. Agent Ridge, get in touch with the district ME and see if he's got any new information about how the victims died."

She thought for a moment.

Then she said, "Agent Huang, you're the point man for the team. Stay in touch with everybody and keep track of their progress. Also see what you can do about handling the media. This whole thing is liable to get out of control if we're not careful."

Huang asked, "Shouldn't we close off the whole park to visitors, especially around the time in question?"

"Good idea," Riley said. "Call Chief Belt and get that underway. Also help him send out a general warning to the community."

Riley breathed a little easier now that she'd assigned jobs to everybody.

Meanwhile, Sam Flores had finished his search.

He said, "I've found an hourglass maker with a workshop near Colonial Williamsburg. His name is Ellery Kuhl. I'll email you the address."

"Good work," Riley said. "Flores, I also need you to search for any similar murders that have been committed anywhere else recently—live burials, I mean. Now get started, everybody. The clock is running out. Literally."

She ended the meeting and said to Bill and Jenn, "Stop dusting for prints and take lots of detailed pictures and send them to Sam Flores. I'll drive us to Colonial Williamsburg."

As she started to drive, she remembered something else that Rags Tucker had said.

"You can't turn back time, as they say."

She glanced at her watch and saw that the meeting had taken about a half hour.

She hoped it hadn't been a waste of time. It was thirty minutes they weren't going to get back.

And it could mean the difference between life and death.

CHAPTER TEN

Riley could feel her anxiety rising as she drove toward Williamsburg. During the hour-long trip, she found herself obsessing about every passing second.

It was still early afternoon on the very first day of this investigation. Although she always worked as fast as she could to stop a killer, the pressure of time had never before been so relentless.

Maybe, she kept reminding herself, this killer would be thwarted by the actions they'd taken so far. Soon the entire Belle Terre property would be closed. Soon the public around Sattler would be warned that a killer was at large.

Wouldn't that be enough to slow a killer down, at least for the time being?

Perhaps, but Riley knew better than to count on it. And in a way, the uncertainty only added to her anxiety.

The worst of it was, she couldn't do anything except drive right now. She felt a desperate need to be actively engaged with the case—searching for clues, interviewing suspects and witnesses, anything that might actually contribute to stopping to these murders. Driving felt strangely, unnervingly futile.

But she'd assigned those usual tasks to other agents back at the BAU. They would be on their way to carry out those on-scene investigations even as she drove her team away from the scene.

Fortunately, Bill and Jenn were able to keep working while she drove. They took detailed pictures of the hourglasses and sent them on to Sam Flores to analyze, then communicated with the rest of the team to keep track of how things were going.

Everybody was doing everything they possibly could.

Still, Riley's anxiety continued to mount.

For one thing, she wondered whether this trip to Colonial Williamsburg was anything more than a detour—perhaps even a fatal waste of time. What did she expect to find out, anyway?

She hadn't called ahead to tell the hourglass maker that they were coming. She didn't want to give him advance warning.

But did she seriously think he might be the murderer?

That would be awfully convenient, she thought. But it was the only thing resembling a lead they had, at least for the moment.

Her thoughts were interrupted by the sound of Bill's voice. He had moved up from the back of the SUV into the seat next to Riley. He was staring at his cell phone.

"Damn," he said.

"What's the matter?" Riley asked.

"I just checked the news," Bill said. "Word has gotten out about the sand timers found at the murder scenes. The public knows."

Riley's heart sank. This was just about the last thing she wanted to hear.

Jenn said, "How could that have happened?"

"One of two ways," Riley said. "Either one of the local cops told a reporter, or a reporter got it out of Rags Tucker."

Bill said, "It doesn't really matter which way it happened. What matters is that we've got a bigger mess on our hands than we did before."

Riley silently agreed. She also couldn't help blaming herself. She shouldn't have taken it for granted that Chief Belt's cops would have the sense to keep quiet. She should have laid down the law while she was still at the beach, told them all to keep their mouths shut. Maybe she should have done something to keep Rags Tucker quiet.

She tried to drive such thoughts from her mind. Self-blame would only distract her from the task at hand.

As she drove into the city of Williamsburg, Riley followed GPS directions to the address that Sam Flores had given her. She knew that the famous Colonial Williamsburg Historic District was surrounded by more ordinary business and residential areas. The address they were looking for turned out to be a small storefront with a sign that said "Sands of Time."

Riley parked the car on the street, and she, Bill, and Jenn walked toward the shop. The window was full of elaborate and beautiful hourglasses of various sizes, although Riley didn't notice any as large as the ones they'd found at the murder scenes.

A little bell rang as they stepped into the shop. In addition to various hourglasses on display, the space was cluttered with carpentry tools and equipment. The floor was untidily littered with wood shavings and sawdust. No one came at the sound of the bell, which was somewhat muffled by the sound of a machine running.

Riley saw that a small woman wearing coveralls and goggles was working at a lathe at the back of the room. She looked like she was ten years or so older than Riley—perhaps in her mid-fifties.

After a moment, the woman glanced up and noticed her visitors. She turned off the lathe and lifted her goggles.

"Oh, I'm sorry," she said in a pleasant voice. "I didn't hear you come in. Can I help you with something?"

Riley produced her badge and introduced herself and her colleagues.

Then she said, "We're looking for the owner of this business—Ellery Kuhl."

The woman smiled.

"That would be me," she said.

Riley was slightly startled, but realized that she shouldn't be. Why hadn't it occurred to her that Ellery might be a woman's name? If she'd known that simple fact, would she have brought her partners all the way here?

What was the likelihood that the killer was a woman?

It's not impossible, she reminded herself.

After all, the last killer she and Jenn had brought to justice had been a woman.

Still, this woman was much smaller than she'd expected the killer to be. She didn't look frail by any means. Riley knew that she had to be in reasonably good shape to do the kind of work she did. Even so, Riley found it hard to imagine her carrying out the arduous tasks involved in the two murders.

Ellery Kuhl got up from her chair and walked toward them, her smile fading into a look of concern.

She said, "But something must be wrong to bring the FBI to my door. What is it?"

Riley said, "There have been two murders at the Belle Terre Nature Preserve. One early this morning, the other early yesterday morning. Both victims were buried alive."

The woman's eyes widened.

"Oh, my!" she said.

Riley studied her reactions. Her shock seemed perfectly sincere. But Riley knew from hard experience that psychopaths were brilliant at faking sincerity.

Riley decided to challenge her directly.

"Ms. Kuhl, could you tell us your whereabouts at around six o'clock on the two mornings in question?"

The woman staggered slightly with alarm.

"I don't understand," she said. "Am I … a suspect? Why on earth would you think …?"

Riley said, "Two enormous sand timers were found at each scene—twenty-four-hour timers. One of them was running when we found it. We expect the killer to strike again when it runs out."

The woman was squinting as if trying to understand Riley's words.

"And because I make sand timers, you think that maybe I …?"

The woman's voice was shaking now.

"I was upstairs in my apartment asleep. I don't know how I can prove it, though. I live alone. I've never been to Belle Terre. I seldom go anywhere. I'm actually a bit agoraphobic. I pretty much stay right here in my shop. I even get groceries delivered to me. I don't even have a car."

Riley kept holding the woman's uneasy gaze. She reminded herself yet again that time was of the essence.

She had to make up her mind about this woman quickly.

In her mind, she imagined what Ellery Kuhl's neighbors might say about her if Riley and her partners only had time to interview them.

She had a pretty strong gut feeling that they'd describe the woman as kindly and reclusive, someone whose entire life was centered right here in her store. She probably seldom talked to other people except here.

Nevertheless, Riley knew that serial killers sometimes impressed their neighbors as perfectly gentle, harmless people.

Riley said, "Ms. Kuhl, I wonder if you'd come outside and have a look at something."

"Of course," the woman said.

Riley, Bill, and Jenn took her to the SUV and opened the back, revealing the two enormous sand glasses inside.

A look of delighted surprise crossed the woman's face. She climbed into the SUV to get a closer look.

"Oh, these are impressive," she said. "Very impressive indeed."

She took a small magnifying glass out of her pocket and began to examine the objects in detail.

Any lingering doubts Riley may have had about the woman's innocence pretty much disappeared. She felt sure that even the most hardened psychopath couldn't fake the pleasure the woman was exhibiting at the sight of these sand timers.

Riley said, "These aren't your work, I take it."

"No, but I wouldn't mind taking credit for it. This is very good work. They're twenty-four-hour timers, you said?"

Jenn said, "Can't you tell by looking at them?"

Riley detected a lingering note of suspicion in Jenn's voice. Perhaps Bill, too, wasn't yet convinced of Ellery's innocence. But Riley was quite sure of it now.

Ellery said, "Well, I'm willing to take your word for it. It's not an exact science, you know. There's no formula for the amount of sand needed to measure a certain amount of time. When you make one of these, you just have to keep trying different amounts until you get it right and seal it up."

Ellery chuckled a little and added, "Imagine how hard that must have been before clocks were invented!"

For a fleeting moment, Riley felt disappointed that they hadn't found their killer. But that feeling quickly passed. Perhaps this woman could help in other ways.

"What can you tell us about these timers?" Riley asked.

"Well, for one thing, the frames are made from excellent wood. The empty one looks like black walnut. The one that's still running is probably mahogany. And they're expertly carved."

"What about the glass?" Riley said.

Ellery sat back from the timers a little.

"Well, I'm hardly an expert on that. I only make the frames, like most other people who make timers like these. I order the glass bulbs I use from China. There's really nothing very special about the glass. It's the same you might use to make vases and pitchers and such."

She leaned toward the timer again and peered at it.

"This sand, though—it is rather unusual."

"How so?" Riley asked.

Ellery was examining the sand with her magnifying glass.

"Well, because it's actually *sand*. Most people use other materials—marble dust, tin or lead oxides, rock flour, pulverized burnt eggshell, powdered glass. Materials with better flowing properties. When sand gets used at all, it's usually river sand, because of its smooth, round granules. This looks like regular quartz sand—the kind you'd find on a beach. That's unusual, because the granules are angular and don't flow as smoothly."

Bill asked, "Does that mean these two timers don't keep good time?"

"No, I wouldn't say that—not at all. Whoever made these timers sifted the sand very carefully, removed any larger grains so that the rest are uniform. Anyone who went to that kind of trouble probably tested these over and over again to make sure they kept perfect time."

Ellery paused and scratched her chin.

"It's not unheard of to use regular sand. Sometimes people use sand from specific areas for sentimental reasons."

She shrugged. "Maybe the sand had some kind of significance for the maker. I really don't know."

She began to peer closely at the timers again.

"It's the woodworking that really impresses me, though—the decorative knobs and grass-like fronds on the spindles, the wavy ridges on the tops and bottoms. So distinctive, such excellent craftsmanship."

Bill asked, "Do you have any idea who might have made these?"

The woman chuckled again.

"Someone who works and lives in this area, you mean? How many sand-timer makers do you think there are around here? And yet …"

She fingered the wood admiringly.

"This woodwork *is* so remarkable. And it does remind me …"

A dark look crossed her face.

She shuddered deeply.

She said, "I think I know someone you should talk to."

CHAPTER ELEVEN

Riley was struck by the woman's expression of extreme distaste—and perhaps of something worse.

Still stroking the woodwork, Ellery said, "This *could* be the work of Otis Redlich. He also lives and works in Williamsburg. Pretty close to here, in fact."

Riley watched the woman's reaction as she said, "I take it you don't like him very much."

Ellery shuddered again. She spoke in a distinctly gloomy tone.

"I used to like him. We were once good friends. Rivals, but friends. He's a woodworker too, you see. Specializes in furniture restorations. He also makes sand timers."

Ellery fell silent for a moment.

"He was a good man, back while his wife was still alive. Charming, funny, intelligent, a wonderful conversationalist. As you can see, I don't get out much, don't socialize. But I did like to spend time with Otis and Peyton, his wife. We'd get together for dinner from time to time. But Peyton died of ovarian cancer about ten years ago and …"

Ellery shook her head slowly.

"Otis changed. Completely changed. He got bitter … and mean."

Ellery shivered deeply. Riley sensed she was remembering some personal wrong he'd done to her.

She asked, "Did something happen between you?"

Ellery seemed to be trying to shake off a memory.

"Nothing I'd rather talk about," she said. "It wasn't anything important, just petty—and hurtful. That's the way he got—hurtful and manipulative."

"And violent?" Riley asked.

Ellery squinted in thought.

"No—at least not that I was aware of. The truth is, maybe I shouldn't … Well, I hate to speak ill of people, but …"

Riley was tingling all over with keen interest.

"I'd like for you to give me his address," she said.

A few moments later, Riley was driving Bill and Jenn across Williamsburg toward Otis Redlich's house.

Jenn asked Riley and Bill, "Do we have any reason to think this could be our guy?"

"I don't know," Bill said. "A lot of this job is about chasing bad leads to dead ends, but we have to do it. What do you think, Riley?"

Riley didn't reply. But she kept flashing back to Ellery's expression when she'd been talking about Otis Redlich.

She also kept thinking about how Ellery had described how he'd been before his wife's death.

"Charming, funny, intelligent, a wonderful conversationalist."

Riley remembered her own impressions back at the two crime scenes—her sense that the killer had been charming and likeable.

She also remembered words Ellery had used to Otis Redlich after he'd changed.

"... bitter ... mean ... petty ... hurtful ... manipulative ..."

Riley couldn't be sure, but it was starting to seem likely.

Or was that only wishful thinking? But of course Bill was right. They had to follow all their leads.

Riley couldn't see the sand timers from the driver's seat. But she could see them clearly in her mind—especially the one that was running now, its fine trickle of sand continuing to flow, with every granule marking the possible difference between life and death.

As she drove through town, she passed a pair of women walking along in wide, full-length skirts and fancy hats. No doubt they were workers in costume for their jobs in the restored colonial area. At least there, Riley thought, they could create an appearance of time turned back. She and her companions didn't even have the luxury of that illusion.

When they arrived at the address Ellery Kuhl had given them, it was quite unlike the little storefront they'd just visited. It was a two-story brick house with decorative shutters beside each window in the classic Williamsburg style. It was a well-kept property in a reasonably prosperous residential area. It appeared that Otis Redlich was markedly better off than Ellery Kuhl.

Riley parked the car, and she and her colleagues walked up to the front door and rang the doorbell. The man who answered was tall and imposing, with big arms and a jutting chin. He carried himself in a rather stiffly dignified manner, and he looked like he was in his fifties.

"Can I help you?" he asked.

"Are you Otis Redlich?" Riley asked.

His thin lips twisted slightly at Riley's question.

"I am. I wasn't expecting customers. I'm sure you must know that I do business by appointment only."

Riley produced her badge and introduced herself and her colleagues.

The man's mouth broadened into a smile.

"The FBI!" he said. "What a pleasant surprise! Do come in!"

Riley was taken a bit aback. She couldn't remember ever paying an unexpected official visit to anyone who'd actually been happy to see her. But on her last case, a pair of killers had feigned delight that the FBI was there. This man's enthusiasm made her suspicious.

Riley glanced at Bill and Jenn and could see that they felt the same way.

They followed the man into a living room decorated with elegant furniture.

Otis Redlich proudly fingered the fine dark woodwork on a settee.

"This is an original Chippendale. The demilune table over there is a genuine Sheraton. The mahogany desk is Victorian. Everything here is museum-quality, I assure you—although I do make reproductions. Very good ones, if you happen to be so interested. Indistinguishable from the real thing to the untrained eye. But of course, I don't suppose you've come here for that kind of thing."

Riley's eye was caught by a sand timer sitting on the fireplace mantel. Although it was much smaller than the ones they'd found at the murder scenes, it looked somewhat similar.

Redlich said, "Oh, I see you're interested in my hourglass. No, that's not an antique, it's my original creation. I quite like hourglasses. I make them as sort of a hobby. Would you care to look at my workshop?"

Without waiting for an answer, Redlich exited through a door in the back of the room. Riley and her colleagues followed him through a hallway and into a workshop filled with benches, tools, and pieces of furniture in different states of restoration or construction. On one shelf was a row of sand timers of various sizes. Several glass globes were lined up on another shelf, ready to be put into wooden frameworks. Here and there, tiny glints of light sparkled on the smooth surfaces.

Unlike Ellery Kuhl's workshop, this one was almost painfully neat and clean—as was Redlich himself. If it weren't for his large, calloused hands, Riley would find it hard to believe that he ever did any carpentry here or anywhere else. The man struck Riley as weirdly obsessive.

Redlich said, "Now—how can I help you?"

Riley said, "Mr. Redlich, could you tell us where you were at around six o'clock this morning and yesterday morning?"

The man's smile twisted into a slight sneer.

"Around the times of the murders, you mean?" he asked. "The ones down at Belle Terre?"

Riley felt a jolt of surprise.

How does he know that's why we're here? she wondered.

CHAPTER TWELVE

Redlich's words left Riley speechless. This man was a step ahead of them.

But if Otis Redlich noticed her surprise, he gave no sign of it. He just kept talking.

"That *is* what you're here about, isn't it?" he said. "After all, weren't sand timers found at both of the murder scenes? And how many craftspeople in this vicinity are known to make timers of that sort? Oh, there's Ellery Kuhl, of course, but I'm sure you've already eliminated her as a suspect. A harmless little woman, obviously."

Redlich let out a growl-like chuckle.

"Now where *was* I during the times in question? Well, I could tell you that I was here at home in bed. But would you believe me? I can't prove it."

Riley's brain clicked away as she tried to figure out what was going on. Redlich could easily have found out about the murders from the media—the hourglasses too. But he seemed determined to ask the questions as well as give the answers. She knew that guilty people sometimes behaved this way when they felt overconfident.

This man was obviously very self-confident. But was he guilty?

And what the hell did he think he was doing?

Without any change in his condescending smile, Redlich sat down on the only available seat in the room, leaving Riley and her colleagues awkwardly standing.

He said, "Tell me—in your line of work, is this sort of crime common? A murderer obsessed with time, I mean? I would think that it does happen now and again. After all, the obsession with time is as old as human thought."

Riley had to bite her tongue. In fact, she and Bill had dealt with such a killer just last October—the so-called Clock Killer in Delaware, who had posed the arms of his dead victims to signify times on a clock.

Did Redlich know about that?

Surely not. He was just enjoying lecturing his audience. And he probably realized that he was successfully pushing Riley's buttons.

Apparently Bill was finding the man annoying too. He said sharply, "I think you'd better answer Agent Paige's question."

Redlich raised his eyebrows.

"Didn't I answer it already? I thought I did. Yes, I'm quite sure I did. I was here at home in bed. It's a fact."

He crossed his arms and looked smugly at Riley and her colleagues.

He added, "So you'd better run along, shouldn't you? Time is of the essence, after all. Literally running out, like sand through your fingers."

Riley glanced at Jenn. She saw that the younger agent didn't look at all disturbed by the man's torrent of words. She seemed to be listening with great interest.

Ignoring Bill's demand, Redlich leaned back and stared at the ceiling.

He said, "There must have been a magical moment in history—I wish I could have been there—when someone first became aware that they lived *in time.* That there was a past behind them that they might or might not remember, and a future ahead that they couldn't predict."

He pointed at the sand timers on the shelf.

"In fact, you could say that humankind has been at *war* with time all along, trying to conquer it with one invention after another—sundials, candle clocks, oil lamp clocks, water clocks—*clepsydra,* I believe those are called. And now we have atomic clocks of extraordinary accuracy. But even so, time always wins the battle. No clock can tell us what's going to happen tomorrow, or an hour from now, or a minute …"

He leaned forward and whispered …

"Or a second! We're helpless against the future. It's a lost cause. But there's something heroic about lost causes, isn't there? And beautifully tragic."

Riley recognized the anger behind the man's words. His cool determination to control the situation was built on an underlying fury with the world.

She could feel her own temper rising. He could easily bait her into physical action, but she was determined not to let that happen.

She realized that Redlich probably hadn't always been like this. As Ellery Kuhl had told her—he had changed for the worst after his wife had died.

But had his anger turned him into a murderer?

Riley glanced at her watch. She almost shuddered to see how many precious minutes they'd spent here already. If Otis Redlich wasn't the murderer, they were already overdue to eliminate him.

Whatever was going on, Riley couldn't let him get the best of her. And if he wanted to play games, she could play them too.

She took out her cell phone and brought up photos of the two sand timers.

She said, "Tell me, Mr. Redlich—what do you think of these two timers?"

Redlich peered closely at the photos.

He said, "In terms of craftsmanship, you mean? Quite good, I would say. Not unlike my own work. You'll notice some of the same sorts of patterns on my sand timers—similar images based on plant life."

He squinted at the photos.

"Of course, if the maker was trying to make the two timers identical—well, that's another story. In that case, I'd consider it quite sloppy. When I choose to make matching pieces, they're utterly indistinguishable. If that's what this craftsman intended, he failed."

Riley knew she had to make her next tactic do the trick.

She pointed to the images on her cell phone.

She said, "What impresses me is the *delicacy* of the detail. It's hard for me to imagine the person who made these doing anything ungraceful and vulgar—much less brutal and cruel. For example, breaking all the limbs of his victims before burying them alive—forearms, upper arms, shins, thighs. It strikes me as—inconsistent."

"Yes," Redlich said. "That does seem rather jarring."

Riley saw no change in his expression at these phony, made-up details—none at all.

And that told her everything she needed to know.

He knew nothing of the murders except what he'd picked up from the media.

Again she felt a knot of anger rising up in her throat. Since they'd arrived, he'd been giving them a performance for his own sick entertainment.

She could hardly believe he'd manipulated her for even this long. She should have seen through him from the very moment she'd set eyes on him. After all, he hardly fit her own instinctive profile of the killer.

This reptilian man could never have charmed his victims into trusting him.

She said, "I don't like being taken for a fool, Mr. Redlich. And I don't like the way you've wasted our time."

Redlich's face twisted into an expression of counterfeit hurt.

"I'm sure I don't know what you mean, Agent Paige."

"Oh, I'm sure you do," Riley said, her voice shaking a little with anger. "You also know that another life is at stake if we don't find the killer on time. You really get off on this, don't you?"

Redlich shrugged.

"I regret any misunderstanding," he said. "I thought we were having a rather pleasant conversation. In fact, I—"

Riley didn't wait for him to finish his sentence. She stormed back through the house with Bill and Jenn right behind her. When they got outside, Riley was practically hyperventilating with anger and frustration.

Bill said, "He played us. He played us all along."

"He sure did," Riley said. "And here we are, wasting our time in Williamsburg. What kind of sick bastard gets his kicks playing with life and death like that? I wish to hell we could bring him in for obstruction of justice."

"Fat chance of that," Bill said. "How could we prove it? It would just be our word against his."

They had just gotten back to the SUV. Jenn was smiling now.

"I wouldn't be so sure of that," Jenn said.

Riley's spirits quickened. She remembered how Jenn had seemed during the interview—as if she knew something that nobody else did.

"What do you mean?" Riley asked.

Jenn reached into her pocket and took out a pocket recorder.

She pushed a button, and Riley could hear Redlich's voice loud and clear …

"Time is of the essence, after all. Literally running out, like sand through your fingers."

"Damn!" Bill said. "That's pretty good evidence! Let's go back and arrest him."

Riley shook her head.

"We don't have time. Not right now. He's not the one we're looking for."

"Okay," Bill muttered. "But let's nail him when this whole thing's over."

Riley said, "Jenn, please send me that recording for future

66

reference."

"I'll do that," Jenn said.

As she and her colleagues got into the car, she couldn't help remembering something Redlich had said.

"Time always wins the battle."

As she started the car, she hoped to hell that Redlich was wrong about that.

CHAPTER THIRTEEN

As they all got back into the SUV, Riley looked at her watch again.

She felt a flash of despair as she saw that it was after three o'clock.

She couldn't help doing the math in her head.

There were less than fifteen hours left before this killer would most likely strike again.

And they were getting nowhere toward catching him. They'd just been wasting precious time.

It had taken an hour to drive here from Belle Terre, and they'd lost almost two more hours interviewing two irrelevant people in Williamsburg.

It would take another hour to drive back to Belle Terre.

But should they drive back to Belle Terre? Was there anything for them to do there that nobody else was already doing?

The truth was, Riley had no idea what to do now.

From the passenger seat, Bill asked, "Are you OK, Riley?"

Riley saw that he was watching her with an expression of concern.

Do I look that bad? she wondered.

"I'm just stymied," she said. "Don't know where to go next. I'm open to ideas."

"I think we should get something to eat," Bill said.

Riley stared at him with surprise.

Bill shrugged and said, "You're acting like it's some kind of crazy idea."

"Well, it kind of is," Riley said. "We're running out of time."

Bill said, "Which is why we've got to keep ourselves sharp. I haven't had anything since breakfast. Have you eaten anything at all today?"

Riley didn't reply. But she remembered how she'd rushed out of her house that morning with a bagel in her hand after taking a few sips of coffee. That had been many hours ago. She was hungry and groggy. Bill was right. She wouldn't be able to do her best work if she tried to keep on this way.

"Food would be OK with me," Jenn chimed in from the back seat.

With a sigh, Riley started the car and followed a main road until she found a fast food place. As they all went inside, she said, "I need to check in with Huang and find out what's going on there."

Leaving the others to wait for her burger and coffee, she found a booth and got out her phone. She knew that Craig Huang was now at the Sattler police station running the activities of the BAU team.

When Huang answered, he asked Riley whether she and her colleagues were having any luck in Williamsburg.

Riley sighed.

"We've hit not one but two dead ends," she said. "Please tell me you've got some good news."

Riley heard Huang clear his throat. Right away she sensed that the answer to her question was no.

Huang said, "Agent Ridge talked to the medical examiner, who is now positive that both victims died from asphyxiation from being buried alive."

Riley drummed her fingers on the table.

"That's hardly news," she said. "What else?"

"Agent Geraty is still out talking to the people who found the bodies. Agent Whittington interviewed Courtney Wallace's family, and also her boyfriend. Agent Craft interviewed Todd Brier's folks. They're both back, and I'm going over their reports. But it doesn't look like they found out much."

While she listened to Huang, Bill and Jenn arrived with the tray of food. When they passed her burger over to her, Riley realized that she was hungry after all. And even this coffee smelled good.

Bill and Jenn sat on the other side of the booth. Riley noticed that they seemed to be discussing pictures on Jenn's cell phone. She was pleased to see them working together.

Riley asked Huang, "Any connection between the two victims?"

"None that we've been able to find. Todd Brier was a pastor at Redeemer Lutheran Church in Sattler. But it doesn't sound like Courtney Wallace was the church-going type. She worked as an office manager for a local accounting firm, but Brier used a different accountant. If they knew each other through any other venue, we still don't know about it."

Riley swallowed down a groan of discouragement.

She said, "Keep at it, Agent Huang. You and your whole

team."

"We'll do that," Huang said.

"You'd better," Riley said. "The clock is running."

Riley ended the phone call and unwrapped her burger. She took a big bite and then sipped some coffee. Bill and Jenn were both still looking something at on the cell phone.

She asked. "Have you found something?"

"Maybe nothing," Jenn said.

"Or maybe something," Bill added. He pushed Jenn's cell phone across the table toward Riley. The photos on the cell phone were the close-ups they'd taken of the tops of the sand timers. He pointed to the wavy lines carved into the woodwork.

Bill said, "Agent Roston remembered something that Otis Redlich said about the patterns."

Jenn nodded and added, "He talked about basing his own patterns on images of plant life. But these wavy lines don't look like plants to me. They look more like … well, have you ever noticed what sand looks like on a beach at low tide? It gets rippled just like that."

Riley looked at the image closely. She remembered how the beach at Belle Terre had looked when they were there discussing the body. Jenn was right, it had been rippled just like that.

"So what does it mean?" Riley asked.

Jenn shrugged and said, "Well, it's seeming more and more like our killer has some kind of obsession with sand. He used ordinary beach sand in the glasses, which Ellery Kuhl thought was unusual. She said he might have used it for 'sentimental reasons.' One of the victims was buried in sand and the other in very sandy soil."

Riley didn't know what to say.

In an ordinary case, this might seem like a small but important insight, and worth the time of following up on. But how would anybody follow up on the possibility of an interest in sand?

And time was exactly the thing they didn't have much of right now.

Riley said, "Jenn, I don't know …"

Jenn just nodded. Rather abruptly, she excused herself and headed for the restroom.

Riley sighed as she watched the younger agent walk away. Obviously Jenn had picked up on her lack of enthusiasm.

Riley said to Bill, "What do you think of her?"

"Agent Roston, you mean?" Bill asked.

"Well, she insists that I call her Jenn, and she now calls me Riley."

Bill's face twitched a little. Riley had the odd feeling that she'd just said the wrong thing.

Bill said, "She's smart, all right. It was a shrewd move, recording our conversation with Otis Redlich. She's also got a good eye for detail, as she proved just now. But …"

Bill's voice trailed off.

"But what?" Riley asked.

"Well, her focus seems to come and go. It's like she's got something else on her mind. Is she always like that?"

Riley shook her head.

"No," she said. "On our last case together, she stayed perfectly focused."

"Maybe it's just me," Bill said.

Riley didn't say anything in reply. But the truth was, she had been feeling the same way about Jenn today. She'd sometimes seem to drift away with a far-off look in her eye.

Riley remembered Jenn's rather odd visit to her office yesterday, when she'd stood in the doorway and said …

"Riley, I don't know whether I should tell you …"

But Jenn hadn't told Riley what was on her mind.

"It's nothing for you to worry about," she'd said, and left.

Now Riley was wondering—maybe it *was* something she should worry about.

In the short time since she'd known Jenn, she'd sensed that her new partner harbored some dark secrets. Most likely, those secrets were none of Riley's business.

But were they going to start adversely affecting Jenn's work?

Other things were starting to worry Riley as well.

She knew that Bill and Jenn had never worked together and barely knew each other. Although they didn't seem to dislike each other, they didn't seem to have hit it off especially well either.

Bill was pulling himself together now, doing better than he had for a while, and he was obviously eager to get back to work. It wouldn't be good if he and Jenn wound up at odds with each other.

On a case as urgent as this one was, a distraction like that would be a disaster.

As Bill sat quietly finishing his sandwich, Riley wondered if he might be feeling like a bit of a third wheel because she and Jenn already had a pretty good rapport.

What could Riley do to fix that?

After years of friendship, she'd long since learned that she could talk to him about anything.

Maybe I should just ask him how he feels about things, she thought.

But before she could think of what to say, Jenn came back from the restroom. She seemed to be fully engaged again.

As soon as she joined them, Jenn said, "I'm wondering whether it's a waste of time looking for connections between the victims. Isn't it possible that he chooses his victims purely at random? Have you ever known that to happen?"

Riley looked at Bill. She could tell that he was thinking of the same case she was.

Bill said, "Last November we took down a killer named Orin Rhodes. He was a real sadist—shot his victims again and again, making sure they were in tremendous pain before they died. But there wasn't any real rhyme or reason to how he picked his victims. He just killed whoever was handy."

Riley shuddered at the memory.

"You're forgetting something, Bill," she said. "Orin Rhodes *did* have a specific victim in mind. It was me. I was his ultimate target. He wanted revenge for my killing his girlfriend in a gunfight sixteen years earlier. His killings were meant to draw me out and make me suffer until he could kill me and my family."

Jenn looked at Riley sympathetically.

"I read about that case," she said. "That must have been hard for you."

Riley gulped hard as the horror of that case came back to her. Orin Rhodes had come perilously close to killing April and Riley's ex-husband, Ryan.

You've got no idea, she thought.

Then Jenn said, "Still, Orin Rhodes *did* also choose random victims. So it's not unheard of. Some overriding purpose or motive or obsession is what really matters to some kinds of killers. In fact, that's something serial killers all have in common, even when it *is* focused on specific types of victims."

"So our killer is obsessed with sand?" Bill asked.

"Definitely," Jenn replied. "But probably most of all with burying people alive."

Both Bill and Jenn looked at Riley expectantly.

Again, Riley didn't know what to say. It was a good insight, she couldn't deny that.

But how were they going to make use of it in the time they had left? How could they research records for anyone who had ever been traumatized by sand? Or who had reason to obsess about being buried alive? That kind of thing probably wouldn't even be in any records.

She wasn't concerned about making Walder's silly six p.m. deadline. But she was getting very worried about stopping the next early-morning murder.

Before Riley could think things through, her cell phone rang. Her heart jumped when she saw that the call was from Chief Belt.

When she answered, she put the call on speakerphone so that Bill and Jenn could listen in.

"What have you got?" she said.

"A real break, I hope," Belt said, sounding quite excited. "A local woman, Hope Reitman, just came into the station here in Sattler. She says she was jogging on that beach around the time of the murder. She hadn't thought she'd seen anything, which is why she hadn't contacted us earlier. In fact, she hadn't realized how close she'd been to the scene of the murder. She thought it had happened someplace else."

"And?" Riley asked.

"Well, when she went out for her run, she saw a man putting a big sand timer among Rags Tucker's stuff at about the time in question. She hadn't thought anything about it at the time. Lots of people bring odds and ends to Tucker's wigwam, including her. But when she heard on the news about how the killer had left sand timers at the murder sites, she came right here to tell us about it."

Riley felt a tingle of excitement.

"Where is she right now?" she asked.

"Right here in the station, working with a composite sketch artist. We should have a facial image to work with pretty soon."

Riley looked at Jenn and Bill and sensed that they shared her excitement.

She said to Chief Belt, "We're on our way back right now. We should be there in an hour."

As soon as Riley ended the call, she, Jenn, and Bill sprang to their feet and headed out to the SUV. None of them spoke, but Riley knew that they were all getting their hopes up.

How could they help it?

They were finally getting a break in this case.

CHAPTER FOURTEEN

There was a feeling of excitement in the stuffy air of the little conference room when Riley and her colleagues arrived. Chief Belt had called his own cops and other members of the FBI team together in the Sattler police station. The meeting was already in progress.

Chief Belt got up from his chair at the end of the table.

He said, "Agents Paige, Jeffreys, Roston—you got here just in time! I think we've got something."

Projected on a screen behind Belt was a composite sketch of a youngish man. Riley guessed it was the drawing that had been made from the eyewitness's description.

Chief Belt said to one of the cops sitting at the table, "Officer Goodner, bring the agents up to speed on what you just told us."

Goodner was a young police officer with a roundish face. Riley recognized him as one of the cops who'd been at the beach.

"The sketch looks to me like Grant Carson. He's an ill-tempered creep that I recognized from a previous encounter." With a smirk, he turned to another cop and asked, "And you remember him too, right, Bryant?"

Bryant was middle-aged and balding. Riley had also seen him at the beach.

"I sure do," Bryant said. "He's been in and out of trouble since he was a kid—shoplifting, vandalism, getting into fights, public intoxication, cruelty to animals ..."

That last detail really caught Riley's attention. Killers often spent their early years mistreating animals. It was a well-known warning sign.

Bryant continued, "Goodner and I busted him for burglary some four or five years ago. And you're right, Goodner, he wasn't pleasant about it."

Chief Belt scratched his chin and looked carefully at the face on the screen.

"I think I remember him too," Belt said. "Yeah, he was convicted of one count of Class Three felony burglary. The last I heard, he was serving a five-year sentence."

"He got paroled a few months back," Goodner said. "He's in vocational rehab now, working at Droullard Building Company as a carpenter."

A carpenter! Riley thought.

After all, the killer was almost certainly skilled at woodwork. Could the identification be right?

She told herself not to get her hopes up.

"Are you sure that this is him?" Riley asked the two cops, pointing to the picture.

Goodner shrugged.

"It sure looks like him to me," he said.

Bryant tilted his head, looking less certain.

"Could be," he said. "I remember him as having a bigger chin. Otherwise, it's pretty close."

"Pretty close," Riley thought.

Those were words she'd rather not hear right now. But of course, sketches made from eyewitness accounts were seldom accurate portraits. They usually just provided a general idea of what to look for.

She walked toward the picture for a closer look. The truth was, this one wasn't much of a sketch. Or maybe the suspect just didn't have a very interesting face. The man pictured here looked extremely plain and ordinary, with short dark hair and no distinguishing features. She could actually think of several guys who looked a little like that.

Riley asked Chief Belt, "Is the witness still in the building? The woman who gave the description, I mean?"

Chief Belt shook his head.

"We sent her home. She told us everything she could remember."

Riley was tempted to say …

"I wish you hadn't done that."

Instead she suggested, "Maybe the witness would recognize your mug shot of Carson."

Belt seemed to hesitate. Then he told Goodner, "Just get Ms. Reitman on the phone. Show her the mug shot and see what she thinks."

Goodner went to his desk and started working at his computer.

Riley asked Belt, "How close was the witness to the suspect when she saw him?"

"She said about twenty feet," Belt said.

Riley asked, "And where was she in relation to him? Between him and the water, or farther up the beach?"

Belt looked slightly puzzled.

He said, "I don't know why it matters. But she said she was coming from the beach road, passing near the wigwam to get to the harder sand where she could run more easily. She saw him put the hourglass down and then jog away along the beach."

In her mind's eye, Riley tried to recreate the scene near Rags Tucker's wigwam and the clutter around it. It was high on the beach, above where any high tide would reach.

At around six in the morning, the sun wouldn't have been up yet, but there would have been traces of light to the east over the water.

It sounded like the suspect must have been between the woman and the light.

From twenty feet away at that time of morning, could she have made out more than his silhouette?

Perhaps.

After all, she'd seemed sure enough of what she'd seen to come in and give a description. But Riley would have felt more confident if the woman had seen the suspect from closer up or in brighter light.

Goodner returned with a grin on his face. "She says it looks like him," he reported.

"She's sure?" Belt asked.

"She wasn't sure at first, but then she said 'Oh yes, I remember now. That's the man I saw.'"

Riley said, "Then we need to talk to Grant Carson."

"I agree," Chief Belt said. "Let's try to find out where he is."

He picked up the phone on the table in front of him, dialed a number, and put the call on speakerphone so that everyone present could hear.

A man's voice answered.

"Droullard Building Company. Quincy Droullard speaking."

Chief Belt spoke in a friendly tone.

"Hey, Quincy. This is Parker Belt. How're things going?"

"Could be better, could be worse," the man said in what sounded like a chronically sour voice.

Belt leaned back in his chair.

"Listen, this is a conference call, Quincy. I need your help with something. Does a guy named Grant Carson work for you?"

Quincy Droullard let out a gruff laugh.

"In a manner of speaking, I guess you could say that. He's not been much good to me lately. I don't know what's with him these days."

Glances were exchanged all around the table.

"What do you mean?" Belt asked.

"Well, his work has gotten erratic. So has his attitude. When he's not apathetic, he's got a bad temper. It's the last time I hire a parolee, I can tell you that. Has he done something wrong?"

"We just want to talk to him," Belt said. "If he's at work today, maybe we could stop by and ask him a few questions."

Droullard grunted.

"Sorry, he called in sick today. He's been doing that a lot lately."

"Have you got a home address for him?" Belt asked.

"Sure," Droullard said.

There was a sound of shuffling papers.

Then Droullard said, "He lives right here in Sattler, at 14 Hale Street."

Belt thanked Droullard and ended the call.

He said, "The address is only a few blocks from the beach. I've got a feeling Grant Carson is our guy."

Riley said, "Let's stop by his house and pay him a visit."

Belt shook his head.

"Not so fast," he said. "This guy could be dangerous. If we show up at his house and politely knock at the door, it might give him a chance to arm himself. Somebody could get killed. I say we get a no-knock warrant."

Riley felt uneasy. She couldn't deny that a no-knock warrant might be a good idea. It would allow a team to storm Grant Carson's house without taking time for a prior warning or announcement. But was it really feasible?

She asked Belt, "How are you going to get a warrant?"

"That shouldn't be any trouble," Belt said.

As he spoke, he was already dialing another phone number. In a few moments, he had a local judge on the phone. The judge sounded eager to send the warrant. All Belt had to do was fax him an affidavit, and the judge would fax a warrant back to Belt right away.

Riley had to admire the man's ability to speed through paperwork.

Belt ended the call and looked around at the officers and agents seated at the table.

"Now we need to pick a team for the raid. From my guys, I want Goodner, Bryant, Moon, and Robinson. Agent Paige, who do you want to take—aside from Jeffreys and Roston?"

Riley looked around at the faces of the FBI people in the room.

She said, "Give me Huang, Whittington, Craft, and Ridge."

Belt nodded and got up from his desk and added, "I'm going to my office to get the paperwork ready for the judge. The rest of you, get ready. We're headed to Grant Carson's house as soon as I have that warrant in my hands."

Belt headed for his office, and the meeting broke up.

Riley, Jenn, and Bill stood looking at each other. Jenn had an expectant expression on her face.

"This could be it," Jenn said.

Bill nodded slightly, not looking quite so sure.

As for Riley, her instincts hadn't clicked in, and she had no feeling one way or the other. She wasn't really comfortable going ahead without some sense that this was the right thing to be doing with their time.

But right now, they had no other possibilities.

She looked at the clock on the wall and saw its second hand sweeping mercilessly around the dial.

Again, she couldn't help but hear Otis Redlich perversely philosophizing about time …

"No clock can tell us what's going to happen tomorrow, or an hour from now, or a minute … or a second!"

She shuddered deeply. She knew this case was wearing on her nerves in a way that few other cases ever had.

She wondered …

Am I really at my best? Am I up to this?

But what choice did she have?

"Come on," she said to her colleagues. "This had better be it."

CHAPTER FIFTEEN

Bill eyed Riley uneasily as the group of FBI agents headed to their SUV. Besides Riley and Jenn, four other agents had joined the team for the raid. He was glad to have the extra support.

As the frustrations of the day had mounted, Bill thought Riley had been looking more and more stressed out. Now he moved up beside her and asked softly, "Are you doing OK?"

Riley looked at him with a defensive expression.

"Why do you keep asking me that?" she said.

"I just wondered," Bill said.

"Well, stop wondering. Get your head in the game."

Bill felt stung. Riley didn't snap at him like this often.

Still, it's not bad advice, he thought.

The truth was, Bill didn't think he was at his best either. He'd been feeling strangely displaced all day, ever since this morning when he'd made the sudden decision to work on this case.

At first he'd been concerned that his own PTSD might kick back in. He still had occasional flashbacks of Lucy's death and of his own shots bringing down that poor innocent kid back in California. But that hadn't happened, at least not so far.

He felt more than eager to get back to work.

So what was the problem?

He had to admit that it was something new. He felt strangely unsure of where he stood with Riley and her new partner, Agent Roston.

Jenn, she calls her, he reminded himself. He had been taken aback to find out that they were on a mutual first-name basis.

He didn't like to think that he was feeling jealous or resentful. But after so many years of working with Riley as a partner and a friend, of trusting her with his very life and much, much more, how could he help feeling strange about such changes?

The situation had been different when he and Riley had been working as a team with Lucy Vargas. They both had liked Lucy immensely, and Lucy had fit in with them perfectly. The three of them had shared a wonderful chemistry together.

But that didn't seem to be happening right now, at least not yet.

For one thing, Bill had an odd feeling that something wasn't entirely right with Jenn Roston. She struck him as downright secretive. Even worse, sometimes she seemed to be unfocused.

More than once, he'd noticed that her mind seemed to be elsewhere when she needed to be concentrating on the case. Something was on her mind, and Bill had a feeling that it wasn't something good.

That kind of thing could get an agent killed. And it could be equally dangerous for anyone working with her.

And as for Riley, he could see that she was letting the unique pressures of this case get to her.

And that wasn't like her at all.

When Bill, Riley, Jenn, and the four other FBI agents arrived at the van, they put on their Kevlar jackets. They prepared themselves for the impending raid on Grant Carson's house, and waited for Chief Belt to get his no-knock warrant from the local judge.

After a while, Chief Belt and his four cops came out and climbed into their own vehicles. Riley got behind the wheel of the SUV and followed them to Grant Carson's address.

It was a short drive that took them into an older community of small, weathered houses. The neighborhood was close to the beach, and the soil was visibly sandy. It reminded Bill of Jenn Roston's observation earlier.

"Our killer has some kind of obsession with sand."

Bill's nerves quickened.

This really could be it, he thought.

Carson's address, 14 Hale Street, was a house like any other in that modest neighborhood—a small white cottage with a picket fence.

Right away, Bill noticed signs of activity. Parked in the driveway was a battered little hatchback car with its doors and back open.

As the vehicles parked, Bill said, "Looks like somebody's getting ready to go on a little trip."

"Not if we can help it," Riley said.

Everybody got out of their vehicles and gathered around Riley. She quietly gave commands for some of the local cops and agents to head around the sides and back of the house, and for others to cover the house from the front. The group moved into their positions with their weapons drawn, surrounding the house and watching all of its possible exits.

Bill was starting to worry a little.

Surely Grant Carson must have noticed their arrival.

So much for a no-knock tactic, he thought. They didn't have to give the resident any warning, but they were making themselves pretty obvious.

Bill, Riley, Jenn, and Chief Belt walked up to the front door. A local cop with a battering ram followed behind them.

Standing slightly to the side of the door in case someone fired through it, Riley rapped on the door and called out, "Grant Carson?"

No reply came.

Riley called out again, "This is the FBI. Come out with your hands up."

Again there was no reply.

Riley gestured to the cop with the ram. He stepped forward and swung the heavy metal form against the door, which popped open easily.

Overkill, Bill thought. A *good kick would have done the job.*

With Riley in the lead, the four of them stepped inside the house. The snug interior was cluttered with bags and other signs that the occupant was getting ready to leave. The sparse furnishings looked like they'd been bought at a thrift shop.

Riley called out, "Grant Carson, we know you're here. Show yourself. Keep your hands up."

A voice replied from an adjoining room.

"OK, OK. Jesus, what's the big deal, anyway?"

Grant Carson stepped into the room with his hands above his head. He was a vigorous-looking but nondescript guy. Bill thought he looked at least somewhat like the man in the composite sketch. But then, so could lots of men his age.

Carson had a smirk on his face. He looked anything but surprised.

He said, "Hey, Chief Belt. It's been a long time, it's good to see you. I see you brought along the whole gang. It's a good thing I'm naturally humble. All this attention could go to my head. What's up?"

"You tell me," Belt said. "It looks like you're getting ready for a little trip."

"Yeah, I'm taking a little vacation leave from work," Carson replied.

Belt shook his head.

"That's not what Quincy Droullard told me," he said. "He said you called in sick."

"Did he, now? Sounds like we had a genuine communication problem."

Carson's smirk broadened.

He said, "What else did old man Droullard happen to tell you?"

Belt pulled out a pair of handcuffs as he said, "Grant Carson, you're under arrest for—"

Carson interrupted him with a chuckle.

"Yeah, I kind of get that. Relax, I'll come along quietly."

Bill's nerves suddenly tingled as Belt took a couple of casual steps toward Carson.

Something's about to go wrong, he realized.

He opened his mouth to warn Belt to stay back from Carson. But before he could speak, there was a blur of motion.

Carson reached downward with one hand and out toward Chief Belt with the other.

Suddenly, Carson was holding Chief Belt with a knife to his throat.

It took Bill a couple of seconds to grasp what had just happened.

Carson had drawn a hunting knife from an ankle sheaf while simultaneously grabbing Chief Belt.

It had been an incredibly deft maneuver. The man was both swift and strong.

Bill guessed Carson's reflexes had been sharpened for survival when he was in prison.

Belt's eyes bulged with shock and terror.

Carson chuckled grimly and said, "And now, if y'all don't mind. I'm going to take that little vacation I had planned. And I'm taking this nice police chief along with me. Maybe we'll do some fishing together."

Bill's teeth clenched. He deeply hated hostage situations.

And at the moment, he couldn't see any way to separate Carson from his victim without Belt getting badly hurt—perhaps fatally.

Then Bill heard Riley's voice.

"Grant—may I call you Grant?"

Carson looked at Riley with a perplexed expression.

"You don't want to do this," she said. "You're just making things worse for yourself."

She held out her hand.

"Just give me the knife," she said.

Carson drew sharply back.

"Stay away from me, bitch," he said.

Riley smiled uneasily and took a step toward him.

"Surely we can work something out," she said.

Bill heard a fearful tremor in Riley's voice.

He saw her hand shake as she holstered her weapon.

Was she scared?

This didn't seem like Riley at all.

Then Bill realized …

It's an act.

She was acting as if she was desperately afraid but naïvely trying to do something brave despite her fear.

She was pretending to be a green rookie who had no idea what she might be getting into.

She was trying to bait Carson into something.

Bill looked at Jenn. Would the actual rookie realize what was going on? If she tried to step in and help, she'd be sure to ruin whatever Riley had in mind.

Jenn met his gaze. She raised a questioning eyebrow.

Bill shook his head slightly. He was relieved to see the younger agent take a step back. He had stopped her just in time.

Then he realized what Riley was doing. She wanted Carson to take her hostage in Chief Belt's place.

Bill saw Carson's expression turn into a sneer.

Riley's gambit was working!

Carson said, "Why sure, little lady, we can work something out. Just come over here so we can talk better."

Still looking terrified, Riley moved closer to him.

And in another blur of movement, Carson let go of Belt and grabbed Riley.

Now he held the knife to her throat.

As Belt staggered across the room to safety, Riley's terrified expression changed to one of smug satisfaction.

"I was hoping you'd do that," she said.

Bill almost smiled.

From his own training, he now knew exactly what to expect, move for move.

Riley threw her upper body backward, striking Carson sharply in the chin with her head.

His head recoiled from pain and surprise.

Riley then leaned swiftly backward, creating an opening between her and the knife-wielding hand.

She grabbed hold of his wrist with both hands. She threw her hips back into his body, throwing him off balance.

She pushed the knife away with her right hand, at the same time hitting him directly in the groin with her left forearm.

As Carson let out a huge groan of pain, Riley elbowed him in the abdomen and pushed the knife away with both hands. She rotated her body out of his grasp until she faced him.

Then she landed another solid blow to his groin with her foot.

Still in motion, Riley stepped farther backward and twisted his arm painfully, causing him to let go of the knife and drop to his knees on the floor. She delivered a kick to his chin, sending him flat on his back.

Riley grabbed up the knife and planted one knee on his chest.

Suddenly, Riley's expression changed to one of wild rage.

She let out a howl of triumph as she raised the knife as if to slam its handle into Carson's face.

She's going to kill him! Bill realized.

He plunged forward and grabbed Riley by the arm, snatching the knife away from her.

She whirled and glared at him, her eyes wide with fury. It was an expression Bill had seen on her face, but never directed at him before.

For a moment, he was afraid she was going to attack him.

"Riley, it's me!" he cried. "Stop! It's over!"

Riley's face and body slackened. She looked dazed with shock, as if she had no idea what had just happened. Then she stood up and stepped away from Carson's fallen body.

She was shaking all over—and Bill knew that she wasn't pretending anymore.

Chief Belt hurried over to Carson, handcuffing him and reading him his Miranda rights.

Bill seized Riley by the arm and led her to the other side of the room.

"Riley, what the hell just happened? What did you think you were doing?"

Riley stared at him dumbly, as if he'd just awakened her from some nightmare.

He said, "Go out to the car and stay there. I'll take care of things here."

Riley nodded and staggered out of the house toward the SUV.

Bill went outside and summoned the team, giving them orders to search the house and immediate area. He noticed that some neighbors were standing in their doorways, looking frightened and alarmed.

He called out to them, "It's OK. Everything's under control. It's all over." He knew that the team would ask some of them what they knew about their neighbor who was being taken away in a police car.

At least I hope it's all over, he thought, still wondering what kind of demon had taken control of Riley.

CHAPTER SIXTEEN

Riley felt weak all over as she climbed into the SUV. She sat down in the back and shivered, feeling cold all over from sheer shock.

She knew she was coming down from a terrible flood of adrenaline.

But what had just happened?

Little by little, the truth began to dawn on her.

In the violence of the moment, she had flashed back to the single most vicious act she had ever committed.

It was when she had killed Peterson, a psychopath who had captured and tortured her, causing her own severe bouts with PTSD. He had kidnapped her daughter, and then she had finally caught up with him and killed him.

She had savagely smashed his head with a rock, time and time again.

And she had enjoyed doing it.

When she'd crouched over Carson's prone body just now, she'd been reliving that moment again.

She cringed as she realized ...

If Bill hadn't stopped her, she would have killed Carson.

What's wrong with me? she wondered.

What was it about this case that was making her react this way?

She tried to tell herself that it was over now, the case was solved, they'd caught the killer and stopped him from committing any more murders.

But somehow, the relief she usually felt at such a moment refused to surface.

She turned in her seat and saw the two sand timers in the back of the vehicle—one of them empty, the other still running. A trickle of sand was still passing through the narrow neck between the two glass globes, a relentless reminder of passing time.

But why did that matter now? Why was the flow of sand still gnawing at her psyche?

It's just sand, she tried to tell herself.

And besides, it no longer signified any danger.

It's over, she tried to tell herself.

Even so, that trickle evoked a feeling of helplessness she'd seldom experienced, not even after years of facing almost every conceivable kind of threat or danger.

She felt a deep, irrational need to stop that flow of sand.

It looked easy enough to stop. Just inserting a single finger below the narrow neck of glass to plug it up—that was all it would take.

But she couldn't do that.

There was a taunting wall of clear glass between her fingers and the flowing sand.

That puny trickle might as well be a massive avalanche or mudslide for all she could do to stop it.

Of course, she could turn the timer over and reverse the flow. Or she could lay it on its side and the sand would stop completely.

But she couldn't make herself reach out and move the thing at all.

Why not?

What was stopping her?

After all, it was over, wasn't it?

The case was closed.

But for some reason, she didn't dare interrupt the flow of sand.

Don't look, she told herself.

With what felt like a superhuman effort, Riley managed to shut her eyes. Then she turned her head away.

She realized that she was hyperventilating. She deliberately slowed her breathing and tried to control it.

It's just stress, she told herself, keeping her eyes shut.

It had been a uniquely stressful case, after all. That's what had taken such a toll on her.

But neither Bill nor Jenn seemed to have been as worn down by it as she was. And Bill had been particularly fragile lately.

She was the one who had almost killed a suspect for no good reason.

What's wrong with me? she wondered.

Why had this case pushed her buttons in such a personal way?

She opened her eyes at the sound of approaching voices. She saw the team coming toward her from the house. Chief Belt wasn't among them. Riley realized that Belt and at least one of his cops must have already driven back to the station with Grant Carson in custody.

The remaining group clustered around the SUV. None of them looked happy—especially not Bill.

Riley asked, "Have you conducted a search?"

"Yeah," Bill said, shuffling his feet impatiently. "We didn't find any solid evidence—no shovel, no wheelbarrow, no carpentry equipment, no sand timers or any sign that he'd been making them."

Jenn added, "But we did find a bundle of money in his car, about five hundred dollars. And he was all packed up and ready to drive out of here. And when we got here, it seemed almost like he expected us."

Bill nodded and said, "He's guilty, there's no question about it. But he's smarter than the average psycho. He's got another lair where he keeps everything incriminating. And my guess that place is going to be pretty hard to find. Until we do, it's going to be hard to prove that he's guilty."

Jenn said, "Well, at least we've got him in custody—and with hours to spare before he planned to kill again."

Bill said nothing, but Riley could see the disappointment on his strong features. Riley knew what he was thinking, and she shared his discouragement. They had found nothing to prove Grant Carson's guilt. If he wound up going free, what kind of threat would he pose in the future? Especially if he left the area and put down new roots in some unsuspecting neighborhood? How many lives would he take on yet another sinister schedule?

She glanced at the other team members who were still gathered around the SUV. They all looked expectant. They were awaiting further orders.

But at the moment, Riley had no idea what to tell them.

Before she could think things through, her cell phone rang. The call was from Chief Belt. Riley put the call on speakerphone so the team could listen.

Belt asked, "Did the team find anything useful?"

"I'm afraid not," Riley said.

"Well, it might not matter," Belt said. "Grant Carson says he's ready to confess."

A murmur of excitement passed among the team.

Riley simply couldn't believe her ears.

"Say that again?" she said.

"Carson says he'll tell us everything," Belt said.

Riley exchanged eager glances with Bill and Jenn.

She said, "Don't let him get started until we can get there."

"Nothing to worry about there," Belt said. "He insists on having a lawyer present when he talks. Just try to get over here before the public defender gives him too many ideas."

The call ended. The local cops headed back to their vehicles. Bill and Jenn climbed into the SUV along with Huang and the other three FBI agents.

Riley just sat still, so Jenn climbed into the front seat and Bill took the driver's seat.

As Bill drove back toward the police station, Riley kept waiting for relief to kick in.

It didn't happen, and she wondered why.

It seems too easy, she thought.

Why was Carson so ready and eager to confess so quickly after his arrest?

It hardly made sense.

During the ride, she kept thinking about the sand timer in the back of the SUV, still marking lost time with its steady trickle of sand. It seemed to contradict the news they'd just heard.

Riley couldn't shake off the feeling that the timer still spelled trouble.

CHAPTER SEVENTEEN

When Bill parked the SUV in front of the police station, Riley saw a group of reporters outside. She also saw that Chief Belt was standing in the front doorway waiting for them. She was relieved to shift her focus from the flow of sand in the timers to the man who had probably placed them with his victims.

Riley and Bill pushed past the noisy reporters, ignoring them as they walked toward Belt.

"Carson's lawyer is here," Belt said. "Come on in, we're ready to get started."

Riley and her companions followed Belt into the building and to the interrogation room. She could see that the chief was excited about the prospective confession.

Carson was sitting manacled to the table in the little room. A rather bored-looking middle-aged man was seated next to him. When the FBI agents entered the room, Carson glanced up at Riley and recoiled.

"Keep that crazy bitch away from me," he squealed.

Riley just smiled and stepped back against the wall. She wasn't proud of the fury that had overtaken her at the arrest, but she thought it might be helpful for the suspect to be a little frightened.

Chief Belt ignored the prisoner's comment. He just nodded to the man at the table to go ahead.

The man introduced himself to Riley and her colleagues as Ralph Craven, the public defender who had been assigned to represent Carson.

Also sitting at the table was a female stenographer armed with pen and paper and also a recording device.

Then Craven said, "My client is willing to talk—but I want you to know that I've advised him not to."

Belt said, "Your client knows his rights. Let him talk if he wants to."

Craven nodded reluctantly at the stenographer, who started the recording machine and sat poised with her pen ready.

Carson just sat there in silence for a moment. Gone was the smirk he'd worn back at his house. Now his expression seemed to be completely blank. Riley had no idea what he was thinking or feeling.

Finally Carson said, "OK, I did it. I'm guilty."

Riley said, "You're going to have to give us more than that."

Carson shrugged.

"Why? You've got me dead to rights. Didn't you find the money in my car?"

The money? Riley thought.

She glanced at her colleagues and saw that they were just as puzzled as she was.

Carson's eyes darted from person to person around the room. He swallowed hard, then started up again.

"You said you talked to old man Droullard," he said. "I figured he'd told you …"

Carson's voice trailed off for a moment. For the first time since Riley had set eyes on him, he looked somewhat alarmed.

He said, "Shit, you mean you didn't know?"

His lawyer let out a growl of dismay.

"I told you not to talk," Craven said. "Now listen to me—not another word. Do you hear me?"

Carson lowered his head.

Riley now worried that he wasn't going to talk after all. She thought hard and fast, trying to figure out what was really going on.

She said, "You've been pilfering money from your workplace, haven't you? Little by little, probably since you started working there. Probably from petty cash. That's how you got the five hundred dollars in the car. You were getting ready to leave town with it."

"Not another word," Craven said again, more sternly this time.

But Carson's patience seemed to be at an end.

"I'm sick of this town, OK? Everyone here has treated me like shit all my life. I've been planning to get out of here since I got out of jail. I'd chew my leg off to go somewhere else. And why not take that money? What's five hundred bucks to a guy like Droullard?"

He shook his head and added quietly, "Hell, he didn't even notice it was gone. And you guys didn't even care about that money. I should have known. I should have kept my mouth shut. I just thought you'd go easier on me if I confessed and saved you a trial and all. I thought maybe you wouldn't send me back to prison, you'd let me off with a slap on the wrist. Maybe I could just give the money back. But now … Jesus, I really screwed myself over, didn't I?"

Craven let out a grunt of angry agreement.

Riley planted her hands on the table and leaned toward Grant Carson. He drew back from her as far as he could.

She said, "Grant, you know perfectly well that you were arrested for a lot more than petty theft. We can add resisting arrest, attacking a police officer and—"

Craven interrupted her, saying to Carson, "I really mean it. Don't say another word."

But Carson seemed more nervous, and more eager to speak his mind than ever.

"Yeah, I know. You guys keep telling me. Two counts of murder. Look, I'm a goddamn social deviant, and everybody knows it. But I'm not a murderer. I had nothing to do with those two people getting killed. You'll never prove it, because I didn't do it."

Suddenly, Chief Belt let out an exasperated snarl and left the room.

Riley was startled. She'd never seen any sign of anger out of the good-natured police chief until now. Of course, the chief did have good reason to be angry with Carson but he'd been acting as though that attack had never happened.

She suddenly felt that she, too, had had enough of this scene. They were getting nowhere with the suspect. This was going to take longer than she had expected.

She hurried out and joined Belt in the booth outside the interrogation room. They could hear Bill and Jenn still prodding away at Carson with questions, trying to get him to confess to the murders rather than to a minor theft.

Chief Belt paced back and forth in the booth.

"I should have known," he said. "He pulled a bait-and-switch on us."

"What do you mean?" Riley asked.

"Well, it's obvious, isn't it? He knows we don't have evidence linking him to the murders, at least not yet. He's confessing to petty theft to throw us off the track. You can see that too, can't you?"

Riley didn't reply.

The truth was, Belt's conclusion wasn't nearly so obvious to her.

She turned and watched through the two-way mirror and listened to what was still going on in the interrogation room. Bill and Jenn were pounding the man with questions, doing everything possible to turn the situation around. But they were obviously getting nowhere. And Riley knew that she couldn't do any better if she were in the room doing the interrogation herself, not even if she threatened the man again.

Riley stepped closer to the window and studied Carson's expression carefully. She now saw genuine panic in the suspect's face.

She heard genuine confusion in his voice.

She swallowed hard.

Still staring through the window, Riley said quietly to Belt, "Carson's not our killer."

"What?" Belt said with a gasp. "What the hell are you talking about?"

"It's not him," Riley said firmly. But before she could begin to explain, her cell phone rang.

She saw that the call was from Carl Walder.

She remembered what he'd said the last time they'd talked …

"I expect you to apprehend the killer before six o'clock."

She looked at her watch and saw that it was six on the dot.

Riley suppressed a sigh of despair.

A bad day was about to get a whole lot worse.

CHAPTER EIGHTEEN

Riley brushed past Chief Belt and stepped out into hallway to take the call from Carl Walder.

When she answered, she was surprised at Walder's cheerful tone of voice.

"Well, Agent Paige, I understand that congratulations are in order."

"What?" Riley asked. "Why?"

"Chief Belt called me just a short time ago. He said you tracked down the killer and that they have him in custody."

Riley's heart sank. This call was going to be even harder than she'd expected.

She said, "Chief Walder, I'm afraid that news was a trifle premature."

A tense silence followed.

Riley said, "I don't think Grant Carson is our killer."

Walder now sounded incredulous.

"You don't *think* he's the killer?"

"No, I don't."

"From what Belt told me, you had him cold. Belt said he was even getting ready to confess."

"He confessed, all right," Riley said. "He confessed to stealing five hundred dollars from his employer. When we caught him, he was just getting ready to split town with the cash."

Another silence fell.

Then Walder said, "According to Chief Belt, Grant Carson is a lifelong criminal with a history of violent behavior who recently got out of prison and just happens to be trained in carpentry—a skill you might expect from a killer who makes sand timers. Do you have any reason to think there's been some mistake?"

Riley gulped hard.

"Well, we haven't found any physical evidence linking him to the murders, and ..."

"And what?"

Riley remembered the expression on Carson's face when she'd looked at him through the two-way glass.

She said, "It's a gut feeling."

"A gut feeling?"

"That's right."

A longer silence fell.

Then Walder said, "I want to talk to your whole FBI team. Right now. A conference call."

Walder abruptly ended the call.

Riley felt crushed and discouraged.

It was bad enough that she was all but sure they'd wasted precious time catching the wrong man. Things weren't going to get any easier with Walder breathing down their necks.

But Riley obediently went back to the interrogation room and called Jenn and Bill away from questioning Grant Carson. The three of them went into the conference room, where all six members of the FBI team were already awaiting further orders.

Reluctantly, she called Walder back on the table phone. She put him on the speaker so the others could participate in the call.

Walder was making no attempt to mask his impatience.

He said to the group, "I guess you've all been fairly busy today—at least I *hope* you've been busy, although I've seen little to show for it. So you probably haven't had time to keep up with the news. The media is going crazy about this killer. I'll spare you some of the bizarre theories that are kicking around. Suffice it to say that the public is still trying to pick a nickname for the killer. Right now the most popular choices seem to be 'Father Time' and 'The Sandman.'"

With an audible sneer in his voice, Walder added, "Which nickname do you people prefer?"

Everybody at the table glanced at one another and said nothing.

Walder waited for several long moments before speaking again. Riley found herself eyeing the clock on the wall, its second hand clicking along in its ruthless circle.

Finally Walder said, "The BAU is looking like a gang of idiots right now. To make things worse, your team leader tells me that she has a *gut feeling* that you've caught the wrong man, and Grant Carson isn't the murderer. Would anybody else like to weigh in with their opinions?"

The mood in the room was growing more uncomfortable by the second. Huang, Whittington, Craft, and Ridge were sitting there slack-jawed. After all, they hadn't been in on the interrogation, and this was the first they'd heard about any doubts of Grant Carson's guilt.

But Bill and Jenn looked less unsure of themselves.

Bill said into the phone, "Chief Walder, this is Jeffreys. I've got some of the same doubts as Agent Paige."

Jenn said, "This is Agent Roston. And I feel the same way."

Walder let out a growl of irritation.

"What about the rest of you?" he asked.

The other four agents looked at one another nervously. Then one by one, they answered.

"This is Whittington, and I've got no idea."

"This is Ridge, and I don't know either."

"Craft here. I don't know."

"This is Huang. I have no basis on which to form an opinion."

More silence followed.

"Listen to me, all of you," Walder said at last. "Your team leader, Agent Paige, seems to be leading you into the middle of nowhere."

Riley winced during yet another silence.

Was Walder about to fire her—again?

No, surely not, she thought.

After all, just last month she'd received a special commendation from FBI Director Gaven Milner himself.

Walder couldn't fire her without making a lot of trouble for himself.

That didn't mean he wasn't going to try to humiliate her.

She sat waiting for the blow to fall.

Walder finally said, "Agent Huang, I want you to take over the leadership of the team."

Huang looked stunned.

"Yes, sir," he said in a rather tentative voice. "I'll do that, sir."

"That will be all for now," Walder said. "I'll be checking in with you frequently. And I'm expecting results, damn it. Remember, the clock is running."

He ended the call, and the team members sat looking at one another.

As though we didn't know that time is tight, Riley thought angrily. She focused her eyes on Agent Craig Huang.

Huang was new to the BAU, and Riley hadn't worked with him very often. In fact, they hadn't gotten along well at first. She hadn't liked his work very much, and he hadn't seemed to like her.

But they'd grown on each other over the months, and she'd

come to admire his dedication and sharp mind.

Nevertheless, she knew perfectly well that Huang was one of Walder's favorites. She also knew that Huang was ambitious. He would surely relish this opportunity to take command.

She couldn't help but feel hurt that this was going to be his big break—now in the middle of a case that she'd been working so hard to solve.

Trying to keep a note of bitterness out of her voice, Riley said, "Well, Agent Huang—what are your orders?"

Huang sat staring at the table for a moment.

In a small voice he said, "My orders are …"

His voice drifted off. Then he looked up at Riley. He grinned ever so slightly.

"My orders are that *you* give the orders, Agent Paige. Now and always. So tell us what to do next."

There was a murmur of agreement from everybody at the table.

Riley was thunderstruck. She could hardly believe her ears.

She was touched beyond words by the loyalty and trust of her colleagues.

She was also humbled and daunted. Was she worthy of their loyalty and trust right now?

She remembered how she'd gone berserk while arresting Grant Carson. She still didn't understand what had come over her.

All she knew was that she wasn't at her best right now, and she didn't understand why.

Whatever demons were nagging at her, she had to shake them off.

Somebody's life might be in danger very soon.

And as Walder had just said …

"The clock is running."

CHAPTER NINETEEN

Before Riley could start giving orders to the FBI agents sitting at the conference table with her, Chief Belt burst into the room. He looked as exasperated as he had when she'd left him back at the interrogation room.

"Would someone please tell me what's going on?" he barked. "Agent Paige, the last thing you told me was that Carson's not our killer. Then you took off without explaining a damn thing."

"Please sit down, Chief Belt," Riley said.

Belt sat down across the table, looking expectant and impatient.

Riley said, "As you just heard, Grant Carson confessed to a completely separate and unrelated crime. And the truth is, we've got absolutely no evidence to connect him with the murders. And if we waste time trying to find some connection that isn't there—"

Belt interrupted.

"What do you mean, waste time? Isn't he the only suspect we've got? We'd better keep putting pressure on him until he talks."

Riley stifled a sigh. This wasn't going to be easy to explain.

Then Craig Huang spoke up.

"Chief Belt, Grant Carson is almost certainly not the killer. And I'm afraid you're going to have to take Agent Paige's word for it. At the BAU, we've all learned to respect and trust her instincts. She's more than earned our trust. And she's got plenty of commendations to back up her gut feelings. If she says Grant Carson's not our man, I'll stake my career that she's right."

There was a murmur of agreement from the other agents present.

Riley felt another burst of humble gratitude.

I hope I'm not wrong this time, she thought.

She was keenly aware that her gut feelings had been known to fail her on just a few occasions. But she sensed that this wasn't one of those times.

Belt's expression softened. He seemed to accept Huang's judgment.

"What do we do now?" Belt said.

Riley said, "First, keep Carson in custody. He's definitely guilty of stealing from his employer, and he might have broken the terms of his parole in other ways. After we've caught the murderer, you can sort out all of that. But for the time being …"

She paused and thought for a moment.

Then she said, "Agents Whittington and Craft, you've already met with the victims' families. Pay them another visit and show them the composite sketch. See if the portrait reminds them of anyone they might know. Then go to the beach and show the sketch to Rags Tucker. Maybe he'll recognize who it is. Take a couple of Chief Belt's people with you."

She looked at the other faces at the table.

"Agent Engel, go deal with the reporters outside. Use your judgment as to what to tell them. Be truthful, but try not to say anything to stir up further rumors or panic. We're in the middle of a PR disaster as it is."

She thought for another moment.

"Agents Ridge and Geraty, drive the two sand timers back to Quantico. Turn them over to Sam Flores so his people can examine them more closely. Be careful with the one that's still running. Don't jar or shake it more than you can help—and whatever you do, don't turn it over."

"How about if you take my car back," Bill said. He pulled a set of keys from his pocket. "I drove down here by myself but I'll stick with the agency SUV now."

Ridge nodded and took the keys. "Yessir," he said. "We can take the timers in the car."

"Good," Riley said. Then she turned to Craig Huang.

"Agent Huang, organize with Chief Belt's people to deal with the public. And make sure that the Belle Terre Nature Preserve is thoroughly closed off, and that everybody knows to stay away from there."

Huang nodded.

He said, "We'll close it up and stake it out. With some luck, that'll be enough to keep the killer from striking again—at least on the schedule he's set for himself."

With some luck, Riley thought to herself.

In fact, she saw no reason to think otherwise.

But luck was a thing she'd long since learned not to count on. Besides, she couldn't persuade herself that luck was on their side right now.

Once they had their orders, Engel, Whittington, Craft, Ridge, Geraty, and Huang all left the room. So did Chief Belt. Riley was left alone with Bill and Jenn.

"What about us three?" Jenn asked.

Riley focused on one idea that was nagging at her mind.

None of her team had actually interviewed the witness. In fact, it seemed that few questions had been asked of the woman. The police unit had been intent on getting the sketch made. But that had been so generic that it had led them on yet another mistaken chase. The man's guilt was infinitesimal compared to the one they were actually seeking. And if anybody could lead them to the actual killer …

Riley said, "We've got to go talk to the witness who saw the suspect at the beach. Maybe we can jog her memory, get more detail than the local sketch artist was able to get from her."

Jenn sat drumming her fingers on the table.

Riley asked her, "Have you got another question?"

Jenn said slowly, "Riley, where are we when it comes to profiling the killer? What do we know about him, really?"

Riley didn't know what to say. All along she'd felt sure that the killer had been able to charm his victims, get them to trust him at least briefly.

But beyond that …

What? she wondered. *What do we really know?*

Riley suddenly realized something.

She was shaking slightly, and her hands were cold and sweaty.

What's wrong with me? she wondered.

Once again, she felt mystified by her own feelings and behavior.

She was still trying to figure out why she had gotten out of control back at Grant Carson's house and had almost killed him.

And now her body seemed to be in a state of low-grade panic.

But why?

She gulped hard, then said to Bill and Jenn, "I need to talk to Mike Nevins about this profile. Could the two of you leave me alone for just a few minutes?"

Jenn looked at Riley with surprise.

"Is something wrong?" Jenn asked.

"Good," Bill said. He nudged Jenn with a quiet grunt, obviously trying to tell her to do as Riley said. Jenn nodded, and without asking any further questions, the other two agents left the room.

Riley sat alone in the silent meeting room for a few moments.

A profile, she thought.

Why was she having so much trouble coming up with one? She didn't know. All she knew was that she kept coming up blank. Surely that was why she was feeling so troubled and anxious.

She needed help getting into the killer's head—the kind of help she couldn't get from Bill or Jenn.

She took out her cell phone to send a text message to Mike Nevins. At Riley's insistence, Bill had gone to the well-known psychiatrist for help with his PTSD. It was also true that Mike had helped Riley through her own share of rough times.

But Mike Nevins was, first and foremost, a brilliant forensic psychiatrist who frequently consulted for the FBI and had given Riley crucial insights into some truly baffling cases.

And this seemed to be one of them.

She typed …

Mike? Have U got a few minutes?

In just a few seconds she got a reply …

Sure Riley. What's up?

Riley thought for a moment, then typed …

Could we talk on video?

Mike replied …

No problem. Give me a second.

Riley got out a pad and pencil to make notes. She quickly saw Mike's face on her cell phone, and she knew that he could see her face as well. He was a dapper, expensively dressed man with a meticulous, fussy personality. As usual, he was a welcome sight.

"What can I do for you, Riley?" he asked with a smile.

Riley sighed and shook her head.

"Mike, I'm really beside myself right now. I'm working on a case that's driving me crazy."

"Oh, yes. The killer people are calling 'Father Time' or 'the

Sandman.' I've been following the case all day on the Internet. I'm sure it doesn't help that he's caught the public's imagination."

Riley stifled a growl of dismay.

"You've got no idea."

"Is it true that he's leaving sand timers to show when he'll take his next victims?"

"Yeah, and the one that's running now is going to run out at around six o'clock tomorrow morning. The trouble is, I'm having an awful time profiling him. At the murder scenes, I got hit with a gut feeling that he's a likeable guy and easily trusted. But that's about all."

Mike stroked his chin thoughtfully.

"Who are you working with on the case?" he asked.

"Jenn Roston and Bill Jeffreys."

Mike chuckled with satisfaction.

"So Bill is back on the job! I'm glad to hear it. I've been encouraging him to get involved in a new case. It's high time for him to get back on the horse. How's he doing?"

Riley shrugged.

"Better than I am at the moment."

Riley found herself idly doodling on the paper in front of her.

She said, "Jenn Roston is really interested in his obsession with sand."

"Yes, he's obviously got a thing about sand. And about time as well. But the sheer cruelty of burying people alive like that …"

Mike shuddered. "That suggests revenge to me," he said.

"I think so too," Riley said. "Still, how can that make sense? We can't find any connection between the two victims. It's as if he picks his victims at random. But revenge is personal, directed at someone specific. Or at least at a specific group or type."

Mike squinted and tapped on the frame of his glasses.

"Not necessarily," he said. "His revenge might be more—how can I put it?—*vicarious* in nature."

Mike paused and thought for a moment.

"Perhaps the *true* subjects of his revenge—the people who wronged him in some way—are now absent from his life. Maybe whatever they did to him happened long ago. Maybe he doesn't even completely remember what they did, or even remember it at all. All he knows is that something long suppressed keeps welling up inside of him—some wild kind of rage that he sometimes feels for human beings in general."

"With that kind of rage, would he be able to pass as a normal person?"

"Possibly. He's a very sick man and exceptionally dangerous to anyone who comes his way at certain times, but he could appear more ordinary under other circumstances. It's quite likely that he doesn't fully understand his own actions or motives."

Riley tried not to groan aloud.

"But I've got to understand him," she muttered. "How am I supposed to do my job if I can't even …"

Riley's voice trailed off. She couldn't think of words to express her frustration.

Mike peered more closely at her, looking deeply concerned.

"Riley, I'm afraid you're on the wrong track altogether. You're trying to profile the killer, you're trying to understand what makes him tick. But you're analyzing the wrong person."

Mike paused, and Riley held her breath.

She sensed that he was about to say something she really wasn't going to like.

Finally he said …

"I think you should look in the mirror."

CHAPTER TWENTY

Mike Nevins's words cut through Riley like a knife.

"Look in the mirror."

What could he possibly mean?

Was he accusing her of something?

It sure sounds like it, she thought. At the very least he was implying that she had overlooked some fault of her own.

Mike wasn't saying anything now. He was waiting for her reply.

She forced a smile and tried to laugh.

"I haven't got a mirror handy," she said. "Maybe you should be my mirror."

Mike heaved a deep sigh.

"Riley, it's been obvious since I started talking with you. I can see it in your face, I can hear it in your voice. This case isn't just getting to you, pushing your buttons. It's hitting you much harder than most cases do. Harder—and deeper."

Riley felt a lump of emotion form in her throat.

"Something happened today, didn't it?" Mike asked. "Something that especially shook you up."

"I pretty much lost it," she admitted. "I … I went way too hard on a guy we were interviewing."

Riley hesitated and then blurted out, "It was a flashback to fighting Peterson, and that kind of thing hasn't happened for a long time. I don't understand why I did that. I don't understand why this case is getting to me like this."

"I don't completely either," Mike said. "But it has something to do with *time*, Riley," Mike said. "This case is all about time in a way that's getting the best of you."

Mike paused, then added, "I want you to do something for me. I want you to do something for yourself."

Riley gulped hard.

"What is it?" she asked.

"I'm going to ask you a question, and you're going to answer it without stopping to think, even for a single second. You're just going to let your thoughts spill out."

Riley felt slightly reassured.

She'd done this kind of thing with Mike before, and it had always been helpful.

"OK," she said.

Mike held her gaze for a moment.

"What does *time* mean to you?"

Riley was shocked by how quickly her thoughts welled up and overflowed.

"I hate it," she said. "I hate time's guts. There's never enough of it. It cheats me at every turn. There are a million and one things I have to do, but never even a fraction of the time I need to do them in. Everyone expects so much from me. I expect so much from myself. I've got to be the best damned agent in the world—and the best mother too …"

An image of Blaine Hildreth suddenly popped into her mind.

"… and even the best girlfriend. Because I sure failed as a wife. Am I going to keep failing again and again whenever I try to have a relationship with a man? It makes me want to scream. And time …"

Her words trailed off.

Mike spoke again, his voice soft with concern.

"Riley, you just said that time *cheats* you. That sounds kind of personal. How is that?"

Now she remembered something else Otis Redlich had said …

"Humankind has been at war *with time all along."*

… and she remembered the twisted sneer on his face when he'd said it.

Yes, she thought. *Time looks and sounds like just like him.*

She said, "Sometimes it's as if time has a face and a voice, mean and spiteful, looking at me and mocking me, smirking at me, laughing at me. 'You can't have it all,' it keeps telling me. 'You can't *do* it all. Something has to give, someone has to suffer—your kids, your colleagues, or innocent victims who'll die because you're busy doing something else. There just isn't *time* for everybody.' Yes, it does feel personal. I feel like I'm the butt of some awful, sick practical joke that time is playing on me."

Riley felt a stab of anger and despair.

She said, "And I want … I don't know … fairness or justice or …"

Her voice trailed off again.

Mike said quietly, "Payback?"

She gasped aloud.

"Yes, I think maybe so. I want to get back at time. I want to get even. But I can't. The idea is ridiculous. Time is just too ... big for me."

A cascade of confusing emotions poured over Riley. She struggled to control herself.

She told herself that bursting into tears would be no help at all. She had to keep her wits about her.

"What ... what does it mean?" Riley stammered. "Is this how the killer feels? Does he feel the same despair and anger?"

"Maybe," Mike said. "If so, maybe you'll be able to use this as an insight. But he could be quite the opposite. He could feel like he's controlling time. He could be enjoying that. But this isn't really about him."

Mike held her gaze for a moment.

Then he said, "What we've been doing is profiling *you*."

Riley shook her head anxiously.

"But why? Why right now? Why not on my last case or my next one?"

"Because this is an unusual case, with unusual pressures. It's already pushing you into emotional exhaustion. And I don't think you're going to get through it unless you understand how it's affecting you."

Riley nodded silently.

It made sense.

She wished it didn't, but it did.

"What do I do now?" she asked Mike.

"Pay attention," Mike said. "Pay as much attention to yourself as you do to the details of the case. More ugly stuff is liable to surface inside you before this whole thing is over. You need to be ready to deal with it."

A silence fell over the two of them.

I guess that's all for now, Riley thought.

There seemed to be only one thing left to say.

"Thanks, Mike."

But the truth was, Riley wasn't sure how grateful she felt at the moment.

"Any time, Riley," Mike said. "And I do mean that. Day or night, I'm right here, and I'll do anything I can to help."

Without another word, Riley just nodded and ended the video chat.

She sat in the quiet room for a moment, breathing slowly,

trying to gather her nerves.

Then she got up from her chair and left the room. She walked out into the hallway where Bill and Jenn were waiting for her.

There was an awkward, quiet moment among them. Riley didn't know what to say.

How could she explain what she'd been doing for the last few minutes?

Fortunately, neither Bill nor Jenn was asking any questions.

As the three of them walked out of the building toward the SUV, Riley noticed that
Bill was watching her with a concerned expression. By contrast, Jenn had a faraway look on her face.

Riley found herself wondering what was nagging at Jenn today, sometimes even distracting her.

Bill seemed to be doing all right today, but he was undoubtedly still frail from his own recent traumas.

Are they up to this? she wondered.

Was she going to have to be strong for Bill and Jenn as well as herself?

And am I up to it?

"Come on," Riley said. "Let's go interview that witness."

CHAPTER TWENTY ONE

Riley was still badly shaken from the troubling conversation she'd just had with Mike Nevins. She sat silently in the passenger seat as Bill drove the SUV through Sattler toward the address they'd been given for the witness. She was glad that Jenn, in the back seat, wasn't asking any questions right now.

Riley was wondering if calling Mike had been such a good idea after all. She certainly hadn't expected to be psychoanalyzed.

She remembered something he'd said …

"What we've been doing is profiling you."

The very idea made her terribly uneasy.

She had no doubt that their conversation had provoked some valuable insights into her own psyche. It had also disturbed her deeply. Was looking inward something she really ought to be doing while working on a murder case—especially one that was so dire and so very urgent?

Mike had seemed to think so. He'd also warned her …

"More ugly stuff is liable to surface inside you before this whole thing is over."

Riley shivered at the thought. She quickly decided that dwelling on her feelings about time itself hardly seemed productive at the moment. Her own anger and fear could wait. There were plenty of other things to do.

For example, she decided, it would be good to let the witness know they were on their way. This was hardly going to be a raid, and the element of surprise wasn't needed. Besides, with time so tight it was a good idea to make sure the witness was home.

She punched in the number Chief Belt had given them for Hope Reitman.

When a cheerful woman's voice answered, Riley introduced herself.

Then she said, "My partners and I would like to ask you a few more questions if we may."

"About what?" the woman asked.

The question seemed a bit odd to Riley. Wasn't the answer pretty obvious?

"About the description you gave of the man at the beach this morning," Riley said.

"Oh," the woman said.

A short silence followed.

"I answered a lot of questions earlier. I don't think I left anything out."

"Even so, we'd like to go over a few things."

There was another pause, followed by an awkward-sounding laugh.

"OK, I guess," Hope Reitman said.

"Great. We'll be there in a few minutes."

The call ended. Riley already sensed something odd about Hope Reitman, something a bit strange in her voice. But she couldn't put her finger on just what.

As the drive continued, Riley brought up the composite sketch on her cell phone. Again she looked in vain for any distinguishing features.

From behind her, Jenn said, "He sure looks bland and ordinary."

Riley agreed. The sketch lacked any sign of individualism or personality.

There has to be something, she thought.

Surely the sketch artist had failed to ask the right question to trigger the witness's memory.

Riley hoped that she, Bill, and Jenn could do better.

The drive took them into a neighborhood not far from Belle Terre. It was more upscale than the area where they'd found Grant Carson. The address itself was in a gated community. A uniformed man stationed in a little booth at the gate asked who they wanted to see.

Bill produced his badge and introduced himself and his colleagues.

"We're here to talk to Hope Reitman," Bill said. "She's expecting us."

The man looked a little surprised.

"That's odd," the man said. "Ms. Reitman didn't mention you."

He turned away to talk on a phone for a moment, then turned toward the car again with a smile.

"You can go on in," he said, pointing. "You'll find her place in the row at the far end of the parking lot."

The man opened the gate, and Bill drove them on in.

They were surrounded by rows of pleasant townhouses, some with brick fronts, others of wood. Dusk was setting in, and windows were cheerfully lighted everywhere. A few people moving about the parking lot and green areas glanced their way and then went on about their business. It was clearly a place where inhabitants felt secure.

Bill parked, and the three agents got out. When they reached Hope Reitman's unit, Jenn rang the bell and the woman buzzed them inside.

Hope Reitman was an imposing, athletic-looking woman wearing loose, comfortable clothes. She had short hair and a warm, welcoming smile. Riley guessed that this witness was just a few years older than she was.

The woman invited Riley and her colleagues inside, where they were greeted by a large, friendly dog—a Malinois, Riley felt pretty sure.

"This is Neptune," Hope Reitman said, patting the dog's head. "Don't worry, he loves visitors. It's a good thing I've got good security and don't need a watchdog. If burglars showed up, Neptune would just wag his tail happily and show them around the place. Sit down, make yourselves comfortable."

Riley and her colleagues sat down in large, comfortable chairs. Hope Reitman sat with the dog lying beside her chair. Riley saw that the townhouse was simply but tastefully decorated—and probably expensively. She noticed that much of the decor seemed to have to do with water. There were large original canvases of soothing ocean scenes, countless seashells, and enormous pieces of coral.

Droning, restful New Age music was playing, mingled with the sounds of gulls and waves.

The woman chuckled a little as she followed Riley's gaze.

"I guess you've noticed a water motif here," she said. "Pisces is my zodiac sign, and I own a chain of gyms throughout the state called Pisces Fitness. Maybe you've heard of it."

Riley nodded. She'd heard good things about the gyms.

She said, "Ms. Reitman—"

"Please, call me Hope."

"Hope, then—like I said on the phone, we want to talk to you about the person you saw on the beach early this morning. We were wondering if you could give us any further information."

An odd expression crossed Hope's face, as if she were a little disturbed by Riley's query.

"How do you mean?" Hope asked.

Riley said, "The man in the mug shot the police sent to you earlier—it turned out not to be the killer."

"Oh?"

Riley took out her computer pad and brought up the composite sketch. She got up from her chair and showed it to the woman.

"This is the sketch the artist made from your description," Riley said.

Hope squinted at the picture.

"Is it really? That's odd, I … remember the man looking a little different."

"How so?" Riley said.

"I'm not sure," Hope said. "Lighter hair, maybe."

Riley began to worry a little. Had the sketch artist botched the job?

Still holding the sketch in front of the woman, Riley said, "I'd like you to describe exactly what happened this morning. What were you doing on the beach?"

"Oh, Neptune and I go jogging there three mornings a week, at least when the weather is nice. It's a lovely, peaceful place in the morning. Although I'm afraid it's been ruined for me after what just happened. I guess I'll have to find a new place to jog."

Hope shuddered deeply.

"What an awful thing to have happen," she said. "And in such a beautiful place, too."

Jenn asked, "Your dog was with you?"

Hope laughed.

"Oh, yes. Neptune keeps me from getting lost. I don't know what I'd do without him."

Riley glanced at Jenn, then at Bill. She knew what they both were thinking. Chief Belt hadn't mentioned that the woman had had a dog with her. It might be an important detail. Just how thorough had the interview been?

Riley said, "I'd like you to talk me through exactly what happened. Which way were you jogging along the beach?"

"South. The sun hadn't come up yet, but I saw …"

Hope got a faraway look in her eye.

"I saw Rags Tucker's little hut some distance ahead of me. I saw a man walking around there. I figured it must be Rags. I thought I'd stop by to say hello. I like to talk to Rags. Everybody does. Sometimes Rags and I even do a little business."

She pointed to a gray twisted piece of wood on a nearby cabinet.

"I got that piece of driftwood from him. Traded an old vase for it. Quite a bargain, really."

"And then?" asked Riley, anxious to keep the woman focused.

"As I got closer, the man didn't seem to look like Rags at all. He looked bulkier and too neatly dressed. I wondered what he was doing there. There was seldom anybody else out and around there at that time of morning."

Hope paused for a moment.

"Then I got a good look at his face."

She looked again at the composite sketch.

"I'm afraid this just isn't right. I'm sure the man had lighter hair. And a ruddy complexion."

Suddenly something didn't seem right to Riley.

She asked, "You got a good look at his face, you said?"

"Pretty good."

"How close did you get to him?"

"Oh, pretty close. Ten feet, maybe."

Riley felt jarred.

She remembered clearly Chief Belt telling her that the witness had been about twenty feet away.

What was wrong here?

She asked, "And you could see his face clearly?"

"Oh, yes."

"How?"

"Well, it wasn't very light out yet. But the light definitely fell on his face."

Riley felt another small jolt. She remembered asking Chief Belt where the witness had been in relationship with the suspect.

She asked, "But wasn't he between you and the light?"

"No, not at all."

"So you were running close to the water? Between the water and the wigwam? Not higher up on the beach?"

"I think so. At least I was running nearer the water this morning."

Riley sat staring at her.

"Is something wrong?" the woman asked, smiling pleasantly.

A strange feeling was starting to come over Riley.

It was as if she were being lulled by her surroundings—the

pastel colors of the walls and the peaceful paintings, the soothing music.

Even the woman herself was somehow a lulling presence.

Lulling, Riley thought. *And likeable.*

A tingling possibility occurred to her.

This woman was large and strong—strong enough to have committed the murders.

Riley flashed back to her impressions of how the murderer had lured the victim on the beach through personal charm, then smiled down into the hole in the woods while pouring dirt over the victim.

With a shock she realized—she could easily visualize this woman's face in those situations.

Was it possible?

Of course it is, Riley thought.

After all, the last murderer Riley had brought to justice had been a woman.

Her brain clicked away, trying to figure out how to draw out Hope's guilt.

She asked, "When you run past Rags Tucker's wigwam, do you always run between it and the beach?"

"I really don't understand why—"

"Just answer my question, please."

The woman's brow crinkled.

"Not always. It depends."

"Depends on what?"

Hope shrugged.

"The tide, I guess. If it's high I run higher on the beach, if it's low I run close to the water."

Riley sensed that Hope was getting nervous.

"Hope, could you tell me where you were the morning before last at about six o'clock?"

Hope's eyes widened.

"Why … I was here. In bed asleep."

"And not out running?"

Hope smiled nervously.

"Probably not. I don't go running every morning."

Riley's voice got sharper.

"Probably not? Are you saying you can't remember what you were doing two mornings ago?"

Now Hope was starting to look angry and defensive.

"Maybe I don't. Why is it any of your business? You don't

need to get pushy about it."

Pushy? Riley thought.

The response struck her as downright weird.

Riley said, "I think you'd better start answering my questions in a straightforward manner."

Hope crossed her arms.

"Why should I? You're acting just like my family. And my friends. And the people who work for me. Acting like I don't know what's what, like I don't know what I'm doing. What's with everybody, anyway? Why are you treating me like this? I don't even understand what you're doing here, asking me all these questions. I've got half a mind to call the police."

The police? Riley thought.

Riley was suddenly baffled. What on earth was Hope even talking about?

It began to occur to Riley that the woman was deeply insane— and possibly very dangerous.

As Riley tried to think of what to ask next, her hand hovered near her handcuffs.

One way or the other, she felt sure that she was going to make an arrest in the next few seconds.

Then Riley felt Bill's hand on her shoulder.

He said, "Riley, we're through here. Let's go."

CHAPTER TWENTY TWO

Riley could hardly believe her ears. She turned and looked at Bill, who was standing right behind her. His expression was serious, but it gave her no clue to why he had suddenly decided to leave.

She opened her mouth to protest, but Bill spoke first.

"I mean it. Let's go."

As Bill escorted Riley to the front door, she heard Jenn saying, "Thank you for your time, Ms. Reitman. We're sorry for the inconvenience. Please call us if you remember anything pertinent."

The three agents left the house. Without comment, Bill took the driver's seat of the SUV again, so Riley got in front next to him. She heard Jenn climb into the back.

When Bill spoke, Riley was startled by the sharpness of his voice.

"Riley, what did you think you were doing back there?"

Riley glared at him. She felt her anger rising.

"What was *I* doing?" she snapped. "I was doing my job. What about you? We almost had her, Bill. She was almost ready to talk."

She pointed to the front door of the townhouse.

She said, "Let's get back in there. We can finish this thing in minutes."

"Finish what?" Bill growled. "She's not our killer."

"Like hell she's not," Riley said. "She's strong enough, she's got no alibi, and she fits my profile. Best of all, she's practically gift-wrapped. She can't keep her stories straight. Give me just another few minutes with her and—"

"And what?" Bill snapped. "You'll beat the truth out of her?"

Riley was startled by Bill's indignation.

"I won't have to," she said. "Just a few more questions. I'm sure to break her."

"She's broken already!" Bill almost shouted.

His voice reverberated through the car for a moment.

Riley's mouth dropped open.

"What do you mean?" she asked.

Bill just shook his head. Riley heard Jenn's voice from the seat behind her.

"Hope Reitman has dementia."

Riley was thunderstruck. She twisted around to argue with Jenn.

"That—that's impossible," she sputtered. "She's so—"

"Young?" Bill interrupted. "It happens. It's called early onset dementia. My sister-in-law had it, died from it just a couple of years ago, and she wasn't much older than me."

Riley glanced back and forth between Bill and Jenn.

She could see by their expressions that they'd come to the same conclusion.

But Riley was still having trouble believing it.

"How do you know?" she asked Bill and Jenn.

Jenn said, "I just got a feeling right from the start. Remember what she said about running with her dog?"

Riley did remember …

"Neptune keeps me from getting lost."

Riley had thought it was a joke.

Had Hope meant it?

Bill said, "And did you hear about what she said about her friends, family, and coworkers? They've all noticed her lapses. They're worried about her living alone. They think she needs someone to take care of her. And she's defensive about it. She's in denial. The same thing happened with my sister-in-law."

Riley's heart sank. She laid her head back on the headrest and ran images of the interview through her mind.

Now that she thought back on Hope Reitman's words, her actions, it seemed perfectly obvious.

It had certainly been obvious to Jenn and Bill.

Why hadn't it been obvious to her?

She was sure that she'd normally pick up on something like that. Her gut would tell her that the woman was too incapacitated to be a murderer.

Why didn't her gut tell her that this time?

She had to stop herself from asking aloud …

"What's wrong with me?"

Instead, she simply said, "I'm sorry."

Bill shook his head.

"This has already been a long hard day," he said. "Let's go get something to eat."

Bill started the car and drove them to a fast food place in the same chain as the one in Williamsburg where they'd eaten earlier.

Inside, everything looked the same. Riley couldn't shake off the feeling that they'd gone nowhere, made no progress at all today. They all ordered burgers again, but Riley didn't feel hungry. She sat staring at her food, feeling frustrated and tired.

"OK, then," Bill said when they all got seated. "What do we do now?"

All three agents sat and thought for a few moments.

Finally Riley said, "I guess we'd better check in with Craig Huang and find out how everybody else is doing."

She dialed up Huang's number and put her cell phone on speaker.

When he answered, Huang asked, "Did you get anything more from the witness?"

"Less than nothing," Riley said. "The witness is completely unreliable."

"Unreliable? How?"

Riley suppressed a sigh.

"I'll explain it some other time. How are things going with your people?"

"There's not much to report. Whittington and Craft are back from meeting with the victims' families. They didn't get any new information. Engel's doing his best to keep the reporters from spreading crazy rumors. Ridge and Geraty are on their way back to Quantico with the sand timers. Chief Belt and I are getting ready to put out an APB warning people to stay away from Belle Terre."

Riley thought for a moment.

"Are you and Belt sending out the sketch with your APB?"

"We're planning to."

"Don't," Riley said.

Huang sounded surprised.

"Isn't it better than nothing?" he said.

Riley thought for a moment.

She remembered what Hope Reitman had said when she'd looked at the sketch.

"I'm sure the man had lighter hair. And a ruddy complexion."

The woman's memory was obviously completely unreliable.

She said to Huang, "It's likely to be really inaccurate and that might do more harm that good. Anyhow, the face is so innocuous, we might start getting false identifications again. Worse, it might give people a false sense of security. They might not recognize the killer if they really see him. It might even put people in danger."

"We'll scrap it, then," Huang said. "What else do we need to do?"

Riley paused again.

She said, "Just do everything you can to secure Belle Terre. Put all the local cops to work, even those who aren't usually on night duty. Send out some drones with night vision to survey the area. Make sure that nobody is in Belle Terre who shouldn't be."

Bill said, "What about Rags Tucker?"

Riley was slightly startled. She'd almost forgotten about Rags, who might be in danger all alone in that area. She was glad Bill mentioned him. But she was also a little disconcerted that she hadn't thought about him first.

She said, "Agent Huang, send a couple agents to pick up that vagrant we talked to on the beach and find a safe place for him to spend the night. He might not be happy about it, but get him out of there anyway."

Huang chuckled a little.

He said, "Should I send a couple of heavies, or agents with good people skills?"

It seemed like an odd question, but Riley knew it was a good one.

"Go with people skills," she said. "I don't think he'll put up a fight but he won't be happy and there's no point in provoking him. But tell whoever you send not to take no for an answer. We've got to get him out of there."

When she finished giving Huang instructions, Riley ended the call.

Jenn said, "What about the three of us? What do we do now?"

Riley shrugged.

She said, "We'd better head back to the police station and give Huang a hand with things."

Bill was looking at her steadily.

"Riley, I'm not sure that's such a good idea."

Riley stared at him for a moment, wondering what he meant.

She quickly realized from his anxious expression …

He's worried about my mental state.

That really made her angry.

She said, "What do you think I'm going to do? Beat somebody else up? Or just generally make a mess of things?"

Bill shook his head.

"Can you really say you're at your best right now, Riley?" he said.

Riley stared at him in stunned silence for a moment. She knew perfectly well that the answer to his question was no.

Bill added, "Riley, we're not needed there. Huang's got things completely under control. Let's head back to Quantico, check in with Meredith and see if we can give Flores and his team any help with their forensics work or computer searches. It's a better use of our time."

Riley couldn't disagree.

She noticed that Bill and Jenn had finished eating. She had barely touched her burger at all. She took one bite, chewed, and swallowed fast.

"Come on, let's go," she said.

As the three agents walked toward the SUV, Jenn said, "Let's not get too worried. With the park closed off, he's not likely to kill tonight."

"If we're lucky," Bill said, getting into the SUV on the driver's side.

If we're lucky, Riley thought as she buckled herself into the passenger seat.

But she couldn't help thinking about that sand timer, still trickling away the seconds.

CHAPTER TWENTY THREE

Felix Harrington leaned on the handle of his shovel and looked over his work with a sense of satisfaction. He had just finished digging a sufficiently deep hole here inside the abandoned storage building. The sandy soil of this dirt floor had been perfect for digging—and a diverting change from his previous two efforts, both of them outdoors.

At least I'm not predictable, he thought.

And that was important.

He'd been following the news all day and knew what a stir he'd caused throughout the area. He knew that the Belle Terre Nature Preserve was closed off to the public, which meant that the cops expected him to strike there again.

He smiled with satisfaction.

No one could possibly guess that this would be his next spot. He wouldn't have guessed it himself until his explorations had turned up this suitable site.

His killings were as random as the patterns made by water in the ocean sand—the very patterns he had portrayed in his woodwork on the sand timers. Yes, they were like those patterns, similar but never exactly the same.

He stabbed his shovel into the pile of dirt next to the hole and walked over to admire the new sand timer sitting nearby. He'd made it just for the occasion. Right now, all the sand lay quiet in the bottom globe. But soon enough he would turn it over and the sand would flow, marking the hours and minutes left in someone's life.

He knew that word had gotten around about his other two timers, especially the one that was still running. The cops, the FBI, and even the public understood his message.

He knew that he'd even gotten a couple of nicknames.

What were they?

Oh, yes.

"Father Time."

"The Sandman."

His smile disappeared. The truth was, he didn't much care for all this publicity.

He wasn't doing all this for fame.

The truth was, he still didn't know quite what drove him to kill.

He only knew that something dark had welled up in him recently—some sort of irrational terror and pain. The only way to expel that pain was to inflict it upon other people—not just the people he buried, but the many other people he shocked and frightened.

People would lie awake tonight, wondering who would die when the timer he'd left behind ran out.

It gave him a feeling of power that relieved his own agony and fear. It also gave him a sense of purpose, of destiny. He was linked in some important way to that falling sand. It fascinated him and it drove him to complete his actions before it ended.

It gave meaning to his life.

He turned away from the timer beside the empty hole. This was not the time to turn it over and start its flow of sand. That would be hours from now.

I've got nothing but time, he thought, brushing off his hands again.

He stepped outside the building and strolled to the water's edge, looking out over the brackish creek that flowed into the Chesapeake Bay. He stood still and admired the nighttime view. It was never completely dark on the water, and lights along the shoreline highlighted the gently lapping waves.

It had been a warm day, a lovely day. And he was truly enjoying the coolness of night on the water.

Off to his right, new and substantial houses boasted their own private piers and boat slips. Those were the lights that illuminated the water. Back to his left, the shoreline was darker. Since this little marina had fallen into disuse, only a few bare bulbs shed their weak light in that area.

Of course, all these old marina buildings and rotting piers would soon be cleared away. No doubt a new and larger marina would spring up with facilities for boats owned by the wealthier families that were moving into the area.

Gentrification, he thought.

The thought troubled him, because it meant that people would soon be encroaching upon this quiet area. People were even moving closer to his own isolated home on a different waterfront.

He shuddered at the thought.

People.

He'd always been shy, but he could remember, when he was little, not being so deeply alarmed by the presence of other people.

For some years now he'd been deliberately reclusive. He could spend days at a time without seeing another living soul.

Or at least he could not long ago.

Machines were disturbing the sandy earth just a mile from his home. He could already feel the pressure of people moving in … setting off pain and terror that he couldn't understand.

Even now, just thinking about it, he could feel his heart beating faster, his breath coming short. He didn't understand why, but he did know what he had to do about it.

He slowly breathed in the damp night air to calm himself down.

After all, there were no people in sight here, and he could bask in the solitude.

And he wasn't in a hurry.

He could spend an hour or so hanging around here before he got into his pickup truck and drove through this little town looking for his next random victim.

Suddenly, a wandering flash of light caught his eye among the other buildings.

He quickly realized that someone was approaching him with a flashlight, walking across the open area between the marina buildings.

Who was it?

He felt a rush of panic at the thought of encountering another human being.

But then he realized, maybe he wasn't going to have to go driving in search of a victim after all.

Maybe he was going to be especially lucky tonight, and a victim was about to fall right into his hands. That was the way he preferred things to happen anyhow—the way the two joggers had come to him during the previous mornings.

The flashlight came closer and hurt his eyes. He couldn't see the person who was holding it. But he heard a man's voice.

"What are you doing here?"

Felix grew anxious. The man seemed to be a night watchman. Felix hadn't spent enough time here to realize anyone came around to check on the abandoned marina at night. Was he about to get kicked out without fulfilling his plans?

That would be a disaster. After all, the twenty-four-hour timer that he had left on the beach put him on a strict schedule. If it emptied without anybody dying, all of his elaborate plans and preparations would be utterly pointless. His life would be off schedule and he didn't know how he could stand that.

Nevertheless, Felix smiled. All his life, he'd known that he had a charming smile that easily won people over, even when he felt anything but outgoing. Surely he'd be able to win this man over as well.

"Just enjoying the night air," Felix said.

The flashlight continued to shine in his eyes.

"This is private property," the man said.

"Is it? I didn't know."

A tense silence fell. But Felix kept on smiling.

Finally he said, "Look, I don't mean any harm. This is a nice place to enjoy the night, that's all."

The man lowered his flashlight, but Felix was still temporarily blinded.

"It is a nice night, isn't it?" the man said.

Felix noticed an odd slur in his voice. Had the watchman been drinking?

Felix's eyes quickly adjusted, and he could see the watchman's face. He was a middle-aged man, of short but stocky build. His face was puffy and tired. It looked like he drank a lot.

The man said, "Well, you don't seem to be causing any trouble. You're not here to steal anything, are you?"

Felix laughed and gestured at their surroundings.

"Is there anything around to steal?"

The man laughed as well.

"Good point. It's a funny sort of job I've got—a night watchman with nothing much to watch out for."

"As long is it pays," Felix said. He had long ago discovered his own funny sort of skills that allowed him to work at home.

"Yep, as long as it pays," the man said.

Felix moved closer to the man. Sure enough, he could smell liquor on his breath. He must be quite drunk.

Felix winked at him.

"Hey, you wouldn't happen to have a nip of whiskey you could share with me, do you?"

The man let out an embarrassed chuckle.

"As it happens, I do," he said. "Don't tell anybody, though."

"Who would I tell?"

"Good point."

The watchman produced a flask from his pocket and passed it to Felix. Felix opened the flask and took a sip, then handed it back. The watchman took a good swallow and put the flask back in his pocket.

Felix said, "I've never come around here before. Maybe you could show me the sights."

The man laughed more heartily. Felix could tell that he was winning over his trust.

"The scenic Lorneville marina, you mean?" the watchman said. "It never occurred to me I might have a future as a tour guide. Sure, let's go have a look around. I'll show you some of the docks. Watch your step, though. Some of the boards are getting rotten, and they're liable to give out from under you."

"I'll watch my step," Felix said.

As the two men started walking side by side, Felix started planning his next move.

Unfortunately, he'd left his leather-covered billy club back in his truck.

But as luck would have it, they were walking toward a wall built out of loose stones of every possible shape and size. Surely he could use one of those to knock the man out cold. The man wasn't too big for him to drag back to the hole in the building. Then he could get an early start on his deadly task. He'd have to take his time, though. He mustn't finish until six o'clock on the dot, when the sand ran out of the timer.

Now that he thought of it, taking his time really appealed to him.

They were walking alongside the wall now. Felix spotted a rock that would fit in his hand perfectly. He reached out and surreptitiously grabbed it, then held it low at his side, out of sight of the watchman.

He'd wait for the perfect moment to use it.

Meanwhile, it occurred to him that this killing was unfolding rather differently from the others. He was striking up something of a personal rapport with his victim, which he hadn't had a chance to do with the other two victims.

For some reason, that also appealed to him—the thought that the man's death wouldn't be merely terrifying and painful but a betrayal of newly found trust.

"What's your name, mister?" he asked.

"Silas Ostwinkle. What's yours?"

Should I tell him? Felix wondered.

Why on earth not?

It wasn't as if the man was ever going to get a chance to identify him.

"Felix Harrington," he said.

"Pleased to make your acquaintance," the watchman said.

"The feeling is very mutual," Felix said.

CHAPTER TWENTY FOUR

Riley felt deeply exhausted by the time Bill pulled the SUV into the BAU parking lot.

Why? she wondered. She looked at her watch and saw that the hour was approaching midnight.

That wasn't really terribly late.

She noticed that Bill and Jenn both looked as tired as she felt.

They had all been working since early this morning, but that didn't explain the way she felt. She'd worked for much longer hours at a stretch on other cases in the past. And while that might not yet be true of Jenn, it certainly was true of Bill.

So what was it about this one that was so especially tiring?

Why was she experiencing this deep, internal feeling of exhaustion?

As if in answer, an image flashed in her head …

That sand timer, its sand still trickling inexorably toward …

What? Riley wondered.

Another murder?

Another burial before an agonizing death?

Riley sighed as she and her companions got out of the car and headed toward the building.

It was hardly any wonder that this case was wearing them down. The flowing sand timer made all the difference, eating away at their energy and morale.

And of course, that was what the killer had in mind.

Riley wondered what he was thinking at that very moment.

Was he feeling happy with himself?

She didn't like the idea that he probably was.

When she and her two colleagues entered the BAU building, Riley felt oddly comforted to see a familiar bustle of activity. The BAU was always vigilant, with personnel working day and night. And vigilance was exactly what was needed right now.

The three of them headed straight toward Meredith's office. Sure enough, the team chief was still here, putting in his own long hours to supervise this especially challenging case.

He got up from his chair as they entered and glared at Riley.

"Agent Paige, Walder stopped by before he left the building earlier," he said. "He sounded pretty pissed off with you. He said he'd relieved you as the leader on this case. I take it that Huang is now in charge."

Meredith crossed his arms.

Riley was about to explain what had happened when she noticed a slight smirk form on Meredith's face.

He knows! she thought.

Somehow, Meredith knew that Huang had shrugged off Walder's orders and left Riley in charge.

Had Huang called and told him so?

Or had her wily superior figured it out for himself?

She didn't dare ask.

Meredith's smirk widened.

He said, "I'm glad to hear that the case is in good hands."

Riley gulped.

"Yes, sir," she said. "Me too, sir."

"Now tell me what's going on," Meredith said.

Riley, Jenn, and Bill filled him in on the day's activities, from their arrival at the two murder scenes to their fruitless interview with Hope Reitman. Meredith listened attentively with his fingers steepled together.

When they finished, he sat in silence for a moment.

Riley held her breath, waiting for the chief to pass judgment on their work. Meredith could be downright savage in his criticism. Surely he couldn't be happy that they hadn't yet apprehended the killer.

Finally Meredith spoke with a note of resignation in his voice.

"You've done well. I wouldn't have done anything differently in your situation."

Riley breathed more easily.

Meredith added, "This case is a bitch, though. Are you assuming there's going to be another victim when the timer runs out?"

Riley exchanged glances with Bill and Jenn.

Jenn spoke up. "Maybe not. The public in that area has been alerted to the danger. And Huang is making sure that nobody gets in or out of Belle Terre. And so far, that seems to be his stomping ground."

Bill added, "There's a good chance that location is a strong element in his MO."

"We still don't know much about him," Riley commented. "But it's a possibility."

"Let's hope we've thwarted him," Meredith said. "The three of you had better check in with Sam Flores, find out how he and his people are doing."

Riley and her colleagues agreed. They left Meredith's office and headed toward the tech center where Flores was in charge. The place was bustling even more than the rest of the building.

Sam Flores was sitting at his desk surrounded by computers. When he looked up and saw Riley and her colleagues, he asked how they were faring with the case.

"We're still coming up blank," Riley said. "Have you found out anything here?"

Flores said, "I've handed the timers over to some of my specialists. So far, they've only been able to confirm that the wood was hand-carved. They'll run tests on the composition of the glass and wood to see if they can find any sources for those. They won't be going home tonight. I won't either."

Flores pointed to newspaper articles he'd brought up on his computer screens.

"I've been running some searches, trying to find out if our killer might have done the same thing someplace else. It doesn't look like it."

Riley was a bit surprised.

She asked, "You mean there aren't any other instances of people being buried alive?"

"Yeah, sure, but they're not like these killings. I don't see any cases where the burials are carried out for their own sake, for the sheer sadism of it. There's always some other motive."

Riley and her colleagues stood behind Flores looking at the stories he'd found.

Flores began pointing at different articles.

"I've found one who buried his victim because she knew he'd murdered somebody else in a more conventional manner. Others bludgeoned or shot their victims first, and weren't even sure whether they were alive or dead when they buried them. Coroners discovered it after the bodies were found."

Riley pointed at one of the stories.

She said, "That one seems to have been initiated by a robbery."

Flores said, "Yeah, the killer buried an elderly couple after emptying their bank accounts."

Riley shuddered at the thought of the victims' terror.

"Do these killers sometimes have accomplices?" she asked.

"Some of them, yeah," Flores said. "It's a lot of work for one person—both the digging and the cleanup. Have you ruled out the possibility that the killer's got a partner?"

Riley said, "Not yet."

The truth was Riley had a gut feeling that this killer worked alone. But she was having trouble trusting her gut right now.

Jenn suggested, "It's all about literally 'covering up' with these killers that you've found, isn't it?"

Sam nodded and asked, "Isn't it the same with your guy?"

"No, I don't think so," Bill said. "He expects us to find his victims. And he expects us to know that he's planning another one. Otherwise, there'd be no point in leaving the sand timers."

Flores sat thinking for a moment.

He said, "When you think about it, what our guy is doing is downright counterintuitive—burying victims when part of the point is for someone to find them."

Riley nodded.

"Almost a contradiction in terms," she said.

Flores pointed to an article and added, "And these aren't your garden variety sociopaths. This one was so overcome with guilt that he tried to kill himself with a drug overdose."

Riley silently agreed. One thing seemed certain—remorse wasn't part of their killer's makeup.

Jenn asked Flores, "So what are you going to do next?"

Flores shrugged.

"I'll keep searching, looking for more insights," he said. "And I'll wait for my guys to come up with some info about the sand timers."

Riley had a sinking feeling.

More insights, she thought.

Normally, insights were exactly what were most needed in a case like this.

But what good were insights into a killer who might be preparing for his next murder at that very moment?

It was the same with researching the source of the sand timers.

What possible use could that information be right now?

They didn't need to understand the killer. They needed to find him and stop him and bring him to justice—right now.

Still, the last thing Riley wanted to do was tell Sam Flores that his work was a waste of time. He was doing his job, and he was doing it with his usual skill and professionalism. And it might eventually point them in the right direction.

"Good work, Flores," she told. "Keep at it."

At that moment, Meredith stepped into the doorway.

"I'm heading home for the night," he said. Looking at Riley, Bill, and Jenn, he added, "I suggest you three do the same."

Riley was startled.

This was the last suggestion she expected the chief to make.

"But sir …" she began.

"But what?" Meredith said. "What do you expect to accomplish? Agent Huang's managing things around Belle Terre, and Flores here has got his team handling just everything else. Unless Huang gets some kind of break, whatever happens during the next few hours won't change anything. If there's still a murderer out there tomorrow, it's going to be up to you three to catch him. I need you to be fresh and alert. Go home. That's an order."

Meredith walked away without another word.

Riley and her colleagues stood looking at each other for a moment. Riley could see the exhaustion in their faces, and knew that they could see the same in hers. But she also knew that none of them wanted to leave with so many questions unanswered.

But Meredith was right. What else could they hope to achieve right now?

Jenn shrugged wearily and said, "Well, an order's an order."

"I guess so," Bill said. "I'll see you all tomorrow."

All three of them left the lab and headed on toward the front entrance. But Riley simply couldn't bring herself to go home just yet. She lagged behind, then went to her office and sat down at her computer. She wondered—what could she search for that Flores might have overlooked?

She remembered what Jenn had said earlier today …

"Have you ever noticed what sand looks like on a beach at low tide?"

Without stopping to think, Riley typed two search words …

Beach sand.

Then she sat staring at the images of the sand that appeared.

She was especially drawn to close-up pictures of sand as the tide was creeping away.

Riley stared hard at the photos. The water made ripples that were unmistakably like the shapes carved into the sand timers. She was sure that images like these had been the killer's inspiration.

But so what? she wondered.

As she kept staring, she had the feeling that the key to the whole mystery was right in front of her.

The truth was looking her right in the face.

So why couldn't she make sense of it?

A wave of exhaustion swept over her and she shut her eyes. Even then the sand images lingered in her imagination, the ripples changing and mutating into all sorts of patterns and shapes.

Her eyes snapped open at the sound of Bill's voice.

"What the hell are you still doing here?"

She turned and saw Bill standing in the door.

"What am *I* doing here?" she asked. "What about *you*?"

Bill let out a growl of disapproval.

"I had a hunch you wouldn't leave. I came back to check. And sure enough, here you are—falling asleep in front of your own computer. Go home, Riley. Get some rest. That's what I'm going to do."

"OK, I'll go," Riley said.

She expected Bill to leave. He didn't.

"What are you waiting for?" she said.

"You," Bill said. "I'll walk you to your car."

Riley reluctantly got up from her chair and left the building with Bill.

Before Riley opened her car door, Bill said, "Do you think maybe I should drive you home?"

Riley squinted at him.

"Why?" she asked.

Bill shrugged.

"You're practically asleep on your feet," he said.

Riley resisted the urge to say …

You don't look much better yourself.

Instead she simply said, "I'll be fine."

She got into the car and Bill headed back toward his own vehicle. As she started to drive, she was hit with wave after wave of exhaustion. It was only a half-hour drive to her house, but even so, she wondered whether she should have taken Bill up on his offer. But it was too late to change her mind.

As she drove, she was having a hard time focusing her eyes. The lights from streetlights and other vehicles and surrounding buildings seemed to be mutating, assuming strange shapes and patterns.

Soon she realized what those patterns were.

They were ripples in damp beach sand, left behind by a retreating tide.

She was starting to become alarmed now. She had to keep her mind on her driving. She slapped herself across the cheek to bring herself back to alertness. It worked—at least a little. At least she felt sure she could make it the rest of the way home.

But as she kept driving, manifold details about the case kept crowding themselves into her brain—her vague impressions of the killer, the two murder scenes, a horde of unanswered questions about the killer's obsession with sand …

She also found herself remembering Hope Reitman's serene and distant expression, that lulling smile of hers, her confused recollections.

The poor woman, Riley thought.

And yet …

Riley wondered if she almost envied her.

After all, Hope Reitman could no longer even try to keep so many things in her head. If she would only allow someone to take care of her, maybe she'd even experience a kind of peace that Riley would never know, quietly disappear into a fog of forgetfulness.

Riley gritted her teeth.

No, that must be terrible, Riley thought.

What could possibly be more hellish than losing everything someone had been and done to a wasting disease?

And yet …

Riley wondered how many more things she could cram into her head without losing her mind.

CHAPTER TWENTY FIVE

Liam walked as quietly as he could out of the family room and through to the front of the house. He was carrying a suitcase stuffed with his own belongings.

One question kept running through his mind …

Do I really want to do this?

He stopped in the dining room and pulled his cell phone out of his pocket, looking again at his father's message …

I miss you, son.

His father had sent that message a couple of hours ago. Liam hadn't replied. Then about an hour later, his father had sent another message …

Are you still my son?

As Liam looked at the words, they tore right through him all over again.

He hadn't answered that second message either.

But he'd immediately started packing his things to go home.

And now he put his cell phone back in his pocket and quietly moved forward again.

He knew that everyone else in the house was in bed—the two girls upstairs and Gabriela in her basement apartment. But Gabriela hadn't gone to bed until a little while ago. He worried that she might not be asleep yet. Would she hear the front door when he opened it?

As he went through the living room, he could see car headlights through the front window. It was pulling up in front of the townhouse and he felt sure that it was the cab he'd called to take him back to his father.

He opened the front door and stepped out onto the stoop as the vehicle stopped and its engine shut off. The car door opened.

Liam's heart sank as he stood there in the open doorway holding his suitcase.

It wasn't the cab at all.

Riley had just arrived home.

He'd hoped that Riley's current case would keep her away until much later, at least until well until after he was gone. He'd hoped he wouldn't have to make any explanations he couldn't imagine how to make.

But here she was.

Riley got out and looked at him.

"Liam!" she called out. "What are you doing?"

Liam didn't know what to say. He wanted to run back into the house and back to the family room and just hide beneath the covers in his sofa bed. But there was no point in trying to pretend that this hadn't happened.

Riley dashed up onto the front stoop beside him. She looked down at the suitcase, then straight at Liam.

Her expression looked both confused and hurt. Without a word, she picked up the suitcase with one hand and grabbed Liam's arm with the other. Carrying the suitcase, she ushered him into the house and plopped him down on a chair.

"What were you doing?" she asked again.

Liam opened his mouth, but no words came out.

He had no idea what to say.

Riley glared at the suitcase, then again at Liam.

With a note of alarm in her voice, she asked, "Were you going to run away?"

Liam was still speechless.

"Well, were you?" Riley demanded more sharply.

Suddenly words started to come to Liam in a helpless stammer.

"I—I don't know. I don't know what I was doing, OK? I mean—running away, what does that even mean? As far as I'm concerned?"

Riley looked completely baffled as she stared back at him.

Liam reached into his pocket and took out the cell phone. He brought up his father's messages and handed the phone to Riley. She stared at the messages with her mouth hanging open.

Liam said, "Aren't I running away already? From Dad?"

Riley turned pale. Now it seemed to be her turn to not know what to say.

"I don't think I can do this, Riley," Liam said. "Leave Dad alone, I mean. I'm all he's got. He misses me. He needs me. I don't know what's going to happen to him if …"

His words trailed off.

Riley slowly sat down in a chair and spoke in a hushed, shaken voice.

"Liam, we talked about this. Your dad is very ill. It's a terrible thing, but it's not your fault."

Liam couldn't hold back his tears anymore.

"But he sounds like he's getting worse," he said.

"It's still not your fault," Riley said.

"I feel like I'm letting him down."

Riley suddenly sounded angry.

"Liam, it's *us* you're letting down! It's April and Jilly and Gabriela—and me! We're committed to you! All of us! We're counting on you! You can't go sneaking out on us like this!"

Liam was shocked—not just by Riley's voice, but by her exhausted expression. It suddenly dawned on him his dad wasn't the only person he'd been worried about. He'd been worried about Riley as well.

Trying to keep his voice from shaking, he said, "Riley, I'm grateful for everything you're doing for me. But you've got so much to deal with already. Not just everybody here, but your job. I've got no idea how tough it must be for you. But it can't be good for you, having another kid to deal with."

Riley shook her head miserably.

"I don't have time for this," she said.

"That's just what I mean," Liam said. "Having me around is just too much—"

Riley interrupted him with a wail of despair.

"You don't understand!"

She was shaking all over now, her fists gripping the arms of the chair.

In a choking voice, she cried out, "I don't … have time … for anything!"

Then Liam saw Riley's eyes dart around wildly.

She looked as if she'd just realized something absolutely terrible.

Then she buckled over in the chair and burst into uncontrollable sobs.

Liam was stunned into silence. For a moment he watched helplessly as Riley wept uncontrollably. Finally, he got up and walked over to her. He sat down on the arm of her chair and put his hand on her shaking shoulder.

136

He soon heard Gabriela's footsteps coming up the stairs, and the girls' footsteps coming downstairs. Riley's outburst had awakened everyone in the house.

*

As she sat there weeping helplessly, Riley felt sick and dizzy, and her whole world seemed to whirl around her. Her own words echoed through her head ...

"I don't have time for anything!"

She knew that she had somehow told the truth about herself, and she was struggling to understand what it meant.

She remembered something that Mike Nevins had said.

"More ugly stuff is liable to surface inside you before this whole thing is over."

This was it, and she knew it.

This case was all about *time.* The inexorable flow of the sand through the timer, the measured hours and minutes and seconds between life and death, the thought of victims themselves being buried alive, knowing that they didn't have much time left to live— all these things were triggering fears Riley didn't even know she had held deep inside, never daring to let them surface.

No, she didn't have enough time—not for her family, not for another teenager in her life, not for all the people whose lives she needed to save.

All those people, she thought wretchedly.

For the first time, the truth welled up and exploded inside her.

There were always more people who needed saving, more monsters to stop, while the people she loved needed her more and more and more. There was no end to it all and there never would be.

She really and truly didn't have time for *anything.*

Even if she lived another fifty or sixty years, she'd die leaving an endless mass of work unfinished.

She'd leave the world completely unchanged, as if she'd never lived at all.

She'd never thought of herself as the kind of person who feared death. But deep inside, she'd been terrified by death all along.

Not for her own sake, but for the sake of the people who needed her now, and the infinite number of people who would need her in the future.

They needed her help, and she'd never be able to help them.

She simply didn't have time … to accomplish anything meaningful or lasting in her life.

Riley's sobbing lessened, and she felt her body go slack. The weight of fear she'd been carrying around had been lifted at long last. But the pain was still there. Riley wondered if it would ever leave.

She realized that Liam was sitting on the armrest next to her with his hand on her shoulder.

The poor kid, she thought.

He must be wondering what on earth had come over her.

She also heard noisy, jarring voices. She looked up and saw Gabriela and the girls standing around speaking angrily to Liam. She realized that they were mad at Liam for planning to leave—and especially for making Riley cry.

She looked up at Liam and saw that tears were pouring down the boy's face.

Riley said to Gabriela and the girls, "Don't be mad at Liam. None of this is his fault."

Jilly was pacing back and forth.

"What do you mean, it's not his fault?" she snapped. "He was sneaking out in the middle of the night without telling any of us. Doesn't he care about any of our feelings?"

"He does, Jilly," Riley said. "He cares a lot. He cares about his dad's feelings too. That's the kind of kid he is. He cares about everybody's feelings. He's a really, really good kid."

Riley reached up and pulled Liam into a hug.

"I'm sorry I yelled at you," she said.

"It's OK," Liam said, wiping away his tears. "I guess I had it coming."

"No, you didn't. I've had other things eating at me, and I took it out on you. I shouldn't have, and I'm sorry."

"It's OK," Liam said again.

Riley saw that April had calmed down and was looking at her and Liam with concern.

April said, "Liam, just promise you'll never do this again."

"I promise," Liam said.

Gabriela was standing by with her arms crossed. She nodded with approval at Liam's promise.

She said, "I will go get us something to make us all feel better."

As Gabriela headed toward the kitchen, Riley got up from her chair and hugged April, Jilly, and Liam, telling them over and over again that she was sorry about her outburst and that everything was going to be all right.

A car horn honked outside. Riley realized it was the cab Liam had called for. Jilly hurried outside to tell the driver that he wasn't needed.

*

Riley and her family sat for a little while in the living room sipping cups of a hot, sweet drink that Gabriela had made called *atol de elote*. It was the perfect drink to soothe their shaken spirits. After some comforting chatter and a few more hugs, everybody was feeling better and headed back to their rooms.

Riley herself went upstairs and took off her shoes and flopped onto her bed. After the emotional upheaval she'd just experienced, she was too exhausted to bother to get undressed.

Anyway, she realized she could no longer stay awake, which was surely a good thing. Like Meredith had said, she and her colleagues needed to be fresh and alert for whatever tomorrow might bring.

She closed her eyes and felt waves of sleep washing over her …

Like the tide over sand, she thought.

She sighed with despair. Those images of sand pouring through the timer or rippling on a beach—she simply couldn't get them out of her head.

She also worried about what the killer might be doing right now.

Had they really thwarted his plans by closing off the Belle Terre preserve?

Or was he busy committing yet another sadistic murder at that very moment?

Riley sighed again.

She wondered—which should she dread more?

The nightmares she was about to have during the rest of the night?

Or the nightmares she might face tomorrow?

All thoughts fled from her mind as sleep closed on her like a vise.

CHAPTER TWENTY SIX

Slowly, consciousness returned to Silas Ostwinkle. At first he wondered if maybe he was in Iraq again. He couldn't remember feeling so terrible since he'd been in combat way back in February of 1991.

The nausea, the splitting head pain, the feeling of helplessness …

Can't be Iraq, he told himself, struggling to clear his head.

No. It's just another goddamn hangover.

Surely that was what was going on.

But he wasn't sure exactly where he was. He hoped he'd somehow gotten home safely into his bed and hadn't wound up unconscious in some strange place.

If he was home, there was nothing to do except sleep it off for a few hours, then climb out of bed and heat up some of yesterday's stale coffee and spend the afternoon and early evening nursing his hangover until he had to go on his night shift duties.

But he became aware that a light was shining on his face, penetrating his closed eyelids. That probably meant that he wasn't at home in bed.

He didn't want to open his eyes. But he was going to have to do that to find out where he was.

He cracked his eyelids open just a little. The painful brightness slammed them shut again.

He almost cursed aloud …

"What the fuck?"

… but he couldn't open his mouth and his curse came out as a wordless groan.

He twisted his jaw and his lips hurt as he tried to move them.

He realized that his mouth was taped shut.

He felt a shock of panic charge through his body.

But his body couldn't move. It seemed to be immobile from his chest down. Even his arms refused to move.

Struggling against the brightness, Silas got his eyes cracked open. What he saw in front of him was disorienting. He couldn't make out what he was looking at.

His eyes were adjusting to the light, so he tilted his head upward. Straight above him he saw a metal ceiling with bare light bulbs hanging down from it. It all looked vaguely familiar.

Now he recognized the place. He was in one of those old storage buildings at the marina. He seldom bothered to even check inside the buildings during his nightly rounds. What was he doing here now?

A face abruptly appeared in front of him—a man's face, smiling and vaguely familiar, looking down on him.

The man reached out and ripped the tape loose from Silas's mouth, sharply stinging his lips and his stubble of beard.

The man spoke in a pleasant voice.

"Hey, buddy, how are you doing? You look a little the worse for the wear."

"Who the hell are you?" Silas asked.

An expression of mock hurt crossed the man's face.

"You've forgotten already? Why, we met earlier tonight. I thought we'd really hit it off. I'm kind of disappointed. Well, I remember *your* name. It's Silas somebody. Yeah, Silas Ostwinkle. And I'm Felix Harrington. Pleased to make your acquaintance— again."

He held out his hand as if offering to shake Silas's hand.

Silas then realized that his own hands were fastened behind him and tingling with numbness. So were his legs and feet. And he was down in the dirt, half-buried.

Silas shook his head, trying to make some sense of everything.

The man's face looked worried now.

"Buddy, you've been out for a long time. I mean, hours now. I was afraid you weren't going to come out of it. Sunrise is coming soon. You'd better start waking up."

Silas was able to twist his head enough to check out his situation. He was down in a hole that he could barely see out of. He was buried up to his chest.

The man—Felix Harrington, he'd said his name was—had crouched beside the hole and was looking down at him.

Little by little, Silas started to remember …

He'd been drinking quite a lot before he started his shift, and he'd been more than a little wobbly as he'd made his way through the marina. But he'd figured it didn't matter. What a stupid job it was, anyway—watching over a bunch of buildings that were just going to get torn down sooner or later. He had even left his gun in his truck because he'd never needed it out here and he didn't like to carry it when he was drunk.

He'd been doing his rounds when his flashlight fell on the face of a smiling stranger.

He'd seemed like a nice enough guy, and Silas had decided not to make him leave the marina. After all, the stranger wasn't doing any harm here.

Silas had even given him a sip from his whiskey flask when he'd asked for it.

Then the guy had said …

"I've never come around here before. Maybe you could show me the sights."

They'd started walking, talking about one thing or another, and then …

Silas remembered a sharp blow to his head—and that was all.

And now he was here, more than half-buried by this nut with the perpetual grin on his face.

The man leaned forward and dangled something in front of Silas's face. It was a military medal hanging from a ribbon with vertical stripes of tan, black, white, red, blue, and green.

Goddamn it!

It was Silas's own service medal, awarded to him for his tour in Iraq.

What the hell did this guy think he was doing with it?

The man waved it back and forth in front of Silas's eyes.

"You seem to have dropped this earlier," he said.

Silas knew perfectly well that he hadn't dropped it. He always carried it buttoned safely in his shirt pocket—a reminder of a long-ago time when he'd felt that his life had been of use to anybody.

This bastard had been poking around in his pockets while he'd been unconscious.

Still waving the medal, the man said, "So which war did they give this to you for? Operation Iraqi Freedom? No, you look too old to have served in that one. Must've been Desert Storm. Am I right?"

Silas gritted his teeth.

Now he was getting mad.

"Get your hands off of that," Silas said. "Give it back."

The man kept smiling, unperturbed.

He said, "Anyway, I want to thank you for your service. I mean that, really. Those of us who stayed home ought to be ashamed of

142

ourselves. We don't appreciate you vets enough. And we've got no idea what you went through to defend the freedoms we take for granted. I can't even begin to imagine. So thank you. From the bottom of my heart. I hope you don't mind if I ask one question. If it's none of my business, just tell me to shove it."

The man peered closely into Silas's eyes.

"Were you scared? When you were in combat, I mean? Because I don't know whether I'd have the courage to do what you guys did, to face that kind of danger. I'm afraid I'd turn tail and run. But I guess you find the courage when you need it, right? I wouldn't know. But you do. And I can't help but wonder … were you scared?"

Silas felt his face twist into an expression of sneering anger.

He'd be damned if he'd answer this bastard's questions.

Even so, this question pushed his buttons.

He sure as hell had been scared in Iraq. And he couldn't help but feel some of that same fear all over again right now. It wasn't just that he was mostly buried and completely immobilized.

It was the soil itself—he'd become keenly aware of its grittiness all over him.

Sand, he thought. *I'm half-buried in sand.*

It was the sand that was getting to him most, bringing back terrible memories. His first firefight in the Iraqi desert had been terrifying in ways he couldn't possibly have anticipated.

Before he'd been in combat, he'd expected to be terrified by fierce explosions, muzzle flashes, and blasts of noise from enemy weapons.

But in the thick of gunfire, he'd barely noticed any of those things.

Instead had come the dull, rapid, eerily soft plop-plop-plop of bullets hitting the ground all around him, stirring up tiny bursts of sand in the air.

It had almost seemed harmless at first—until, right next to him, his buddy Asher's body erupted with spurts of blood from gunshots that Silas couldn't even hear, the bullets making that same plop-plop-plop noise in Asher's flesh.

Damn right, I was scared, he thought.

And it really pissed him off that this goon had the gall to stir up that fear all over again.

"Get me out of here," he hissed.

The man who called himself Felix looked all around with mock concern.

"Yeah, you are in an interesting situation here," he said. "And it looks like somebody left this job unfinished. Somebody stopped in the middle of filling up this hole. He's liable to get in trouble if it doesn't get done. I guess it's up to me."

Now the face disappeared from sight. Then the man appeared again, standing at the edge of the hole. He had a shovel in his hand.

The man shoveled a heap of dirt that barely missed Silas's face.

Silas yelled, "Hey, what the hell do you think you're doing?"

"Somebody else's job, it looks like," the man said, scooping up another shovelful of dirt from a nearby pile. "No need for you to worry about it. You're pretty inconvenienced at the moment, I can see that, so don't even bother trying to help. I'll take care of everything."

Silas was seized with real terror now—the kind of terror he often experienced in nightmares, and which he tried for many years to drown out during his waking hours with alcohol.

He was helpless—truly helpless.

His very immobility triggered psychic echoes of that first firefight.

His body had been free then, but even so he'd felt paralyzed, because there was no safe place to move to. There wasn't anywhere to run from the plop-plop-plop of bullets in the sand.

But right now he could do one thing he hadn't been able to do in Iraq.

He could scream his head off.

He screamed at the top of his lungs.

"Help! Somebody help!"

The man threw another shovelful of dirt into the hole, then looked around.

"Odd that somebody bothered taping your mouth shut," he said. "I can see taping your wrists and ankles to keep you from getting too wiggly, but what was the point of taping your mouth? I mean, who's going to hear you? The night watchman maybe?"

With a chuckle, he lifted up another shovelful of dirt.

"Oh, right," he added. "You *are* the night watchman!"

Silas screamed so loud that the inside of his throat felt like it was getting scraped with sandpaper.

"Help! Help!"

But this time he was silenced by a shovelful of sandy dirt right in his face, filling his mouth and making him gag. He coughed and

144

choked and tried to spit it out.

The man above him was loading another shovel full, still smiling as agreeably as ever.

He said, "You just keep right on yelling, if it makes you feel better. It'll help you pass the time."

Silas managed to force a sound out of his throat.

But it wasn't a scream this time.

He couldn't scream now.

Instead of a scream came a horrid, hollow, belching sound.

A resignation started to kick in—a lie-down-and-die response he also remembered from combat when death had seemed a certainty.

There really was no point in screaming.

He only wanted his killer to finish the job quickly. But the man seemed to be taking his good sweet time.

As inevitable as Silas knew death would be, it seemed to be an eternity away.

CHAPTER TWENTY SEVEN

Riley found herself walking along the waterline of a beach.

She was barefoot, and her pants legs were rolled up, and she might have enjoyed the walk if the sea air and the damp sand under her feet weren't so cold.

The sky was dusky, but she saw a glimmer of light out over the water.

Sunset? *she wondered.*

But no—the view from the nearest beach was to the east.

Sunrise, then.

It would be dawn before long. The thought filled her with alarm. She was dimly aware of something terrible about to happen. But for a few moments, she couldn't quite bring to mind just what it was.

Then it came to her ...

Someone is going to die before the sun comes up.

And it was up to her to stop it from happening.

But she couldn't stop the sun.

How could she stop death?

She looked down at her feet as she walked, observing the ripples the retreating tide left in the sand.

It means something, *she thought.*

Indeed, the ripples kept seeming on the verge of taking the shapes of letters. She felt as though, if she could only read the ripples, she'd find out what she needed to know to save somebody's life. But each little ebb of saltwater washed those shapes away before they became fully legible.

She quickened her footsteps as she walked.

Soon her eye was caught by something farther down the beach.

It was a little makeshift wigwam surrounded by a crazy collection of objects of one kind or another ... seashells, vases, driftwood, old toasters, broken lamps ...

It's where Rags Tucker lives, *she realized.*

She felt strangely relieved.

Perhaps Rags Tucker could tell her what she needed to know.

She walked up to the wigwam and pulled back the flap that

hung over the opening and ducked inside.

To her surprise, she wasn't in Rags Tucker's tent. Instead, she found herself inside a prison cell.

Sitting on the edge of a hard narrow bed was a muscular African-American man wearing a prison jumpsuit.

Shane Hatcher, *Riley realized with a shudder.*

It was the brilliant but dangerous man who had for too long been both her mentor and her nemesis.

In the past, he'd helped her understand the minds of some of the most evil killers she'd ever faced.

He could help her now, surely.

But did she dare ask for his help?

Did she want to renew her connection with him—that terrible bond that had caused her so much guilt and shame?

What choice to I have? *she asked herself.*

She crouched down in front of him.

"Hatcher, I need your help," she said. "There's a killer out there, and he's going to take a victim in just a very little while, and I've got to find him and stop him. What can you tell me? What do I need to do?"

Hatcher didn't answer. He just sat there staring blankly at the wall in front of him, seemingly unaware of her presence.

Then she remembered ...

She'd been told that Hatcher hadn't spoken a word to a single soul since she'd found him and arrested him.

It was as if he'd taken some kind of private vow of silence.

As she crouched there looking at him, he reached out and touched the cell wall with his finger. He idly began to make scribbles on the wall with his finger—completely meaningless, random scribbles, not even patterned like the ripples in ocean sand or on the tops of the timers.

The scribbles he was drawing were bright red.

Blood, *Riley realized.*

Hatcher's fingers and hand were covered with blood.

The blood of his victims? *Riley wondered.*

After all, Shane Hatcher had brutally slain many people.

But then she noticed that his other hand was bloody also—and it was clutching a bleeding wound in his belly. He was also bleeding from his shoulder.

Riley recognized the wounds.

She hadn't caused those wounds—hadn't shot Hatcher.

Blaine had done that while courageously defending Riley's family.

But by the time she had tracked Hatcher down afterward, he'd been dying from those wounds—and he'd wanted to die.

But Riley wouldn't let him.

Against his own wishes, she had saved his life.

And so she knew what those wounds represented to Hatcher.

They were symbols and reminders of Riley's betrayal—not just how she'd betrayed his trust and brought him to justice, but how she'd denied him his ultimate wish.

As his finger kept making those pointless scribbles, Riley realized ...

That's all he's got to say to me.

Scribbling like this was all he was going to do from now on.

He wanted nothing more to do with Riley.

She felt a terrible surge of sorrow and loss.

But why?

Why did she even want the friendship of this bloodthirsty monster?

She didn't know—and she didn't think she could ever possibly understand.

But she did know that she needed his help right now.

"Help me, Hatcher," she said. "I don't know what to do."

But Hatcher sat staring with glazed eyes, scribbling meaningless shapes in his own blood.

Riley's eyes snapped open at the sound of her phone ringing.

Suddenly she was wide awake, although her dream still tugged at her consciousness.

She remembered Shane Hatcher's silence—and before that, walking on the beach, dreading the approaching dawn.

And now she saw morning sunlight pouring in through her window.

She sighed with despair.

Together, the sunlight and the ringing phone could only mean one thing.

Someone else had been killed.

CHAPTER TWENTY EIGHT

Riley turned over on her bed to look at the ringing phone. Sure enough, the call was from Brent Meredith.

"What's happened?" she asked when she picked up the call.

"Another murder," Meredith said. "Not in the Belle Terre Nature Preserve, though. This time it was in the town of Lorneville."

Riley remembered that Lorneville was not far north of Sattler and Belle Terre. Although the killer had moved away from his expected turf, he was staying in the general area. But any hopes she and her colleagues had of stopping his grim murders by closing off Belle Terre were now crushed.

Riley had feared this all along.

Meredith added, "The body was found buried in an abandoned storage building in the marina there."

"And there was also a sand timer at the scene?" Riley asked.

"Yeah, right beside the hole—and it's running right now."

Riley suppressed a groan of despair.

She thought of the two sand timers currently in the hands of Sam Flores's team—the one that had emptied and the one that had still been running when they'd found it. Of course that second one had run out of sand a short while ago—with predictably fatal consequences.

It's starting all over again, she thought. *We have less than twenty-four hours to stop another murder.*

Meredith said, "I've already called Agent Jeffreys. He says he'll get in touch with you and Agent Roston and drive you to Lorneville."

Sure enough, as soon as she ended the call, Riley saw that she'd gotten a text message from Bill …

On my way. Will pick you up in 20 minutes.

Riley typed back …

OK

She felt stiff as she scrambled to her feet. She worried that neither her reflexes nor her thinking was sharp. She knew she had to pull herself together. She and her colleagues were most likely in for another long, brutal day.

She headed to the bathroom and washed her face, then stripped off the clothes she'd slept in and put on fresh slacks and a shirt.

Then she rushed downstairs, where she found her whole household up and around, the kids getting ready for school.

Gabriela was fixing breakfast, and Liam was cheerfully helping her. The girls were at the table finishing their homework. Everybody looked perfectly alert and happy, as if last night's drama had never happened.

Resilient, Riley thought.

The kids were definitely resilient, and so was Gabriela.

Riley herself didn't feel so resilient at the moment. She felt tired and discouraged. None of their efforts yesterday had done any good. They had failed to prevent another death.

Gabriela asked, "Will you have breakfast with us, *Señora* Riley?"

"I'm afraid not," Riley said. "I've got to leave in just a few minutes."

Jilly looked at Riley and grinned eagerly.

"Catching bad guys today?" Jilly asked.

Even though both girls often asked her that question, Riley felt slightly jarred by it. It always sounded as though they thought Riley's life was an adventure, like some cop show on TV. She also realized that she hadn't told anybody in the house about her current case. She certainly didn't want to try to explain it right now.

With a forced smile, Riley said to Jilly, "I'll do my best."

"Go get 'em, Mom," April said.

Gabriela handed Riley a bagel and a cup of coffee, which she carried with her outside the front door. She sat down on the stoop and downed as much of it as she could while she waited for her partners to show up.

When Bill pulled up in front of her townhouse moments later, she was surprised to see that he was alone in the SUV. Riley took a final gulp of coffee and left the dishes on the stoop, knowing that the kids or Gabriela would collect them for her.

"Haven't you picked up Jenn yet?" Riley asked as she climbed into the passenger seat.

"I tried," Bill said, starting to drive. "I messaged her, and the messages were marked 'read,' but she didn't answer them. Then I tried to call her, but she didn't answer. After that I drove to her apartment, but when I knocked, nobody answered. So I came on here. I didn't know what else to do."

Riley felt a rush of worry. This didn't sound like Jenn at all.

She asked Bill, "Do you think she's already on her way to the crime scene?"

"I don't see how she'd know where to go. I didn't tell her anything specific. Should we let Meredith know she won't be joining us?"

Riley thought for a moment. Meredith would surely be furious that Jenn hadn't been readily available.

"Bill, I suppose we ought to, but ..."

Her voice trailed off.

"But what?" Bill asked.

Riley was remembering the case she had recently worked on with Jenn in Iowa, and the terrifying text she'd gotten from Bill during that time ...

"Been sitting here with a gun in my mouth."

Riley hated to remind Bill about that, but she had no choice.

She said cautiously, "Bill, do you remember when you had that suicidal spell?

She could see Bill cringe.

"Yeah, I remember," he said.

"When I flew back from Iowa to help you, I went AWOL from the case Jenn and I were working on. Jenn covered for me—lied for me, even. I don't know what she's doing right now or why. But I think I owe it to her to cover for her this time."

Bill nodded grimly.

"I guess we both owe it to her," he said.

As Bill kept driving, Riley was still worrying. She took out her cell phone and called Jenn's number. When she got her voicemail, she said, "Jenn, this is Riley. Where are you?"

Riley waited a moment, hoping that Jenn would simply pick up the call.

But no answer came.

Riley added, "There's been another murder in Lorneville, just north of Sattler. Bill and I are on our way there. We need you to join us."

Riley paused again, then added, "Call me. Right away. Tell me what's going on. Bill and I are worried about you."

Riley ended the call but she kept worrying during the rest of the drive to Lorneville. Should she have seen something like this coming? After all, she'd long sensed that the young agent harbored some kind of secret. And Jenn had seemed uncharacteristically distracted yesterday.

But Riley hadn't imagined that Jenn would shirk her duties.

Was she in some kind of danger?

Surely she's all right, Riley kept telling herself.

*

Jenn was sitting at her desk in front of her home computer, trying to persuade herself not to listen to Riley's message again.

But somehow, she just couldn't help it.

She pushed the play button and began to listen …

"Jenn, this is Riley. Where are you?"

… then Jenn pushed the pause button.

She realized that her eyes were stinging with tears.

"That's a good question," Jenn whispered aloud. "Where am I?"

She was at home in her apartment, of course.

But where was she in her priorities, her loyalties?

Where was she in her life?

Bill had knocked on her door a little while ago. She'd known it was him—she'd seen him through the peephole. It had made her sick at heart not to answer the door, just as it had made her feel sick not to pick up Riley's call.

She ran the rest of Riley's message …

"There's been another murder in Lorneville, just north of Sattler. Bill and I are on our way there. We need you to join us."

Then after a pause, Riley added …

"Call me. Right away. Tell me what's going on. Bill and I are worried about you."

The message ended.

Tears were rolling down Jenn's face now.

What would they think of me if they knew? Jenn wondered.

It had all started yesterday. The woman she had long known as "Aunt Cora" had contacted her to make a demand—a demand that Jenn had spent all of yesterday trying to ignore.

But very early this morning, Aunt Cora had called again. This time, Jenn had realized that she couldn't refuse.

She had to do what Aunt Cora insisted she do.

She'd realized yesterday that Riley and Agent Jeffreys had noticed something was troubling her. She hadn't been able to hide it completely, even though she'd spent the whole day trying.

Today they surely knew that something was wrong, now that Jenn was shirking her duties. Not even answering their calls.

Was it over now—her FBI career?

Maybe if she got in her car right now and drove straight down to Lorneville and joined her fellow agents, she could make up some excuse for her tardiness and all would be forgiven.

But no, she couldn't do that.

Her past had caught up with her, and she had to contend with it here and now.

She hoped she could finish this task today. But what would happen after that?

She felt Aunt Cora's dark, inexorable pull.

She'll never let me go, Jenn thought.

She cleared her head, looked at the string of messages on her computer screen, and set about her task.

CHAPTER TWENTY NINE

When Bill pulled the SUV into the marina at Lorneville, Riley saw that it was a rundown hodgepodge of docks and storage buildings, mostly an abandoned ruin. She was dismayed to see a rowdy gathering of reporters, most of whom she recognized from yesterday.

Some local cops stood along a line of police tape, doing their best to keep the reporters away from the crime scene. FBI Agents Whittington and Ridge were also here, undoubtedly waiting for Riley and Bill to arrive.

Riley looked at her watch and saw that it was nearly eleven o'clock.

She felt a stab of despair. The day was going by much too fast already.

The fact that Riley couldn't stop worrying about Jenn added to the pressure.

Naturally, as soon as Bill and Riley set foot outside the SUV, the reporters surged around them, yelling questions.

"Tell us what you know about the latest victim."

"Why hasn't his name been released yet?"

"Was he buried alive like the others?"

"Is it true the Sandman is going to commit a murder every twenty-four hours?"

"Do you have any idea who the Sandman might actually be?"

The Sandman, Riley thought.

At least the reporters had finally settled on a nickname, and they had eliminated "Father Time." Riley didn't much care for either alternative. Nicknames had an unfortunate way of granting a certain mystique to serial killers, often giving them a fascinating aura of mystery and power. That was never helpful.

Riley and Bill said nothing to the reporters as Whittington and Ridge flanked them protectively and escorted them past the police tape. The other agents led Riley and Bill into one of the storage buildings, where the murder had been committed.

Inside, Riley saw that Zane Terzis, the slender, black-haired medical examiner for the Tidewater District, was here with his team. Parker Belt, Sattler's stocky, red-haired police chief, was standing beside Terzis. The FBI agents who had been working on the case yesterday were also here, including Craig Huang.

Huang was huddled with his fellow agents, looking very much in charge. Riley knew this was a good thing, since as far as Carl Walder was concerned, Huang *was* in charge, and Riley was only following his orders.

When Huang spotted Riley and Bill, he hurried toward them.

"Isn't Agent Roston with you?" he asked.

Riley exchanged uneasy glances with Bill. The time had come for them to start covering for their wayward colleague.

Bill said, "Agent Roston is working on another detail."

Another detail? Riley thought.

What could that possibly mean? But obviously, Bill was being intentionally vague. And Huang just nodded, too busy to ask for specifics.

Huang led Bill and Riley over to an overweight man with an unflattering buzz cut. His hands were stuffed in his pockets and he kept shuffling his feet in a restless manner.

Huang introduced him as Waylon Fellers, the Lorneville chief of police. Fellers acknowledged the introduction with a wordless scowl. He just stood staring into the hole that had been dug in the building's dirt floor.

Realizing that the Lorneville chief wasn't going to be of any help right now, Riley turned her attention to the larger scene. She saw that the entire floor inside the building was of sandy soil. The victim had been buried in a hole dug in the center of the space. A large sand timer was placed at the foot of the hole.

The whole scene gave her a chilling sense of déjà vu. It was different in many details from the first two sites, but the same in its awful eradication of life and prophecy of yet another death.

Terzis's team was unearthing the body with the same delicate care that they might use searching for fossils or rare artifacts. Unearthed from the waist up, the corpse looked even more grotesque than the one at the beach had yesterday. The torso was twisted, the back arched in frozen agony, while the hands remained fastened behind the man's back, bound with duct tape.

Unlike yesterday's victim, this one's eyes were wide open, his gaze permanently fixed upon the tormentor who had murdered him.

Chief Fellers shook his head with disapproval.

He said to Terzis, "Now that the last of the Feds have showed up, can't we get poor Silas out of this goddamn hole? He deserves better than this."

"Soon," Terzis said. "Be patient."

Fellers let out a growl that sounded anything but patient.

"Who found the body?" Riley asked Fellers.

The man finally looked directly at her.

"Stuart Miles, the man who owns this property. Stuart's been fixing to renovate this place for a while now, put a whole new nice facility in this area. This morning Stuart was showing a builder around here, making plans for what they'd have to tear down to get started, when he noticed this building's lock was broken, and the door was standing open, and the lights were burning inside."

Fellers pointed up. Riley saw that the ceiling lights were still on.

Fellers continued, "Well, none of that was normal, so Stuart and the builder came in here to see what was going on. They found a freshly filled hole with a sand timer standing there. He'd heard about the goings-on down at Belle Terre, and figured out what this had to be, so he called me then and there."

Riley saw that this sand timer looked much liked the others. Although the frame was made out of lighter-colored wood, the carvings appeared similar. And of course, sand was trickling from the top globe into the bottom.

Fellers shuffled restlessly again.

He said, "My boys and me started digging, and dug just deep enough to find Silas's face, looking up at us like this. I called Chief Belt right away—and the medical examiner too."

Fellers fell silent. He gulped and wiped his nose.

Riley asked Fellers, "Have you and your men moved the timer at all?"

"No, we left it be. It's exactly where we found it."

"That's good," Riley said.

Riley stooped beside the hole and looked at the body. She saw that the victim was wearing a uniform.

"I take it you knew the victim," she said to Fellers.

"I sure ought to," Fellers said. "Silas Ostwinkle's my first cousin."

Riley looked at Fellers and noticed a flash of guilt in his expression.

Fellers said, "It was my idea, getting this night watchman's job for him. He'd been having troubles with booze ever since he came

156

back from the Gulf back in the nineties. I thought this would be an easy way for him to pay the bills and keep him out of trouble. There's never been any problem here in this marina—until now."

Fellers blinked a few times, apparently trying to hold back his tears.

"If only I'd known," he said in a thick voice.

Still crouching beside the hole, Riley looked around and saw footprints in the surrounding dirt. They looked just like the ordinary sneaker prints they'd found where Courtney Wallace had been buried.

Riley looked at the victim again and shuddered at the horrified, pleading, wide-eyed expression on his face.

She glanced up at Terzis and asked, "Have you found any wounds on this one?"

Terzis said, "There was a blow to the back of his head by some hard, rough object. Maybe he was knocked out for a while."

Riley looked into the victim's eyes again. One thing was certain—he hadn't stayed unconscious.

He'd been all too aware of what was going on when he'd been buried alive—the same as the other victims.

She noticed a distinctive bruise around his mouth and jaw.

Duct tape, she realized.

The killer had taped the victim's mouth shut to keep him quiet.

But then he'd pulled the duct tape off.

Why? Riley wondered.

Obviously, he hadn't been worried that anyone would hear his victim's screaming.

But even so, she wondered—wouldn't his task have been easier if the victim had kept quieter?

She felt a familiar tingle coming over her—a sense of what the killer had been thinking and feeling.

Again, she sensed the man's charming manner as he exchanged mock-banter with his terrified victim—the same behavior she was sure he had shown to the other two victims.

And yet Riley sensed something different about this killing.

What was it?

An icy grip came over her as she saw something in the victim's eyes. It was more than just the terror that he'd surely shared with the other victims.

It was weariness, exhaustion—perhaps even a desire for this ordeal to be over with.

But the killer hadn't granted that wish.

Riley sensed that this burial had been slower than the others—much, much slower, and much more sadistically cruel.

Riley shakily got to her feet.

She whispered to Bill, "He's enjoying this more with every murder. And now he's taking his time to relish every minute of it."

CHAPTER THIRTY

Riley could see Bill shudder with horror at her words.

"Damn," Bill said in a whisper. "You mean he's burying them more slowly? Drawing the whole thing out?"

Riley nodded grimly, and Bill added, "What the hell are we going to do to stop him?"

Riley didn't know the answer. But she did know that the killer was likely to get even harder to stop, now that he was getting a taste for killing in an especially ugly way.

Just then Riley heard Craig Huang's voice from a few feet away.

"Yes, sir … Yes, sir … Yes, sir."

She turned and saw that Huang was talking on his cell phone, looking thoroughly abashed as he kept saying "yes, sir" over and over again.

Riley stifled a sigh. It wasn't hard to guess who Huang was talking to.

With a final "yes, sir," Huang ended the call. He walked toward Riley and Bill and spoke to them quietly.

"That was Chief Walder. He's even more pissed off than he was yesterday."

Riley felt a pang of sympathy for Huang. She'd long since gotten used to being the butt of Walder's frustration. But today it was Huang's turn. After all, Walder was still under the impression that Huang, rather than Riley, was in charge of this investigation.

"Don't tell me," Bill said to Huang. "He's mad because of all the negative media coverage."

Huang nodded. "Oh, he's mad, all right."

Riley said, "Don't let him get to you, Agent Huang. That's pretty much all Walder cares about—whether the agency's getting good or bad publicity. When it's bad, he blames us. When it's good, he takes all the credit."

Huang looked a little relieved. Riley realized that this was probably the first time she'd spoken to him openly about her dislike for Walder. She wondered if maybe she was being indiscreet. It certainly didn't seem very professional of her.

But she liked and respected Huang. She figured it was about time he knew what more senior agents thought about the boss.

Huang said, "Well, you're still in charge as far as I'm concerned, Agent Paige."

By then the other FBI agents—Engel, Craft, Geraty, Ridge, and Whittington—had clustered around Huang and were looking at Riley, obviously waiting for her to give orders.

Riley's spirits sank a little.

These were good agents—some of the best Riley knew. But after a whole day under her leadership, they'd gotten nowhere, and now someone else had been murdered. She simply wasn't at her best right now. Under normal circumstances, she'd hand over the decision-making to Bill at this point. But she sensed that Bill was still shaky from his bouts with PTSD. Was he in any condition to assume authority?

Maybe Walder's right, Riley thought. *Maybe I should just turn the whole thing over to Huang.*

But she could see that the younger agent was still upset about the petty scolding he had gotten from Walder. Riley realized that Huang hadn't yet developed the toughness and resilience it took to give commands in the field, especially when things weren't going well. He was good, and he was getting better all the time, but he was still green.

She gathered her fortitude and told herself …

It really is up to me.

She thought fast and started giving instructions.

"Agents Whittington and Engel, ask Chief Fellers where you can find the two men who found the body this morning. I want you to interview them, see if they can remember anything helpful."

Whittington and Engel nodded, then walked over to Chief Fellers.

Riley continued, "Agent Craft, take lots of photographs of the body while the ME's team keeps uncovering it. Check and see what belongings he's still got on him. If he's like the others, nothing will have been stolen—he'll still have his wallet, money, ID, even his cell phone. Use your own judgment as to when Terzis and his people should take the body away."

Craft took out his cell phone and went straight to work taking photographs.

Then Riley said, "Agent Ridge, work with the local cops to comb the area inside and outside this building, see if the killer left any clues. Agent Geraty, get out and knock on doors and talk to people. Interview everybody who lives near the marina or is connected with it in any way."

Geraty asked, "What about the sand timer? Should we send it to Quantico?"

Riley thought for a moment.

"Not yet," she said. "Get one or two of the local guys to help you take it out to the SUV, then make sure it's secure and safe. Be careful getting it out there. Don't let any of those damned reporters get to it."

Geraty nodded and left.

Riley had now assigned tasks to all the agents except Bill, Huang, and herself.

She walked over to Chief Fellers and asked, "Did Silas Ostwinkle have any friends or relatives you think we should talk to—aside from you, I mean?"

Fellers shuffled his feet and made a slight snorting sound.

"I was figuring you might ask me that," he said. "I got in touch with Silas's kin a little while ago, told them to get together at his house. I'll take you right over there to meet them."

As she and Bill followed Fellers out of the building, Riley gestured to Huang to come with them. More reporters had already gathered beyond the police tape, some accompanied by TV cameras. As the reporters aggressively yelled out questions, the BAU agents and Chief Fellers pushed wordlessly through them to the chief's car.

It was a short drive to Silas Ostwinkle's house—so short that Riley thought maybe they might as well have walked. She could see that nothing in this tiny village of small wooden houses was very far from anything else. Riley guessed that no more than a few thousand people lived in Lorneville.

Riley wasn't at all familiar with fishing villages in this area, but she knew that some of them were closely knit communities that had long been isolated from the rest of the world. Some of them were still rather isolated and she sensed that Lorneville was like that.

Chief Fellers parked in front of Ostwinkle's house, which looked much like all the other little homes in the area, except that it was more rundown than most and its big yard was somewhat overgrown. A handful of old cars were parked nearby.

As Fellers, Riley, Bill, and Craig Huang got out of the car, a stream of people began to pour out through the front door, then crowded together on the porch, staring out at their visitors.

There were some fifteen people. Most of them were middle-aged or older—Riley guessed that young people had a way of moving away from Lorneville. But there were a few younger people here, including a handful of children. The men and boys wore jeans, and the women and girls wore plain cotton dresses.

There wasn't a smile among them. All the faces seemed to be frozen into the same surly frown.

Riley, Bill, Huang, and Fellers stood knee-deep in grass in front of the porch. The group on the porch was a strange sight. For a moment, Riley found it hard to believe it was real. Silas Ostwinkle's relatives seemed to be stiffly grouped and posed, looking weirdly like some old family tintype from the nineteenth century. Riley could see all sorts of family resemblances among them.

Riley was so startled that it took a few moments for her to register that Chief Fellers was in the middle of rattling off introductions …

"… and Ezra Wheeler here is Silas's uncle, and this here's his grandson Ezekiel. Luke Ostwinkle over there is Silas's brother by a different mother, and Delilah Griffin is his sister by a different father. Over to the left is Gage Grady, Silas's brother-in-law."

Fellers put his hands in his pockets and shuffled his feet.

"I guess that's everybody," he said.

Then he said to the family, "These three folks are Feds, from up in Quantico. They came here on account of what happened to poor Silas. They'd like to ask a few questions, if that's all right."

For a moment, the whole family stood there, as still and silent as statues.

Then a man with an impressive beard drawled, "Feds, eh? Well, I'm sorry you wasted the trip. We won't be needing your services."

Riley's mouth dropped open with surprise.

She said, "I don't think you understand. We're trying to find out what happened to Silas."

Another bald-headed man said, "We know sure enough what happened to him. He got murdered. We don't need you to tell us that."

Riley exchanged glances with Bill and Huang, who looked as baffled as she felt.

Bill said, "We're trying to find his killer. We need to stop him before he kills again."

A woman with pinched eyes said, "We'll take care of that, don't you worry. We look out for our own here. Whoever killed Silas, we'll find him an' deal with him as we think good and proper."

Chief Fellers seemed to be getting impatient.

He said, "Now listen here, Luke—and you too, Delilah. I know you think this is a family thing, and it's nobody else's business but ours. But I've been a lawman for a good long while now. I'm telling you that you're going to need these folks' help. They've got all kinds of expertise and skills that I don't have, and you don't either. You can't deal with this on your own."

The crowd of relatives kept standing, still and silent.

Chief Fellers said, "Damn it, folks, this is serious ..."

As Fellers went on haranguing his relatives, Craig Huang quietly led Bill and Riley a short distance away.

"This is a waste of time," Huang said, shaking his head. "This is just a bunch of would-be vigilantes—and the only good thing about them is they don't know enough about what they're doing to even get themselves into trouble. Even if they wanted to talk to us, they've got nothing to tell us. Silas Ostwinkle probably didn't know his killer, had no connection with him. None of these people did either."

Riley couldn't disagree. And yet ...

"It's procedure, Agent Huang," she said.

Bill added, "We can't leave any stone unturned, no loose ends. If there's even a chance that anybody here knows anything, we've got to check it out."

"I know that," Huang said. "But time is running short, and the two of you can make better use of your time. I'll stay here and deal with these folks. If there's any information to be had here, I'll ferret it out."

That made good sense to Riley, and she was grateful for the suggestion. She glanced at Bill and could see that he felt the same way. They thanked Huang and walked the few blocks back to the crime scene.

Riley was glad to see that their SUV was now inside the taped-off area forbidden to reporters. Doubtless the agents had done that when they put the sand timer into the vehicle.

Dodging reporters, she and Bill slipped under the yellow tape and climbed into the SUV. They just sat there for a moment, trying to decide how to reorient themselves.

Riley took out her computer pad and brought up a map of the area, marking each of the murder locations.

"This isn't good," Bill said, pointing to spots on the map. "The first two murders were close together, in Belle Terre. At first the killer seemed to have targeted that particular area, a nature preserve on the Chesapeake Bay. It seemed to be part of his MO, making him at least somewhat predictable,"

Bill pointed to the current location and added, "But Lorneville is more than twenty miles north of Belle Terre, off on a more remote creek. There's no public property out here. Can you see any rhyme or reason to this? Is there any connection among locations now?"

Riley didn't have to think hard to answer his question.

"It's all about sand," she said. "Sand at the beach, sandy soil in the woods nearby. The soil inside that building is also sandy."

"Well, I guess that narrows his options some," Bill said. "Sand makes for easier shoveling. At least we shouldn't expect him to strike farther inland, where he might need a backhoe to dig a hole. But this whole tidewater area is sandy. Even the creeks and rivers have sandy shores. And we've got no idea what new location he's got in mind. It's too big of an area."

Riley sat staring at the map. She simply couldn't think of any way to guess where he might strike next. She could find no clue to how they should proceed.

Just then her phone buzzed. Her heart jumped when she saw who was calling.

It was Jenn!

But where had she been?

And what had she been doing?

CHAPTER THIRTY ONE

When Riley took the call, she heard Jenn speak in an unsteady voice.

"Riley—where are you?"

Riley was taken aback by the question.

"What do you mean, where am I? Jenn, where are *you*?"

Jenn made a choking sound.

Is she crying? Riley wondered.

"I'm in Lorneville," Jenn said. "In your message you said there was another murder here, so I drove here, and I'm right at the edge of town. I'm …"

Jenn let out an audible sob.

She said, "Could you just tell me where the crime scene is? I'll be right there. I'm sorry I'm not there already."

For a moment, Riley had no idea what to say. Jenn clearly wasn't her usual self.

Certainly she and Bill could use Jenn on the job right now—but not if she was too emotionally distraught to function professionally.

Riley said, "Where are you right now exactly?"

Jenn choked back another sob, then said, "I'm sitting in my car in a parking lot outside a restaurant called the Smokehouse."

Riley remembered the place from when she and Bill had driven into Lorneville.

"Stay put," Riley said. "I'll be right there."

As Riley ended the call, she saw that Bill was staring at her with surprise.

He asked, "Was that Jenn?"

"Yeah," Riley said. "And something's wrong with her. Let's go."

Riley got behind the wheel and drove the short distance to the Smokehouse restaurant. Sure enough, Jenn was sitting in her car in the parking lot.

Riley said to Bill, "I need to talk to her alone. Could you …?"

Bill nodded. "I understand."

He got out of the SUV and went on into the restaurant.

Riley walked over to Jenn's car and got in the passenger's side.

165

Jenn was wiping her eyes and nose. She seemed to be trying to pull herself together.

"I'm sorry, Riley," she said. "I'm ready to get back to work now."

"No, you're not, Jenn. What's going on? Why did you ignore our calls and messages?"

"I *didn't* ignore them, I just …"

Jenn's voice trailed off.

Then she said, "I had to take care of something. I got it done. Really, I'm ready to work."

Riley didn't speak for a moment. She sat studying Jenn's expression. She knew that something had happened to her new partner—something serious.

Finally Riley said, "Neither of us is going anywhere until you talk to me."

Jenn still seemed to be having trouble calming herself.

"Riley, there are some things you don't know about me," she said.

Riley waited breathlessly for Jenn to continue.

Jenn said, "When I was a teenager, I spent several years in a foster home. That's in my records. What the records don't show is that it wasn't just any ordinary foster home …"

Jenn shook her head.

"Oh, Riley. I shouldn't tell you. I don't want to mix you up in this."

Riley patted Jenn's hand.

She said, "Look, you know things about me that nobody else knows. About my relationship with Shane Hatcher, especially. I've learned to trust you with some pretty dark secrets—stuff that even Bill doesn't know. Now you've got to trust me. Whatever you tell me, I won't repeat it to a single soul."

Jenn nodded and gulped hard.

"The name of the woman who ran the foster home is Cora Boone—*Aunt* Cora, we kids called her. The thing is … she chose kids carefully. She only took in the ones … who she thought had potential for …"

Jenn's voice faded again.

Potential for what? Riley wondered.

Riley's brain clicked away, trying to figure out what Jenn was trying to say. Then it dawned on her what Jenn must have been subjected to.

Riley spoke calmly. "Do you mean potential to become professional criminals?"

Jenn nodded.

She said, "Aunt Cora runs a criminal network. Most of her accomplices are kids she handpicked and taught. They're grown up now, and they know how to do—all kinds of things. I don't even know all of the criminal activities she's involved in."

Riley struggled to contemplate the implications of what Jenn was saying.

"Jenn," she said, "are you part of her network now?"

Jenn sat in silence for a moment.

"I don't do anything criminal for her," she said. "But … oh, Riley, things are so complicated."

"Tell me," Riley said.

"You know I worked a case in LA before I came to the BAU."

Riley nodded. Jenn's fine reputation had preceded her. Her success in LA had put her on the map as a promising young agent.

Jenn continued, "Aunt Cora—helped me on that case. She gave me insights. Mostly she gave me information."

Riley was shocked. Jenn really was deep into something dark and dangerous.

But she told herself …

Is it any different from my relationship with Shane Hatcher?

After all, she had relied on Hatcher's help even when he'd been at large and she shouldn't have been in contact with him. Jenn was the only person who had any idea of the extent of Riley's forbidden relationship with him.

No, Riley couldn't see any difference at all between herself and Jenn.

She had no right to judge her.

Then Jenn said, "After that, I thought I was free of her. But yesterday she got in touch, and …"

So that was what was bothering Jenn all of yesterday, Riley thought.

Jenn went on, "And this morning—well, I couldn't say no anymore. I had to do what she told me to. I did it, I got it done."

Riley was on the verge of asking …

"Was what you did illegal?"

But it seemed like a stupid question.

Of course it was illegal. That's why Jenn was so badly shaken.

Riley asked, "Are you finished with her now?"

Jenn shook her head.

"I don't think so. And I don't know what she might expect from me next."

Riley was putting more of the story together in her head. She was even able to consider things from the point of view of this "Aunt Cora" woman. Surely Aunt Cora was more than a little pleased that one of her protégés had joined the FBI. Jenn could be a lot of use to her from inside the law enforcement community.

A real resource, Riley thought.

Riley felt a pang of sympathy.

She couldn't begin to imagine the kind of hold this woman still had over Jenn.

But she did know that she owed Jenn a debt of loyalty.

She patted Jenn's hand again.

"Jenn, we'll deal with this. I don't know how, but we will. And you've got to be fair to yourself. We haven't been working together for very long, but I've seen enough of your work to know you're a brilliant agent—with or without Aunt Cora's help. And right now we've got a case to solve. Someone else is going to die if we don't solve it. Can Bill and I count on you to get back to work?"

Jenn drew herself up and sniffed back her remaining tears.

"You can count on me," she said.

Riley was jolted by the sound of a sharp knock against her window. She turned and saw that Bill was standing outside the car. She rolled down the window.

Bill said, "I've got Craig Huang on the phone. Maybe we should all talk to him."

Bill put the call on speakerphone so Riley and Jenn could join in.

Huang sounded flustered and frustrated.

"I'm getting nowhere fast. Asking those people at Silas Ostwinkle's house questions was like pulling teeth, and I don't know anything more than when I started. But I did get names of more of Ostwinkle's friends and relatives. Hell, it's like he's connected with everyone in Lorneville. I need to interview all those people too, whether they know anything or not. It looks like it might take me all day, though."

Riley shared Huang's frustration. Now was no time to get bogged down in dead-end interviews. But there was no way to avoid them.

All the same, Riley sensed an opportunity to ease Jenn back to work.

She asked Huang, "Do you want somebody to take some of those interviews off your hands?"

"Sure, but who's available?" Huang asked.

"Agent Roston's free now," Riley said. "And she's got her own vehicle."

Jenn smiled and nodded, obviously pleased to be offered a task.

Huang sounded hugely relieved. "Great! She can start with a guy named Emmett Sawyer, an old army buddy of Silas's."

Huang read off the man's address. With a whispered "thanks," Jenn drove away to find him.

Riley and Bill walked back to their SUV. Bill had bought coffee and sandwiches inside the restaurant, so they sat in the SUV eating and drinking and reviewing the case.

Between bites, Bill asked, "What do we know about our killer?"

Riley suppressed a sigh.

"Not much," she said. "He's obsessed with sand. And revenge."

"But what did the victims ever do to hurt him?"

"Nothing, probably."

"So why do we think these killings are acts of revenge?"

Riley thought for a moment, remembering her conversation with Mike Nevins. Mike had thought that the killer didn't even know who had wronged him.

"Perhaps the true *subjects of his revenge—the people who wronged him in some way—are now absent from his life."*

Riley spoke slowly, trying to make sense of her own thoughts.

"This is partly based on Mike's input, Bill, and on my own insight into him."

Bill just waited, so Riley plunged ahead.

"Something happened to him a long time ago—probably when he was just a kid. Somebody did something terrible to him—something cruel and awful. He's got no conscious memory of it. It's all suppressed. But lately, his anger has resurfaced. He doesn't know why. But it's driving him to kill."

"But who is he?" Bill asked. "Where is he?"

Riley let out a groan of discouragement. She had those insights into the killer's mind—true insights, she was pretty sure.

But what good were they to her, or to anybody else?

They didn't bring her any closer to finding him, to stopping him from killing again.

Riley felt too restless to sit still. She set her sandwich and coffee down on the dashboard and got out of the car.

"Where are you going?" Bill asked her.

She didn't answer. She really didn't know.

On an impulse, she walked around to the back of the SUV and opened the hatch. Inside, the timer was secured safely in place. Sand was pouring in a relentless trickle from the top globe into the lower globe.

She stood staring raptly at the timer.

He handled this timer, she thought. *He probably even made it.*

Maybe, if she could just look at it closely enough, she could catch a glimpse of …

Him.

It was a weird thought, and it didn't really make any sense to Riley.

Even so, she let herself get lost in the glistening shapes of the glass. She studied the waves of varying thickness, scrutinized how those waves refracted and reshaped surrounding objects as she looked through them.

And then her eyes were caught by a flash of light.

She peered more closely and saw that the flash was caused by a flaw in the glass—a tiny imperfection of some sort.

She gasped aloud.

The flaw looked and seemed insignificant, and yet …

It's important, she thought.

And she had seen that little flash of light from a glass globe before.

Then she remembered exactly where.

CHAPTER THIRTY TWO

As Riley peered at the flaw in the glass timer, the memory came back to her clearly.

She'd seen a tiny flash of light like this from glass globes lined up on a shelf. Of course, she'd thought nothing of it at the time. But those glass globes had been in the workshop of a man who made sand timers. Otis Redlich.

Bill called out to her from the driver's seat.

"Hey, Riley—what are you doing back there?"

Riley could see Bill through the glass, his face almost comically distorted.

"Give me just a minute," she said.

She brought her face to within inches of the glass. Now she could see what the flaw was.

It was a tiny bubble, so small that it didn't make a bulge. But when the sunlight came in at a certain angle, that made it glisten.

Riley thought hard for a moment.

She couldn't remember seeing any such similar flashes among the many timers in Ellery Kuhl's shop, The Sands of Time.

Is there a difference? she wondered.

Of course, she realized, it could be that the light had to hit just right. It could be purely accidental that she'd noticed the bubbles in this glass and at Redlich's, but not in the earlier ones.

She walked back around to the front of the car and sat in the seat next to Bill again. She took out her cell phone and punched in the number for Sam Flores at the BAU in Quantico.

"What's going on?" Bill asked.

"I'm not sure yet," Riley said. "Just bear with me."

When Flores answered, Riley put the call on speakerphone so Bill could listen in.

Riley said, "Flores, I assume that you and your team have gone over every square inch of those two timers that were left at the murder scenes."

Flores chuckled.

"Every square millimeter is more like it."

"And you've been doing a lot of research into timers in

general?" Riley added.

"Lots," Flores said. "What do you want to know?"

Bill was looking at Riley with a very curious expression now.

Riley asked, "Do either of those timers have flaws in the glass?"

"Do you mean occasional tiny bubbles or something larger?"

Riley's heart quickened with excitement.

"Bubbles," she said. "The one I've got here has some bubbles."

"Sure, the ones here have got bubbles too. I don't know why that's especially interesting. Bubbles in that kind of glass aren't unusual, and they're not really considered flaws. It's called an 'included bubble,' because it's one hundred percent below the surface of the glass. It's also sometimes called a 'seed.'"

A handful of words caught Riley's attention.

"You said bubbles *in that kind of glass*," she said. "What kind of glass do you mean?"

"Hand-blown glass. Meaning blown by mouth, of course. They're often seen in antique glass, and they can show up in hand-blown glass that's made today. Bubbles can appear just occasionally and randomly, like they do in the timers here. But some craftspeople like to create clusters of them for decorative effect. Ours aren't like that."

Riley's brain clicked away as she put her thoughts together.

She remembered seeing glassblowers at work, heating glass tubes and blowing hot glass into forms for wine bottles, pitchers, and candleholders. That had been years ago, at Jamestown, where actors portrayed characters in settlers' costumes. There had been a glasshouse, the kind that settlers had used to create glass in the 1600s. Now some modern artisans learned their trade and worked there.

So was a killer now creating glass globes in that same way, blowing tubes of glass into just the right size and shape to mark upcoming murders?

She remembered what Ellery Kuhl had said to them during their visit.

"I order the glass bulbs I use from China."

Riley's breath quickened as she asked Flores, "What about timers made from manufactured glass? Would they have the same sorts of flaws?"

"Probably not," Flores said. "The ones we've been looking at are made by individual craftspeople. The others would be mass produced, machine blown, and they'd be more uniform. Not that there'd be any difference in the glass itself. There's nothing exotic about the material involved, not even in the hand-blown specimens."

Riley knew that the information she was getting was important. She wasn't sure yet just how or why. But there was a difference. The sand timers that Redlich had were not the same as those used by Kuhl.

Flores asked, "Is there anything else you need me to do?"

Riley thought for a moment.

She remembered her discussion with Bill just a little while ago about the killer—how he might be acting out of long-suppressed rage over a long-suppressed trauma.

Yes, there might be something Flores could do.

She said, "Flores, I need for you to run a search for me. It's liable to be difficult, and I'm afraid I can't be very specific."

"Difficult suits me fine," Flores said. "What do you have in mind?"

Riley stopped to think for a moment.

How old is the killer? she asked herself.

The composite sketch had portrayed him as a younger man. But of course, the composite sketch had turned out to be useless because of the witness's early onset dementia. Whoever the killer was, this submerged rage had been building up in him for quite a few years now.

But not for too *many years,* she thought.

If he were well into middle age or older, that rage would have boiled over before now.

Her gut now told her that the killer was somewhere around thirty-five years old.

She said to Flores, "I want you to search events dating back between twenty-five and thirty years ago. Focus on this Tidewater area. I'm looking for a case of a child between five and ten years old experiencing some terrible trauma. A trauma involving sand. It would have been caused by somebody else—I don't know whether deliberately or accidentally."

Riley briefly worried that Flores would balk at such a vague search.

Instead he chuckled, sounding quite eager to take up the challenge.

"I'm on it," he said.

Riley added, "Work fast. We're running way short on time."

Riley ended the call.

Bill had been listening to the call with extreme interest.

"What do you expect Flores to find?" he asked.

"I don't know," Riley said. "Maybe nothing. Or maybe everything."

"What about this whole business of hand-blown glass? What are we supposed to make of that?"

Riley squinted as she thought.

"I'm not sure," she said. "But it seems likely that the killer is making the timers himself. If so, he's making more than just the frames. He's blowing the glass too. And now we know that Otis Redlich's timers were made from blown glass."

"So?" Bill asked.

Riley hesitated, then said, "So—we need to go talk to Redlich again."

Bill's mouth dropped open.

He said, "Do you think Redlich might be our killer after all? Just because he uses hand-blown glass? Isn't that more than a bit of a stretch?"

Riley fidgeted nervously. Her instincts were starting to kick in—but she wasn't yet sure what they were trying to tell her.

She said, "He could be our killer, but I doubt it. My sense of the killer is that he comes across as pleasant and friendly. I don't think Redlich could pull that off. He'd have to be one hell of an actor. Even so, I've got a hunch he can tell us something he didn't tell us before. Something very important. About the sand timers, and where they came from."

Bill shook his head.

He said, "You know I've always trusted your hunches, Riley. But …"

"But what?"

"I'm not sure I like this. We're running way short on time. But you want to drive all the way to Williamsburg to re-interview a guy who's a proven bullshit artist."

Riley gritted her teeth. It was true that Redlich had been uncooperative and downright unpleasant.

"Oh, he'll talk all right," she said. "We won't give him any choice. Now let's get going. We don't have a minute to lose."

Bill started the car and began to drive.

CHAPTER THIRTY THREE

Felix Harrington stood looking proudly into the large pit he'd dug in his backyard on the sandy river shore.

I'm anything but predictable, he thought.

This murder was going to be very different from the others—and more satisfying, he felt quite sure.

He'd been preparing this pit for weeks now. It was twelve by twelve feet square, its sides braced by wooden supports of his own building. He could bury more than one victim here—just how many he didn't yet know.

His newest victim was lying unconscious at his feet at the edge of the pit.

She'd wandered into his trap randomly, just like the others. He'd pulled into a gas station across the river, and she walked right up to his pickup truck asking for a ride. He knew that his charming smile had drawn her to him—although once she was in the car, she had made sure that he saw that she was carrying a pepper spray canister.

At a stoplight, he'd knocked her out with a sharp blow from his leather-covered billy club. She'd been unconscious ever since.

She was a petite young woman, and carrying her all the way out here to the pit had been easy. But he was a little worried that she hadn't yet regained consciousness. Had the blow been too hard? She simply had to be awake when he carried out his plan. It wouldn't work any other way.

He was relieved to hear her whimper.

"Where am I?"

She lifted her head and looked all around.

When she turned her head and saw him, he gave her a sharp kick that sent her backward into the pit. She let out a loud, wordless yelp of protest.

Felix smiled.

The excitement was about to begin.

The pit looked like it was only three feet deep, with a sand bottom.

But as the young woman scrambled to get to her feet, her

trouble began in earnest.

The solid-looking sand started to give under her feet—sponge-like at first. But then it swallowed up her sneakers and her ankles and her shins …

"Hey!" she yelled up at Felix.

His smile widened. The quicksand was working perfectly.

He'd worked very hard, getting exactly the right balance of sand and clay and water so that it would look solid but trap whatever or whoever fell into it. So far, it had just taken a couple of small animals—a rabbit and a stray cat.

The quicksand struck Felix as quite beautiful. Left alone, it thickened and looked solid. But once disturbed, it became more like a living thing, grasping and holding whatever had fallen into it.

As he had with the other victims, he addressed the girl in a friendly manner.

"Hey, looks like you're in a bit of trouble."

Right now she looked more angry than scared.

That didn't bother him. He knew the fear would kick in soon enough.

"What is this, some kind of joke?" she yelled.

He shook his head and clucked his tongue as he crouched beside the pit.

"Wow, that stuff looks sticky. You're going to have to really twist and pull to get out of it."

Of course he knew that struggling was the last thing the girl ought to do. The more frantically she moved, the deeper she sank. But although the quicksand went very deep, he knew that she wasn't going to vanish underneath it.

After all, that would spoil everything!

He knew that quicksand didn't work like it did in the movies, swallowing people whole. In fact, anyone who really knew what they were doing could get out of it. He'd tried it himself. It required just the right kind of wiggling to create a space between the legs to let water flow in and loosen the sand's grip.

But the girl didn't know that—and he wasn't going to tell her.

She would only sink just so deep, because human bodies had less density than quicksand.

But that would be enough.

She'd be here all night, helpless and immobilized and terrified, until the time came for him to finish burying her the rest of the way with ordinary sand.

Meanwhile, he could entertain himself with her terror to his heart's content.

She was up to her waist now—probably about as deep as she was going to get. She pulled her hands free of the grasping sand and fumbled desperately around her shirt pocket.

He held up her cell phone in his hand.

"Looking for this?" he asked.

Her eyes widened.

Of course, he'd snatched it out of her pocket while she'd been unconscious. He'd also turned it off so that nobody could track or call her.

"Give me that!" she yelled.

Still smiling, he shoved it into his own pocket.

The woman seemed to be swept by the full horror of her situation. She began to scream and babble, begging for mercy.

Her shrill voice was music to his ears, a delight to his soul.

In fact, it calmed and soothed him—relieved him of the strange, nameless terror that he always carried inside himself.

Why is that? he wondered.

He didn't know, but he was proud of the many years of sheer creativity—even artistry—that he'd put into coping with that terror.

He closed his eyes and let the screaming take him back through the years.

He couldn't remember how it had started—all that pain and terror.

In fact, he couldn't remember much about his life before age eight.

But he did remember how it had begun as a deathly fear of sand, and also of people.

He'd conquered his fear of sand by learning to control it. And he'd found that the best way to control it was to channel it to a useful purpose—to tell time. So he'd learned to make sand timers.

As for his fear of people—well, he had as little to do with them as possible. But now the lonely, isolated little house he had inherited from his parents was in danger of being encroached upon by development and construction. New houses were springing up just a mile away, so he knew that his days as a solitary hermit were numbered.

But he'd learned that he could conquer his fear of people by making *them* afraid. He struck fear not just in his victims, but in the thousands of other people who had no idea where or how he was going to strike next.

Yes, he was a true artist, and his house was filled with beautiful pieces of craftsmanship.

Still, like all creative people, he yearned for some impossible perfection.

For example, he was sorry that the tides here on this brackish river weren't extreme enough to drown the girl. In some places near the sea, a person stuck in quicksand could drown at high tide.

Of course, it was a foolish wish.

He couldn't control the tides, after all—couldn't synchronize them to drown his victims at exactly the right moment.

He really was exercising the best artistry he possibly could.

And yes, he *was* unpredictable.

He'd meant for the other bodies to be found, and the sand timers with them.

But nobody would find this girl's body—or any of the other bodies he wound up burying here.

Nevertheless, the world would know she was dead.

As soon as he finished burying this girl, he'd start another timer running. He'd take it into some small town early in the morning when few people were up and around and leave it in some prominent place—maybe even in front of the courthouse.

And he'd leave the girl's cell phone with the timer.

Everybody would know that she was dead, and that somebody else would die when the new timer ran out.

Meanwhile, the girl's screaming had waned to more of a whimper. He opened his eyes and saw that she looked tired. Perhaps her voice had grown tired from screaming.

He hoped she would rally soon and start screaming again.

It would be a shame if she stopped.

She had such a lovely voice.

CHAPTER THIRTY FOUR

As Bill parked the SUV in front of Otis Redlich's two-story brick house in Williamsburg, Riley keenly remembered the spiteful mind games the man had played with them when they'd been here yesterday.

Redlich had known nothing about the murders except what he'd picked up from the media, but he'd taken delight in wasting their time. He'd even taunted them with the possibility that he himself was the murderer.

He was, as Bill had said, "a proven bullshit artist." And he played his games for no apparent purpose at all, just out of a deep-seated anger with life.

Riley was determined not to let him play her and Bill like that again.

And she had a trick up her sleeve. She knew how to thwart him.

All the same, she was apprehensive about paying him another visit. Redlich had had a way of getting under her skin with his wry, bitter eloquence. She had remembered how his words had nagged at her …

"Time always wins the battle."

She told herself sternly …

Don't let him get to you.

Riley and Bill strode toward the house and knocked sharply on the door. Redlich opened the door and greeted them with his reptilian smile.

"Well, isn't *this* a surprise?" he said. "I didn't expect the two of you back. I'd been afraid that we hadn't hit it off, and you didn't exactly like me. Of course, you already know that I do business by appointment only. But in your case, I'll make an exception. Come on in."

He escorted them into the living room filled with museum-quality furniture.

"Do sit down and make yourselves comfortable," Redlich said, feigning more hospitality than he had shown them yesterday.

Riley and Bill ignored his offer and stayed on their feet.

179

Riley headed right toward the fireplace mantel, where the small sand timer was still sitting. She looked it over carefully and soon located a tiny bubble in the glass.

She and Bill had been right to come back here.

She said, "You're proud of your timers, aren't you, Mr. Redlich?"

"I am."

"And do you make them completely from scratch?"

Redlich squinted inquisitively.

"I'm not sure I understand quite what you're asking," he said.

"Well, you're an excellent carpenter, after all. But what about the glass? Where do you get it?"

Redlich smiled again.

"Oh, it's of very high quality. Not manufactured. Hand-blown, I assure you."

Riley peered closely at the timer.

She said, "Yes, it does look like very fine work. Do you make it yourself?"

Redlich lowered his head in an expression of mock shyness.

"Oh, I mustn't brag," he said. "Modesty forbids."

"You won't tell us?" Riley said.

"No, I don't think I will."

The bullshit begins, Riley thought.

Once again, Redlich was determined not to give them any straightforward answers, just out of general spite.

But she wasn't going to let that continue. Not this time.

She said, "If you *did* make it, I'm a bit surprised. I guess you're still learning your craft."

She pointed to the little bubble and added, "Because I couldn't help but notice this flaw right here."

Redlich's smile vanished.

He said, "Bubbles are quite normal in hand-blown glass. Desirable, actually."

"Are they? You don't need to get defensive about it. Did you make it?"

Redlich looked dismayed now. Riley sensed that she had taken the fun out of his little mind game.

With a slight growl, he said, "I'd rather not say."

Riley turned to Bill.

"He'd rather not say, Agent Jeffreys. What do you think of that?"

"I'd call it obstructing a criminal investigation," Bill said.

"So would I," Riley said. "Mr. Redlich, are you aware that obstruction of justice is a criminal offense?"

Redlich's lip curled into that patronizing smile of his.

"Oh, I wouldn't call it that. I'm afraid it would be your word against mine."

She didn't reply. She simply took out her cell phone and played a bit of the recording Jenn had made yesterday. Redlich's voice came through loud and clear …

"Now where was *I during the times in question? Well, I could tell you that I was here at home in bed. But would you believe me? I can't prove it."*

Riley clicked the recording off.

Redlich's face sank. Now he obviously knew that they had a full recording of the mind games he'd played with them yesterday. They had solid evidence that he'd interfered in their investigation and wasted their valuable time.

She said, "Now tell me, Mr. Redlich—where do you get the glass for your timers?"

Redlich let out a little chuckle of resignation.

"If you must know, I get all my glass from a craftsman named Kairos."

"Kairos?" Bill asked. "Is that a Greek name?"

Redlich seemed to be starting to enjoy himself again.

"It's his business name. I don't know what his real name is. But it is a Greek word. And I think you'd find its meaning quite interesting. Perhaps even quite pertinent to the case you're working on."

Riley sensed that Redlich wasn't playing games anymore. He was about to share a bit of genuinely useful information—and he was basking in his knowledge.

He said, "In Ancient Greek, there are two words for time. One is *chronos*—meaning chronological time. *Kairos* is the other word, and it's a bit more difficult to define. But it refers to a single moment—an *opportune* moment, the ideal moment to carry out some sort of action."

Riley felt a deep chill.

Kairos, she thought.

The word seemed very significant indeed. After all, they were looking for a killer who wasn't obsessed merely with time, but with the exact *moment* when a sand timer emptied out and it came time to kill another victim.

"Tell us more about him," Riley said.

Redlich shrugged.

"I wish I could. He's quite well known throughout this area for his work, but he's also very reclusive. I've never met him. I order my glass bulbs from him, with exact specifications, and they get delivered here. But as it happens, I *do* have some information you might find useful."

Redlich went to a desk and opened a little drawer. He pulled out a business card and handed it to Riley. In large, decorative letters, it simply said …

Kairos—artisan

There was no phone number on the card, but there was an email address—and also a mailing address.

Riley looked at Redlich, not knowing quite what to say. She knew she ought to thank him, but part of her balked at the idea. He was, after all, a terribly unpleasant, mean-spirited human being.

Finally, through gritted teeth, she said, "Thank you for your help, Mr. Redlich. We'll be going now."

She and Bill went out of the house and got into the SUV. The first thing she did as they sat in the car was to locate the address. It was on a road near Jamestown, about a half-hour drive from where they were right now.

Bill asked, "Do you think this is our guy?"

Riley sat staring at the card.

"He calls himself Kairos—a Greek word for time—and he makes sand timer bulbs. What do you think?"

"I'll bet he's our guy."

Riley could hear a note of certainty in Bill's voice.

Bill added, "He could be dangerous. Should we call in a SWAT team?"

Riley thought for a moment, then said, "That would take time—and time is exactly what we don't have right now."

Bill chuckled a little.

"Then I guess it's just you and me," he said. "That suits me fine. The two of us are more than enough of a team. Let's go get this guy."

CHAPTER THIRTY FIVE

It was starting to get dark by the time Riley and Bill arrived at the address of the craftsman who called himself Kairos.

The changing light gave Riley a chill.

She couldn't ever remember dreading the arrival of nightfall. But the waning light was just another reminder of the passage of time—and every such reminder filled her with dread of what the coming hours would bring.

Bill drove them past an upscale neighborhood and then through a lightly wooded area. He pulled the SUV to a stop at a simple, ornamental metal gate.

Riley got out of the SUV and checked the gate. It was locked and there was no sign of a speaker box or buzzer. Not that they wanted to announce their arrival to the man who lived on this property anyhow. They wanted to take him by surprise.

Beyond the gate, a lane disappeared among the trees. She could see no sign of any building.

She looked back at Bill and shrugged.

He turned off the SUV, got out, and joined her. They easily hopped over the low fence beside the gate and walked along the dirt road.

After a short distance, a bend in the drive brought a house into view. It was surprisingly small for what seemed like such a large property. Its design was modern, which was a bit unusual in this region of colonial nostalgia. Just beyond the house was the James River, wide and glowing in the evening light.

There were plenty of lights on in the house. They quietly walked closer to the building.

Suddenly, security lights flooded the area. A dog inside the house started barking.

"So much for the element of surprise," Bill said.

They both drew their guns and moved ahead. When they were about twenty feet from the house, a door swung open and they could see the barking German shepherd.

"Who is it?" a man's voice called out over the dog's barking.

"FBI," Riley yelled, holding up her badge in the light. "Step into the light and put your hands where we can see them."

There was a moment of hesitation, and then a man's silhouette appeared in the doorway, his hands held straight up.

"OK, OK! Jesus!"

Then he said to the dog, "Quiet, Bozo. Sit."

The dog immediately stopped barking and sat beside the man.

Bill called out, "Are you the man who calls himself Kairos?"

"Sure," the man said with a nervous laugh. "But since you've got me at gunpoint, I'll tell you my real name. It's Alfred Kriley. Come on over here. Don't worry, I'm not armed. Don't worry about Bozo. He's all bark. He wouldn't hurt a soul. His noise keeps intruders away, though."

The man looked big, but his hands were still up in the air, and he really did seem to be unarmed.

Their weapons still drawn, Riley and Bill took a few steps closer.

The man said, "Why don't you come on inside and tell me what this is all about?"

Riley glanced at Bill. She could tell by his expression that he, too, was worried that this might be a trap. The man was still silhouetted against the indoor light. Riley wanted a better look before she went inside.

"Take a few steps back, sir."

The man did, and the light shone on him more clearly.

He was a tall, bald, portly man in his mid-forties. His face looked amiable enough, despite the fact that he was obviously quite scared. Of course, Riley had every reason to expect the killer to look perfectly friendly.

Riley was about to ask him where he'd been at the times of the murders when she noticed something.

His feet were enormous, even for a big man. Riley could remember the sneaker tracks at two of the crime scenes. The killer's feet weren't nearly this big.

She looked at Bill and silently nodded toward the shoes.

Bill looked and then nodded, understanding.

Riley and Bill both holstered their weapons.

Riley said to the man, "Sorry for the misunderstanding, sir. We'd like to come in and ask you a few questions, if you don't mind."

The man lowered his arms and shrugged.

"Sure, come on in," he said.

As Riley and Bill went through the door, the dog got to his feet and bounced happily around them wagging his tail. Riley saw that they were in a well-equipped studio that stretched the whole length of the house.

"Are you here alone?" Bill asked.

"Yes, I am," the man said. "Just about always."

Riley looked around at the space. It was all one long room, and most of it seemed to be a workshop. It was filled with equipment for glassblowing—furnaces, steel tables, blow tubes, and torches fueled by tanks of oxygen and propane. Beyond that was some carpentry equipment. She could see living quarters at the far end, and she went to check that out. There was no sign of anyone being here besides the man and his dog, so she rejoined Bill and the occupant.

"Feds, huh?' the man joked nervously. "Is this about the size of the workspace I claim on my tax returns? Because you can measure it if you like. I'm not cheating, honest. I've got a tape measure if you don't."

Bill said, "Are you aware of three very similar murders that have happened in this part of the state during the last few days?"

The man's eyes widened.

"Murders? That's terrible. Are you saying there's a serial killer?"

Riley nodded.

"My god! No, I don't get any news to speak of. I stay off the grid as much as I can. That's why I bought this out-of-the-way place—years ago, back when it was still cheap. Of course it's worth a hell of a lot now. Not that I'd ever sell it."

With a pleasant laugh he added, "It's perfect for a crusty old hermit like me."

Bill asked, "So your name really is Alfred Kriley?"

"Yeah, but don't let it get around. It's good for business for an artist to stay mysterious. And I'm sure you'll agree that the name Kairos sounds plenty mysterious."

Riley said, "These particular murders seem to have been carried out by a gifted craftsman."

The man's face showed distress but she saw no sign of guilt.

Bill asked, "So you don't know anything about the murders at all?"

"Not a blessed thing."

Riley's spirits sank. She didn't believe that this man was lying to them.

Another wasted trip, she thought.

Then, as she glanced around the workshop again, a new feeling started to come over her—a tingling of intuition.

No, this wasn't going to be a wasted trip, after all.

She didn't yet know why, but she sensed that she was about to get an important clue.

She said, "Mr. Kriley, do you always work alone here?"

"Oh, yeah," Kriley said with a laugh. "I'm too grouchy for anyone to put up with."

Riley could tell that Kriley really was as good-natured as could be. He was just self-effacing, and he obviously treasured his privacy.

"And you don't have any assistants?" Riley asked.

"No. I guess it might make my work easier, but I just don't want anybody else around."

Riley paused. She still had a strong sense there was something to be learned here.

Then she asked, "Did you *ever* have an assistant?"

Kriley's forehead crinkled in thought.

"Now that you mention it, I did once. It was years ago now—some ten or fifteen years. A really odd young man, maybe about twenty years old at the time."

Riley's tingle of intuition grew stronger.

"Tell us about him," she said.

The man sat down and thought for a moment.

"Well, like I said, he was an odd young man. Very peculiar. The first I heard from him was by a letter in the mail. He said he liked my name, Kairos, because he was fascinated by time, and of course I make sand timer bulbs. He said he wanted to be my assistant, wanted to learn my trade. Well, I got curious, so I invited him over."

Kriley shrugged.

"I've got to say, I liked the kid. He was nice, and he seemed awfully earnest, and he really and truly wanted to learn. So I took him on. Taught him glassblowing—and carpentry too, because I do some of that as well."

Riley breath was quickening.

"What was his name?" she asked.

Kriley scratched his head.

"Well, that was the strange thing about him. He always said his name was Bob. That's all, just Bob."

"No last name?" Bill asked.

"No, and I got the feeling Bob wasn't his real name. Not that it mattered much, I paid him in cash. And I liked him enough not to care."

Kriley paused again, then said, "Then one day he just didn't show up. That wasn't like him, he'd always been dependable. I never heard from him again. He was doing good work by that time, so I guess he figured he'd learned all from me that he wanted to. Still, I can't say it didn't hurt my feelings."

Kriley shook his head.

"Odd kid. I wonder what happened to him."

Riley was tingling all over now. This man was very lucky that his friendly apprentice had never returned. If her intuition was right, Alfred Kriley might have become a victim of the Sandman.

She definitely wanted to know what happened to "Bob" too.

"Could you describe him?" she asked.

"Well, he had thick brownish hair, green eyes, a pale complexion, a really winning smile. He was maybe five foot nine, muscular, quite strong. Of course, I've got no idea how much he might have changed over the years. I guess he'd be in his mid-thirties by now."

"Did he happen to say where he lived?" Riley asked.

Kriley knitted his eyebrows.

"As a matter of fact, he did. Not an exact address. But he did say that he lived in Abel's Point, over across the York River."

Riley was almost breathless now. She thought hard and fast. What other questions could she ask Kriley?

That's all he knows, she realized.

There was no point in wasting any more time here.

She said, "Mr. Kriley, thanks so much for your help. And again, my partner and I are sorry for the misunderstanding."

"No problem," Kriley said with a chuckle. "It brought a little adventure into my otherwise boring life." Then he added, "You think it might be Bob that you're looking for?"

"We just have to check every possibility," Riley told him.

She and Bill left the house and headed back the way they'd come.

As they walked, Bill said, "So you're thinking that this 'Bob' kid is our murderer?"

"Aren't you?" Riley said.

"I don't know, Riley. It seems kind of thin to me. And even if it's the same person, how are we going to find him? Kriley's description isn't much to go on, especially after all these years. And we don't have time to go wandering around Abel's Point questioning a lot of people."

Riley didn't say anything. But she remembered the task she'd assigned to Sam Flores—to search for past victims of childhood traumas involving sand throughout this area.

When they got into the car, Riley got Flores on the phone. She put the call on speakerphone so Bill could listen.

"Flores, how are you doing with that search?" she asked.

"I've turned up five incidents so far. I wanted to narrow them down before I got back in touch."

Riley felt sure that the list was about to get narrowed down to one.

She asked, "Did any of those incidents take place in or around Abel's Point?"

She heard Flores gasp slightly.

"Yes, as a matter of fact. I found a police report. It happened twenty-seven years ago. An eight-year-old kid was playing with some older friends on the beach. They were digging sand tunnels, about five or six feet deep and long enough to crawl through. The kid crawled into one of the tunnels and it collapsed on him. The other kids panicked and ran to get help."

Riley's heart was pounding now.

"What happened next?" she asked.

"The kid was stuck there for twenty minutes. It's amazing he survived. The cops who showed up guessed that he twisted around a lot to keep some air in front of his face. But by the time they dug him up, he was unconscious. They managed to revive him and he made a full recovery."

Riley felt a jolt at the those words.

Images and thoughts tumbled through in her mind, connecting with Flores's words.

A full recovery.

Physically, maybe.

But the trauma had remained, possibly repressed but there ever since.

She thought it possible that no one had ever told him what had happened, not even his parents. Everyone had naïvely thought it was best for him not to remember. And he still couldn't remember, not consciously. But his bottled-up fear had forced its way to the surface—and rage, too, at having been abandoned by his friends.

And he was wreaking his misdirected rage on innocent people.

"Agent Paige?" Flores's voice reminded her that he was still on the phone. She brought herself back to the present.

"What was his name?" Riley asked.

"Felix Harrington. And it looks like he still lives at the same address in Abel's Point."

Flores gave her the address. Riley thanked him and ended the call.

"So what do we do now?" Bill asked.

"What do you think? We bring this guy in."

Bill shook his head warily.

"Riley, wait a minute. I'm not sure about this."

Before she could answer Bill, her phone buzzed. It was Jenn.

Riley answered, "Jenn, what are you doing now?"

"Nothing. I've been helping Huang with interviews. We're getting nowhere. I've got nothing to do."

"Where are you right now?"

"Right here in Lorneville."

Riley's excitement was mounting. She had to catch her breath.

She said, "I think we've located our killer. His name is Felix Harrington. He lives on the York River at the end of Hatchet Road in Abel's Point. Bill and I are going there right now."

"Please count me in," Jenn said in an urgent tone.

Riley paused to think about time and distance.

Then she said, "Let's meet at the York River Bridge. It'll take Bill and me maybe forty-five minutes to get there."

Riley ended the call, and Bill started the SUV engine.

"We'd better be right about this," Bill said, with a note of doubt in his voice.

Riley's teeth clenched with determination.

There was no doubt in her mind.

"Don't worry," she said. "We are."

CHAPTER THIRTY SIX

Jenn had called Riley from the Smokehouse restaurant in Lorneville, where she had stopped for coffee. When the call ended, she used her cell phone to look up the location Riley had mentioned.

"... the end of Hatchet Road in Abel's Point."

She was startled to see how close the place was—less than half an hour away. She could get there even more quickly than Riley and Agent Jeffreys if she left right now.

Her pulse quickened.

The last few hours of interminable interviews with Silas Ostwinkle's friends and family had driven her crazy. None of them had known anything useful—not that she'd expected any of them to.

Everybody working on the case was sure that the killer was choosing his victims at random. There was no reason to expect that any of their acquaintances knew the killer or anything about him. Nevertheless, the interviews had been mandatory procedure.

Jenn was relieved that they were over with.

But what was she going to do now?

Well, she had her instructions from Riley ...

"Let's meet at the York River Bridge."

She'd get there long ahead of Riley and Agent Jeffreys. She'd wind up parking there and waiting for them.

But what else did she have to do?

She paid for her coffee, left the restaurant, got in her car, and was on her way.

As she drove, she thought back over the terrible day she'd had—and the shame and guilt she'd felt at not showing up for work when she was supposed to. It had all started yesterday, when Aunt Cora had gotten in touch with her. This time Cora hadn't been pleading with Jenn to help her out. She had been demanding it.

It had been nothing less than ugly emotional blackmail.

Jenn had spent several of her teen years in Cora's supposed "foster home," learning criminal skills along with her ordinary schoolwork. Among her foster brothers and sisters, she'd grown especially close to one. Little Linus Quade never had the instinct for ordinary theft or violence that Aunt Cora valued, but he had grown up to be a very smart Internet criminal. And he had kept on working with Cora's organization.

Jenn hadn't had any contact with Linus for years, but she remembered him fondly.

Yesterday, Cora had told Jenn that Linus had been kidnapped by one of Cora's rivals. Linus was going to be killed unless Cora paid a ransom.

It would have been easy enough for Cora to pay that ransom herself. All she had to do was transfer money through a few accounts until it got to Linus's captor.

But Cora had said she wasn't going to do it. She had demanded that Jenn go through all the steps of paying the ransom herself.

"Or do you want your brother to die?" Cora had asked. *"It's up to you."*

Jenn knew what Cora was trying to accomplish. She did want Linus back, but she was also willing to use him to pull Jenn back into her criminal orbit. That was the kind of manipulation that had driven Jenn far away from the foster home years ago.

And Cora had succeeded, because Jenn couldn't be sure that Cora wouldn't let Linus die.

Jenn herself was skillful enough to carry out the transfers from her own computer at home, and she knew how to cover her tracks. Still, she'd had to get knee-deep into Aunt Cora's illicit accounts and do some money laundering. So her own involvement was illegal, and Aunt Cora now had yet another threat to hold over her. She'd done that just this morning.

The illicit job was finished, but she knew that Cora wasn't finished with her. She had no idea what the woman might demand from her next or how she could respond.

Jenn was glad that she'd told Riley as much as she had—and truly relieved that Riley had been sympathetic.

But was that a good thing or a bad thing?

Now that Riley knew what she knew, wasn't she mixed up in this as well?

Might Cora even gain some leverage over Riley too?

It was a horrible thought. Jenn knew she had to make sure that never happened.

Meanwhile, the shame clung sourly to her. In fact, it had only gotten worse during the string of pointless interviews. Her shame festered with every passing moment of useless activity.

She felt desperate to do something positive, to at least partly redeem herself.

She was eager to stop this killer who had so far eluded them all.

As Jenn came near the big steel bridge—the only public crossing across the York River—she slowed down and found a place to pull her car off the road. She could park here and wait for Riley and Agent Jeffreys to arrive.

She shut off the engine and sat looking along the broad river. The lights of a ship approaching from downstream caught her attention. She knew that this bridge was a double-swing bridge. Was it going to open for the approaching ship?

If so, what kind of delay was that likely to cause?

Jenn got on the Internet and found the website for the Virginia Department of Transportation. According to a notice there, the bridge was scheduled to open ten minutes from now. It was expected to stay open for a half hour or even longer.

Riley and Agent Jeffreys would probably arrive here right in the middle of that time.

Meanwhile, the killer would be doing whatever he liked— perhaps taunting and torturing a new victim.

Jenn felt a surge of impatience.

Could she really put up with any more waiting?

She felt her teeth clench.

I've got to go, she thought.

But should she call Riley and tell her that she was driving on ahead?

No, Riley would just tell her to stay put and wait.

And Jenn simply couldn't sit here doing nothing—not for another minute.

She started the car and drove across the bridge, stopping only to pay the two-dollar toll.

On the other side of the bridge, she took directions from her GPS service. She turned off the main highway, then continued along several curves into the countryside until the road led back toward the river. Finally she turned off onto Hatchet Road. She passed an area where new houses were being built, and then the road narrowed as it continued into some woods.

For a mile or so, there was no sign of habitation. Finally she saw lights from a house just beyond where the road ended. She pulled over and got out of her car. Everything was quiet except for crickets and other night creatures chirping.

Her hand hovering near her weapon, Jenn looked around, carefully surveying her situation.

She was facing an old two-story house with a few lights on inside and a single light bulb over the doorway. The house looked battered and in need of paint. A pickup truck was parked nearby.

She skirted around the lighted area toward the side of the house. She could see the river flowing just beyond a small yard. She stood there trying to decide what to do next, fighting down an urge to charge into the house alone.

As anxious as she was to take positive action, she wasn't crazy or stupid.

It was definitely time to contact Riley and tell her that she'd arrived here. After that, she'd have no choice but to wait.

But just as Jenn reached for her cell phone, she heard a noise.

It sounded like a woman's outcry—but only for a moment. Silence fell again, broken only by the monotonous nocturnal chirping.

Jenn tried to judge where the sound had come from.

Had it been inside the house?

Or had she only imagined it?

She stood dead still and listened.

Then she heard it again—the sound of low, desperate weeping.

And no, it wasn't coming from the house, but from the waterfront somewhere beyond.

The weeping continued—but it was a raspy voice and not very loud. Jenn guessed that the victim's voice was exhausted and raw from screaming. This place was far enough from any other habitation that screams would go unheard except by the killer himself.

Jenn drew her weapon and crept around the house. Then her eye was caught by a floodlight burning a short distance away. It was posted on a stand and turned to shine downward.

Her heart clutched. She knew the light must be shining on a victim caught in a trap. She stopped herself from rushing forward.

Stepping into the illuminated area near the light would reveal her presence, but she saw no sign that the killer was there. The woman cried out weakly again, and Jenn moved toward the light.

She arrived at the edge of a large pit, about twelve feet on each side.

To the side of the pit were a wheelbarrow and a huge pile of sand.

And inside that pit, buried up to her waist, was a young woman.

He's already started burying her! Jenn thought.

But where was the killer? In the glare of the light, it was hard to see anything around the pit.

She called out, "This is the FBI. Show yourself with your hands where I can see them."

No one appeared, and no one answered.

The woman let out a hoarse moan of despair.

Her eyes were half closed, and she didn't seem to be aware of Jenn's arrival.

Jenn stepped nearer the pit and said to her, "Don't worry. You'll be all right."

The woman lifted her head at the sound of Jenn's voice. She looked around, apparently unable to see Jenn in the glare of the light.

She murmured, "No. No. No."

Jenn was seized by pity for the poor woman. She seemed to be completely incoherent from fear, exhaustion, and shock.

The woman kept on saying, "No. No. No."

"Don't worry," Jenn said. "I'm here to help."

The pit appeared to be about three feet deep. Jenn climbed down and stepped out onto its solid-looking floor.

Suddenly, her whole body lurched, and the gun flew out of her hand.

What's happening? Jenn wondered.

It felt as if the sand under her feet had come to life and was fiercely pulling her downward.

Quicksand! Jenn realized.

Her feet and ankles quickly disappeared beneath the sand.

Jenn saw where her gun had fallen. Lighter than a human body, it remained partially suspended on the surface. Jenn tried to reach out for it.

But a shovel appeared from above, flipping the gun out of her reach.

She looked up and saw a man silhouetted against the light.

"You've got a cell phone," the man said.

"No, I don't," Jenn lied.

She knew better than to expect him to believe her.

And he didn't.

194

"Do you think I'm an idiot? You've got a cell phone. I want it."

Still silhouetted against the light, the man lifted his shovel high above the captive woman's head. Jenn knew that one blow from the blade of that shovel would mean death for the victim.

She took out her cell phone and threw it out of the pit in the man's direction.

He smashed it with his shovel. Then he sat down on the edge of the pit, his face catching the light at last.

A weird, friendly smile spread across his face.

"Well, well, well," he said. "Things have just gotten interesting!"

CHAPTER THIRTY SEVEN

The sand was up to Jenn's thighs now, and she could feel herself sinking deeper.

The woman in the pit with her was shaking her head and whimpering miserably.

"You shouldn't have," she said in a slurred, stunned voice. "I tried to warn you. I tried …"

Jenn suppressed a groan. That's what the captive had meant by crying "no, no, no."

She wished the woman had tried a lot harder, but she was obviously debilitated by what she was going through.

Jenn stared up out of the pit at the killer's face.

He was looking down at her with what seemed like a truly sympathetic expression.

He said, "Well, you're in a fix, aren't you? You poor thing. How did you get into this mess, anyway?"

Jenn was disarmed by the man's apparent concern.

"Is there anything I can do to help?" the man asked.

Of course Jenn knew he had no intention of helping her. Even so, she wondered what on earth could be going on in his head.

Then she remembered something Riley had said to Chief Belt at the place where Courtney Wallace had been buried …

"The killer is charming, likeable. People trust him."

Riley's instincts had been absolutely right, as usual. And now Jenn knew firsthand that the man didn't drop his charming persona even after he'd captured his victims. He kept taunting them with smiles, toying with them like a cat with a mouse.

As Jenn's understanding grew, a tactic started to form in her head.

Surely the best way to throw him off guard wasn't to rage or beg or plead or even to struggle.

If there was a way to manipulate him she should be able to find it.

Jenn knew that she could play mind games at least as well as he could. After all, she'd been taught by the best—meaning she'd been taught by the worst.

She'd been taught by Aunt Cora.

Still sinking and almost up to her waist now, Jenn let her shoulders drop into a posture of resignation, as if nothing really dire was happening—as if she'd just lost a card game or something.

"I'm so screwed," she said. "I'm just so, so screwed. I mean, look at me. Can you believe I let this happen? I'm just too damned stupid. Jesus, it's just been that kind of day."

The man's smile faded a little.

"What do you mean?" he asked.

Jenn shrugged.

"Well, for one thing, my partners are both assholes. I mean, imagine—sending me out to this place all by myself. You've probably guessed by now that I'm a rookie. They never give me any respect."

The man looked thoroughly puzzled now.

It's working, she thought.

Jenn shifted her imagination into full gear.

It was time to get really creative, to tell a story that would really mess with the guy's head.

And she knew a story that just might work.

It was a prank that her foster brothers and sisters had played on her years ago—a prank that even Aunt Cora hadn't known about.

She said, "I'll bet anything my partners sent me out here on a goddamn snipe hunt. It's all just a joke to them."

The man looked quite serious now—almost genuinely concerned.

Jenn said, "Never heard of a snipe hunt? It's a kind of hazing ritual. It happened to me once when I was a kid and I wanted to join this club and I had to go through an initiation. The other kids took me way out in the woods—to hunt snipes, they said. They showed me a hole in the ground and gave me a burlap bag and told me to stay right there and wait for a snipe to come out, then catch it in the bag. It would put up one hell of a fight, they said. I had to be tough—and I had to be patient. It might take a very long time, they said. Then they went away—to hunt snipes on their own, they said."

The woman in the pit with Jenn was whimpering again. Jenn knew she must be wondering what the hell the newcomer was talking about.

The man's brow knitted in a curious expression.

He said, "But there are no such things as snipes."

Jenn nodded.

"Yeah, you're catching on. Pretty damned mean, huh?"

Jenn knew it was time to turn on the anguish.

And it wasn't hard to do.

She remembered the betrayal as if it were yesterday. She remembered, too, how she'd refused to take part in Linus's hazing when he'd come to live with Cora.

Even so, Linus had had to go through the whole awful thing just like she had.

Tears came to her eyes now.

"I stayed right there beside that hole for the rest of the day. It got dark, and nobody came back, and I was alone out there in the woods, and it was night, and I was scared half to death. It seemed like forever until I finally gave up. And then I had to find my way out of the woods in the dark. All by myself. I was lost and terrified and I didn't get home until morning."

A sob came out of Jenn's throat.

"And now it's happening all over again. My partners are somewhere having a beer and having a laugh at my expense. Well, maybe they won't laugh so much if I never come back, ever. Or maybe they won't care. Yeah, I'll bet anything they just won't care."

Jenn's tears were coming easily now.

Through her tears, she could see the man's expression pass through a whole range of emotions, as if some dark memory were welling up in his mind.

She knew she was stirring up something in him—she had no idea exactly what.

But if she distracted him enough, maybe she could thwart him somehow. She just had to stay alert, be ready to take action.

"I'll bet you know what it's like," Jenn sobbed. "Getting betrayed, I mean. Getting left behind by people you trust. You've been through it too. It's so awful. It's like …"

Jenn looked around the pit, then at the man again.

"It's like getting buried alive," she said.

Suddenly the man's eyes bulged, and for a moment his whole face froze into a mask of terror.

Oh, God, Jenn thought. *He remembers something.*

But what?

It started to dawn on her that her tactic was about to backfire in some awful way.

Finally, the man threw back his head and let out a long,

howling shriek of despair.

He shouted to the sky, "You … left … me … to die!"

Then he stared down into the pit at Jenn. In a horrible, croaking voice, he said, "You! Die! Now!"

He staggered over to the wheelbarrow, which was already full of sand.

Jenn threw her arms over her face as sand poured over her head.

CHAPTER THIRTY EIGHT

As Bill drove the SUV toward their destination, Riley stayed glued to her cell phone, searching for old newspaper stories about what had happened to Felix Harrington all those years ago. She found absolutely nothing. Apparently the police had kept it quiet to protect the kids who had buried Felix.

It was one more reason for Riley to believe that Felix had never learned what had happened to him.

If he wanted revenge, it could only be for some wrong that he felt deeply but couldn't even name.

As they neared the bridge on the York River, Riley heard Bill grunt with dismay.

"Oh, shit."

She looked up and saw what had annoyed him.

Lighted up in the darkness, the double-swing bridge was wide open, letting a large ship pass through. The ship was most of the way through the bridge, but it was moving much too slowly for Riley's liking.

Bill pulled to a stop in the row of cars waiting for the bridge to open again.

"Be patient," she told Bill. "I'll go find Jenn."

She got out of the SUV and looked around, trying to spot Jenn's car.

She couldn't see it anywhere.

Where is she? Riley wondered.

She took out her cell phone and called Jenn's number. To her alarm, she got an out-of-service message. Then she typed in a text …

Jenn where R U?

But when she sent it, it was marked "undeliverable."

She climbed back into the car with Bill.

"Jenn's not here," she said.

"What do you mean, she's not here?" Bill said. "You told her to meet us here."

"I know," Riley said. "I looked all around and didn't see her car. I can't reach her by phone or text either."

"That's crazy," Bill said. "This is the second time today when she's not been where she's supposed to be. Where is she? What's she doing?"

Riley didn't know what to say. But she had a sinking feeling deep in her stomach.

Bill said, "You had a talk with her back in Lorneville. What was it all about?"

Riley suppressed a groan of frustration. She hated keeping secrets from Bill.

But she remembered all too clearly her promise to Jenn ...

"Whatever you tell me, I won't repeat it to a single soul."

So far, Jenn had kept Riley's secrets. It was her turn to keep Jenn's.

After waiting for a reply, Bill said, "OK, I guess it's something you can't tell me. I respect that. But Riley, something has been wrong with Jenn for two days. And now we can't depend on her to be where we need her. I don't care how you feel about that, but I'm through with her. I'm going to have to report her behavior to Meredith. She'll be finished at the agency."

Riley couldn't argue with Bill. And she couldn't excuse Jenn's behavior either.

But she felt confused about her own feelings.

She knew she ought to feel angry and disappointed.

Instead, she felt inexplicably afraid. She couldn't explain that fear even to herself, so she just kept quiet about it.

The ship moved the rest of the way through the opening, and the huge arms of the bridge swiveled back into place. The barricade lifted, and the row of stopped cars started to move again. Bill turned on the SUV's siren and flashing lights and sped past the traffic, across the arched bridge, and down onto the highway on the other side.

When they turned off the highway onto a smaller road, Bill turned off the lights and siren and followed GPS instructions through the back roads. Finally, they reached the end of the road and saw the house they were looking for. Bill parked the SUV and pointed.

"Hey, isn't that Jenn's car?" Bill said.

Riley was startled. It certainly was Jenn's car, so obviously she had come on alone.

But where was she right now, and what was she doing?

Was she in trouble?

Riley and Bill got out and drew their weapons. As they approached the house, Riley expected to pound on the door and announce their presence. But then a more distant sound caught her ear.

She touched Bill on the shoulder.

He looked at her, then cocked his head to listen.

He nodded—he could hear it too.

It was a man's voice a short distance away, yelling …

"Die! Die! Die!"

They followed the sound around the house until they saw an area lit by a single floodlight illuminating a large, square pit. At the nearest side of the pit, a man stood facing away from them, using a wheelbarrow to dump a load of sand into the pit.

He kept yelling down into the pit …

"Die! Die! Die!"

As she and Bill moved closer, the man didn't notice them. Riley thought he probably couldn't see them there outside his ring of intense light. Finally, Riley could glimpse what was down in the pit.

Two women were partially buried there—one of them about waist deep, the other nearly up to her neck. The pit was large and it would take a long time to fill it. Right now, the man seemed intent on piling sand into one part of it.

He was concentrating his attention on the woman who was already buried more deeply, dumping all of his current load of sand on her. She was writhing weakly, her hands barely free and trying to push the sand away. She was obviously exhausted.

Riley couldn't see the victim's face, but she recognized the haircut from behind.

"It's Jenn!" Riley whispered to Bill.

Still not noticing her or Bill, the man was shoveling more sand into the wheelbarrow to make another load.

Riley stepped into the pool of light, several feet behind him.

"FBI," she yelled. "Put your hands where I can see them."

The man froze for a moment.

Then, in a blur of movement, the man whirled around and the shovel flew out of his hands, spinning through the air. It hit Riley in the stomach handle-first.

She buckled over and the gun dropped from her hand. She felt a flash of anger with herself for miscalculating his possible moves.

But before she could regain her bearings, the man was upon her, grappling with her. She was startled by his enormous strength. She fought back and they spun around together, locked in each other's grip.

Then Riley felt herself falling and knew they had both gone over the edge of the pit. Her back hit the sand at the bottom, with the weight of the man on top of her.

She had expected the blow from the fall to be sharper. Instead, the surface felt strangely soft and cushion-like.

As the man kept thrashing on top of her, the sand seemed almost to come to life, pulling her whole body downward.

And then Riley knew …

Quicksand!

She flailed away at the man, trying to push him off of her.

Instead, they rolled together, then rolled again.

Riley desperately needed help.

She wondered …

Where's Bill? What's he doing?

*

It had all happened too fast for Bill to process.

Before he knew it, Riley and her assailant were locked in fierce combat, and then they'd tumbled into the pit.

And now they were thrashing away down there in a gloppy mix of sand and water.

Quicksand, he realized.

Riley was in danger of sinking and suffocating.

Bill's weapon was still in his hands.

He pointed it toward the figures in the pit, trying to get a clear shot at Riley's attacker.

But as the struggle continued, both of the figures were caked in sand.

Could he even tell which of them was which?

I can't get a clear shot, he thought.

Then he was fighting to keep the memories out of his head …

Memories of Lucy lying on the floor of an abandoned building, and a young man rushing toward her, and himself firing at the man, not knowing that he was only trying to help Lucy …

Don't think about it!

Bill yanked himself back to the present moment.

As he stared downward, the two bodies seemed almost to be a single mass now.

No, it was impossible.

He couldn't get a clear shot.

*

As they rolled together, Riley wound up on top of the man who had attacked her. She pushed hard against his chest and raised her head to get a good breath of air. Beneath her, the man's head and shoulders disappeared beneath the sand.

Then Riley realized …

He's going to suffocate!

She tried to pull him out, but the thick, sticky mass seemed more alive and malicious than before—and devilishly strong. The more she wrestled to pull him loose, the deeper they both went. By trying to help him, she was only hastening his death.

She heard Bill's voice nearby.

"Leave him. Don't even try. Here. Let me help you."

Riley looked up and saw that Bill was crouching on the edge of the pit. He was extending his hand toward her.

She was barely within reach of it. She reached out and grabbed his hand, and Bill tried to pull her toward him.

But her own weight, her entire body, was in the sand's slippery but powerful grip.

It was as if she couldn't help but pull in the opposite direction.

How could she assist him in his efforts to pull her out?

Then she remembered something Flores had said over the phone about the childhood trauma Felix Harrington had endured, and how he'd managed to survive being buried alive for twenty minutes …

"… he twisted around a lot to keep some air in front of his face."

That's it! she thought. She remembered long ago reading instructions on getting out of quicksand, and it all came back to her now.

Instead of struggling against the muck, she needed to create space between it and her body. Space for water to seep in and allow her to get free.

Defying her own fighting instincts, she let her body go slack.

Then she twisted and moved her legs as gently as she could.

Sure enough, she could feel water seeping between her legs and the sand.

She kept moving her entire body in the same manner, feeling the quicksand loosening its grip on her, until at last she was floating on the top of it and Bill was able to pull her out of the pit. Exhausted from her ordeal, she collapsed in a heap.

Solid ground had never felt so sweet to her before.

Bill quickly pulled her to her feet.

"Come on," he said. "We've got to help the others."

Riley and Bill went to the other end of the hole where the two women were partially buried. The killer's intended victim was still up to her waist in the quicksand, staring in silent shock at the struggle that had just unfolded.

Jenn was still neck-deep in the ordinary sand that the killer had poured over her, but now she had managed to get her arms fully free.

Jenn called out to Bill and Riley, "Get her out first. I can wait."

Bill picked up the shovel that the killer had thrown at Riley. He extended its handle to the woman, and Riley started talking her through the process of loosening herself from the sand.

*

About twenty minutes later, both Jenn and the woman were out of the sand. Bill took out his cell phone and called for belated backup. He also notified them that there was a body for the medical examiner's team to pick up, but that it was still partly submerged in a quicksand pit.

Jenn and the woman were now on their feet, although the woman was awfully wobbly and leaning on Jenn for support. They all headed for the killer's house.

As they walked, Bill said to Riley in a miserable voice, "I couldn't take the shot."

Riley saw that his expression was distraught.

"You couldn't, Bill. The killer and I were all tangled up together. There was no clear shot to take."

Bill didn't reply, just trudged along beside her.

Riley felt a pang of sadness. She understood why Bill was upset.

After his recent bitter struggle with PTSD, this felt like a terrible setback to him. Surely Bill would get back to his old self eventually. But now Riley knew it was going to take longer than both of them had hoped.

The door on this side of the house was unlocked. Bill drew his weapon again, in case an accomplice was still lurking somewhere inside. While Jenn kept comforting the distraught woman just outside the door, Bill and Riley crept on inside the house.

They found themselves in what had once been a large and comfortable living room, with a large window overlooking the beach and the river. There was little furniture there now except for tables cluttered with sand timers of various sizes. On one table in the middle of the room were four large timers, nicely carved with rippled, sand-like patterns on the top.

Riley felt a chill.

These were surely the ones the killer had intended to use to taunt authorities over future deaths.

Bill and Riley stepped through another doorway that led into what had once been a kitchen. The only remnants of its former use were an old refrigerator and a hot plate and an old sink. The rest had been turned into a workshop filled with equipment for both carpentry and glassblowing, including a furnace.

"I'll check upstairs," Bill said.

As he headed up the stairs, Riley went to a bathroom and gathered up some towels.

She soon heard Bill's voice calling from above.

"No one's here."

Riley called to the women outside, "It's safe. You can come in now."

Jenn brought the woman inside, and Riley shared the towels with them as they started to rub as much of the sand off of themselves as they could.

Bill soon came back downstairs and said, "There was a computer on in his bedroom. I checked it. It looks like he made pretty good money day-trading."

It made good sense to Riley. Felix Harrington had been able to make a living right here in his house, all the while maintaining his solitude.

As she kept rubbing herself off, Riley stared at the big sand timers sitting on that table.

She felt anger welling up inside of her.

He wasn't going to stop, she thought. *He was going to keep on*

206

killing.

But she realized her anger wasn't just at the killer.

It was the same anger she'd struggled with since she'd started working on this case.

It was anger against time itself.

She and her colleagues had won this little skirmish against time.

But she knew that their victory wouldn't last forever.

No one ever defeated time in the long run.

Sooner or later, everybody had to die.

Riley heard the sound of sirens approaching in the distance.

The wailing noise triggered a burst of rage.

One by one, Riley picked up the sand timers and smashed them to the floor.

CHAPTER THIRTY NINE

Riley woke up slowly.

The sun shone brightly through her bedroom windows.

And from the angle of the beams she knew …

It's late morning!

Where had the hours gone?

Had she been absent from work?

Then she realized—it was Saturday. Felix Harrington—the man known to the public as the Sandman—was dead. He wasn't going to bury anyone alive today. Or any other day.

She remembered getting home just before dawn on Friday and collapsing on her bed. Later that morning, she'd awakened just enough to get rid of her sandy clothes and take a luxurious shower. Then she'd gone back to sleep again until a call came in from Quantico.

To her relief, Meredith had let all the agents on the team join in on a videoconference to make an initial report on how the case had unfolded. Riley hadn't even needed to leave her bedroom to take part in that.

And now, she didn't have to go to Quantico until Monday, but she was looking forward to seeing Walder then. She always enjoyed hearing him choke over the obligatory congratulations after she'd successfully solved a case.

For the rest of yesterday, Riley's sleep had only been interrupted by soup and snacks that the kids ferried up to her from Gabriela. This morning, they had just let her sleep in.

Today there was nothing on Riley's schedule except a late lunch date with Blaine. She had plenty of time to get ready for that.

She got up slowly, relishing a familiar satisfaction in knowing that she and her colleagues had done their work well, and the public was safe from at least one more killer.

Of course, she also felt sore all over after the ordeal in the quicksand.

She shuddered at the memory, then shook it off. She was determined to let nothing spoil the pleasant day that awaited her.

She took her time getting dressed and finally made her way

downstairs. Jilly apparently heard her footsteps and met her at the foot of the stairs.

"Mom, you're up! And are you lucky! There are still some pancakes left!"

Riley was surprised to realize that she was really hungry. She started toward the kitchen, but Jilly stopped her and planted her on the living room sofa.

"Just sit down," Jilly said. "I'll bring everything right here."

"Thanks," Riley said, smiling. "And some coffee too, please."

"Coming right up!"

While Riley waited, Liam and April came in from the family room.

Riley asked, "What do the two of you have planned for today?"

Liam said, "April and I are going to a chess club practice session this afternoon."

"We've been practicing all morning," April said.

"I was giving her a few pointers," Liam said. "She's catching on fast."

Liam and April sat down in the living room with Riley, and Jilly came back with a hot cup of coffee. She put it down and dashed back to the kitchen. In moments she returned with a dish and silverware for Riley. Gabriela followed with a plate full of pancakes and a bottle of syrup.

Liam said, "Mmmm. I know we've already had breakfast, but I could sure eat more of those."

"I'll make some more," Gabriela said, exiting into the kitchen.

April said, "Mom, could I go to chess camp this summer?"

"I don't see why not," Riley said.

April broke into a broad smile.

"Good! Chess will make me smarter, and I have to get as smart as possible! I've made an important decision, Mom."

"What's that?"

"I'm going to be an FBI agent!"

Riley's eyes widened.

"Well, what do you think, Mom?" April asked.

Riley hesitated, then said, "We've got a lot of talking to do, I guess."

As Riley stabbed a piece of pancake with her fork, she wondered—did she want April's life to be like hers? She had always wished a more pleasant and ordinary life for her daughter.

Don't get alarmed, Riley thought.

After all, April might well change her mind—and there was still plenty of time for her to think about it. To apply to the academy, she'd need a college degree and probably some work experience.

A lot could happen between now and then.

Jilly laughed and said, "Hey, I've got big plans too! There are exactly eighteen days left of school before summer vacation starts. If I survive my exams, I'm going to sleep all summer long!"

Riley laughed heartily.

"Well," she said, "it's so nice to know that both of my girls know what they'll be doing with themselves in the future."

*

Awhile later, Riley was sitting on the patio at Blaine's Grill. The restaurant was busy, as was usual on a Saturday. Riley was enjoying the sun and air, the pleasant bustle of servers, the cheerful conversations of customers around her.

This was a very different world from the one she inhabited so much of the time.

And much nicer, she thought.

Blaine soon freed himself of his restaurant duties and joined Riley at her table. Together they sipped white wine and enjoyed a delicious seafood bisque. Riley hoped that Gabriela would understand if she wasn't very hungry for dinner tonight.

Of course, Blaine wanted to know about the case. Riley told him—selectively, as usual. She didn't get into Bill's ongoing struggle with PTSD, and she certainly didn't say anything about what she'd learned about Jenn.

She also skipped over some of the darker details of the case—for example, the grotesqueness of the buried bodies in rigor mortis, and the hideous expressions on their faces.

As always, she harbored a worry in the back of her mind—a worry that, sooner or later, this wonderful man would get scared away by the life she lived and disappear from her life altogether.

He didn't seem scared by what she was telling her right now, though. When she finished talking, he actually seemed pensive.

"I don't know, Riley," he said. "Maybe there's something wrong with me. I can't help but feel at least some pity for the killer. It must have been horrible, carrying that suppressed horror inside of him all those years. And the irony! The whole thing began with him being buried alive in sand—and his life ended that way too."

Riley found it to be an interesting thought. And now that she had put her outrage and anger behind her, she couldn't help but feel the same way.

Still, there was no question that Felix Harrington had been a monster, even if he'd been a victim as well. He'd made the choice to start killing.

Not all victims become monsters, she told herself.

There wasn't a doubt in her mind that Harrington had deserved his fate.

As she ate and tried to enjoy Blaine's pleasant conversation, dark thoughts began to intrude.

For one thing, there was Jenn.

Riley's younger partner had gotten a mild reprimand for rushing ahead of Bill and Riley to Felix Harrington's lair. Meredith had accepted Jenn's explanation that the closing bridge had complicated her decision.

But Riley now knew that Jenn's life was full of dangerous secrets.

She also was sure that she didn't know the full power this "Aunt Cora" might wield over Jenn.

What did it mean for Jenn's continuing work for the BAU?

And what did it mean for Riley?

Of course, Riley knew that she had no right to judge Jenn for all this—not after her own dark involvement with Shane Hatcher.

Hatcher's hold on Riley had been hard and ruthless—and he'd forced her to examine darker parts of her own personality.

And now Riley wondered—was it possible to do this job for long without becoming a bit of a monster?

And did she really want that kind of life for April?

ONCE BOUND
(A Riley Paige Mystery—Book 12)

"A masterpiece of thriller and mystery! The author did a magnificent job developing characters with a psychological side that is so well described that we feel inside their minds, follow their fears and cheer for their success. The plot is very intelligent and will keep you entertained throughout the book. Full of twists, this book will keep you awake until the turn of the last page."
--Books and Movie Reviews, Roberto Mattos (re Once Gone)

ONCE BOUND is book #12 in the bestselling Riley Paige mystery series, which begins with the #1 bestseller ONCE GONE (Book #1)—a free download with over 1,000 five star reviews!

In this heart-pounding thriller, women are being found dead on train tracks across the country, forcing the FBI into a mad race against time to catch the serial killer.

FBI Special Agent Riley Paige may have finally met her match: a sadistic killer, binding victims to the tracks to be killed by incoming trains. A killer smart enough to evade capture across many states—and charming enough to go unseen. She soon learns it will require all of her faculties to enter into his sick mind—a mind which she unsure she wants to enter.

And all with a final twist that is so shocking, even Riley could not expect it.

A dark psychological thriller with heart-pounding suspense, ONCE BOUND is book #12 in a riveting new series—with a beloved new character—that will leave you turning pages late into the night.

Book #13 in the Riley Paige series will be available soon.

Blake Pierce

Blake Pierce is author of the bestselling RILEY PAGE mystery series, which includes eleven books (and counting). Blake Pierce is also the author of the MACKENZIE WHITE mystery series, comprising seven books (and counting); of the AVERY BLACK mystery series, comprising six books; and of the new KERI LOCKE mystery series, comprising four books (and counting).

An avid reader and lifelong fan of the mystery and thriller genres, Blake loves to hear from you, so please feel free to visit www.blakepierceauthor.com to learn more and stay in touch.

BOOKS BY BLAKE PIERCE

RILEY PAIGE MYSTERY SERIES
ONCE GONE (Book #1)
ONCE TAKEN (Book #2)
ONCE CRAVED (Book #3)
ONCE LURED (Book #4)
ONCE HUNTED (Book #5)
ONCE PINED (Book #6)
ONCE FORSAKEN (Book #7)
ONCE COLD (Book #8)
ONCE STALKED (Book #9)
ONCE LOST (Book #10)
ONCE BURIED (Book #11)
ONCE BOUND (Book #12)

MACKENZIE WHITE MYSTERY SERIES
BEFORE HE KILLS (Book #1)
BEFORE HE SEES (Book #2)
BEFORE HE COVETS (Book #3)
BEFORE HE TAKES (Book #4)
BEFORE HE NEEDS (Book #5)
BEFORE HE FEELS (Book #6)
BEFORE HE SINS (Book #7)
BEFORE HE HUNTS (Book #8)

AVERY BLACK MYSTERY SERIES
CAUSE TO KILL (Book #1)
CAUSE TO RUN (Book #2)
CAUSE TO HIDE (Book #3)
CAUSE TO FEAR (Book #4)
CAUSE TO SAVE (Book #5)
CAUSE TO DREAD (Book #6)

KERI LOCKE MYSTERY SERIES
A TRACE OF DEATH (Book #1)
A TRACE OF MUDER (Book #2)
A TRACE OF VICE (Book #3)
A TRACE OF CRIME (Book #4)
A TRACE OF HOPE (Book #5)

9 781640 292284